THE LONG RIDE HOME

Blessings
Christa Scott Rude

THE LONG RIDE HOME

Christa Scott Reide

TATE PUBLISHING
AND ENTERPRISES, LLC

The Long Ride Home
Copyright © 2012 by Christa Scott Reide. All rights reserved.

No part of this publication may be reproduced, stored in a retrieval system or transmitted in any way by any means, electronic, mechanical, photocopy, recording or otherwise without the prior permission of the author except as provided by USA copyright law.

The opinions expressed by the author are not necessarily those of Tate Publishing, LLC.

Published by Tate Publishing & Enterprises, LLC
127 E. Trade Center Terrace | Mustang, Oklahoma 73064 USA
1.888.361.9473 | www.tatepublishing.com

Tate Publishing is committed to excellence in the publishing industry. The company reflects the philosophy established by the founders, based on Psalm 68:11,
"The Lord gave the word and great was the company of those who published it."

Book design copyright © 2012 by Tate Publishing, LLC. All rights reserved.
Cover design by Allen Jomoc
Interior design by Ronnel Luspoc

Published in the United States of America

ISBN: 978-1-62295-099-7
1. Fiction / Christian / Romance
2. Fiction / Christian / General
12.09.14

Dedication

Dedicated to my parents, Elmer and Imogene Fields
and to the memory of Gina Marie Tonge Jacobs

Acknowledgments

To my Lord and Savior, who has gifted me with more than I ever deserved.

To all my family and friends who believed in me.

To my husband, Chris, for supporting me. My love for you grows stronger every day.

To my sons Jacob, my laughter, and Justin, my strength, for enduring my idea long before it was put on paper. I love you both more than you'll ever know.

To my daughter, Moriah, my joy, who'll one day be old enough to read this book. I love you more than words can say.

To my parents, Elmer and Imogene Fields, for showing me unconditional love. I love you both.

To Roy Fields and Cathy Baird, for being my friends as well as my siblings. I love you.

To my niece's, Sarah Baird and Jessica Fields, thanks for being such great sounding boards!

To Karen Dotson, Joseé Hupp, and Michele Crouteau for encouraging me to never stop until it was published! Thanks for your wonderful friendships.

To Jeemes Akers for legal assistance and Imogene Akers for your encouragement. Thanks for being such amazing friends.

To Cyndie Reason for your inspiration. You are an amazing woman!

To Jerry Reason, thanks for the 911 advice on how to deliver a baby.

To Detective Ron Horak, for your assistance with information on the drugs utilized in this book.

And to Jerry Dotson for the initial encouragement to write this in the first place!

Thank you to Tate Publishing for believing in me when others wouldn't. My sincerest gratitude goes out to you all. Especially my editor, Liz McLane, you've been such a wonderful advisor and editor! Thanks for helping me make my characters come to life! And to all my readers, I can't thank you enough!

Prologue

"Why did you turn me in for sexual harassment?" He couldn't believe her accusation. "You know there was no such thing. I never touched you!" He leaned in closer. She could smell the alcohol on his breath as he spoke his expletives. "How dare you report me to the board of directors! Now I've lost my job. All because of you and your big mouth!"

Puffing out a deep breath, he was careful not to touch the woman as he wagged his finger in her face. "I may have lost my job, but you'll lose more." He paused for effect. She flinched when he placed his hand gently on her cheek. "Ha! Miss Goody Two-Shoes, you'll regret the day you snitched on me." He stabbed her shoulder with his finger. "That I promise you."

He grabbed the box of office paraphernalia from his desk and stormed out of what was his office just hours ago. She didn't turn to watch him leave. Relieved, she exhaled audibly.

She had tried to get him to stop with his advances to no avail. It took a lot of courage to go to the board of directors, but she had nowhere else to turn.

During the investigation, he had conceded to flirting with the smoky-blue-eyed beauty. He denied ever touching her, although the thought had crossed his mind on more than one occasion during his tenure. Of course, most every man that saw her must have felt the same way. But this was different. He wanted a real relationship, not one of flirting and occasional, stolen glances. An irrefutable purely carnal relationship.

The flirting began innocently enough. She reciprocated with her own enticing looks and gestures. He knew she wanted him as much as he wanted her. Then, without so much as a warning, she reported him.

The board of directors had passed a verdict, and he was offered to resign his position quietly or be fired. If he chose the latter, she would press charges.

If they wanted him to resign, then fine; screw the job. He didn't need it anyway. Now he wouldn't be accountable to anyone but himself.

Beginning the moment he walked out the door, he would do whatever he wanted. He had some money tucked away. He would use it until his trust fund became available on his thirtieth birthday, which was only a few weeks away. He would have his inheritance from his rich, dead daddy's estate and could live the remainder of his life in pure comfort. If only his tightwad father had not put the money in a trust fund, locked up as tight as Fort Knox, he could have partied daily and still had enough dough to live a life most people only dream of. Only, his father had stipulated in his will not only that he had to go to grad school but in addition had to obtain and work a job for a minimum of one year in the field of his studies.

School wasn't so bad. He'd partied at night and attended classes during the day. Even did a little studying. Academics weren't his forte, but he somehow managed to graduate with a two-point-nine grade point average. He figured he would finish school, land an undemanding job, and coast through it for a year. Only he didn't expect to have such a beautiful young thing as Emily Wilkerson working for him.

Try as he may, she remained adamant in refusing a relationship outside of work. Therefore, innocent flirtation began. She would occasionally tease him. He knew he had to remain in his position so he could get to know her better and one day take their relationship all the way. Then he could quit the farce of a career and move on with his life.

One day he collected his courage and flat-out told Emily, "I want you," and then he tried to kiss her. That was all it took. She up and turned him in just because of three simple words. Well, she wasn't going to get the last word. He promised himself that he would get even one day.

Although working was not his specialty, he only worked as a condition of his father's will. Now he had no job. That was fine with him. Luxury was within sight. After the money was in the bank, he would make his move.

He had only a few weeks to strategize. She would regret her complaint; he would make sure of it. Sentencing had been passed down, but he hadn't committed a crime…yet.

Before he had turned in the key to the office, he made himself a copy and tucked it in the glove compartment of his four-wheel-drive truck. He had also placed a tap on her phone. Every call she made or received, he would listen to. One day, when the timing was right, he would make his move.

He tossed the box of his personal belongings into the passenger's seat and slammed the door shut. Walking over to the driver's side, he promised himself he would get everything he wanted. All he had to do was be patient. The time would come for him to make his move. As he sat in his 4x4 truck, he rubbed the silver key between his thumb and forefinger, promising himself he would get what he wanted, soon…very soon.

Chapter 1

The late afternoon air was stifling as she walked out onto the front porch. The house was the one safe haven she had. Built just four years earlier, she and her grandmother designed each and every inch of space.

The house replicated a Victorian farmhouse with a wide wrap-around porch on three sides. She could walk from the front door to the back door on this porch. She only wished it could have wrapped all the way around, but then they would not have the attached side-load garage. On the east corner of the veranda stood a gazebo with morning glory intertwined in the latticework below and on each column. It overhung from the rooftop. Gram had tended each and every vine to train it to grow where she wanted. It was a glorious and peaceful place—one that the inhabitants enjoyed frequently, even on blistering-hot days like this one.

A breeze would be a welcome relief on this hot and humid Indian summer day in Ashburn, Virginia. Even though there was a huge lake behind their home, it didn't present any comfort today. The area was known for its summer humidity, so thick it could take your breath away. And everyone was struggling to breathe today, especially this little mother-to-be.

Not one to complain normally, Emily Wilkerson braced herself against the terrace post, taking as deep a breath as her crowded lungs would allow. She gently petitioned her dearest friend to allow her to remain home.

"I really don't want to go."

All she wanted to do was relax in the comfort of her air-conditioned home and await the birth of her baby. A baby she had no recollection of conceiving...

Upon graduation from college, Emily took a position with her community association. She adored her boss, who was a jolly old man. Upon his retirement, a younger, more aggressive man took over. George Baxter was not liked among the staff. He was short in temperament and long on conceit. Many times he mentioned how he would like to take Emily out for a good time. Eventually, the comments became daily remarks. With them came flirtation. Emily had repeatedly requested that he quit the statements and flirting or she would have to tell the board of directors. It had developed into harassment, and she was quite tired of the daily pronouncements.

Like all things, it came to an end, or so she thought. It wasn't two weeks before George began again. Emily informed the board of directors, who took the matter into consideration.

After careful investigation and deliberation, George was asked to tender his resignation. Upon his departure, George promised to extract revenge on Emily one day.

For several months, Emily dared not work alone. She only worked evenings when the budget was due, as it required more time than she had during the day.

One evening, while waiting for her friend, Kate, Emily sat in the building alone working on a special project the new manager had requested. She had called Kate, who agreed to come over and stay with her while she worked late. Kate had called to say someone had slashed her tires and was waiting for roadside assistance. Although it had been months since his threat, Emily decided to walk through the building and verify the doors and windows were locked. Once satisfied, she then returned to her desk and the task at hand.

He slipped the key into the lock of the front door where he knew she wouldn't hear him enter. The front door opened quietly. His feet took him to the kitchen where he dumped the drug into the office water decanter, which happened to be low on its supply of water. He slipped into the men's room and waited.

Alcott loves exploring.

Read Alcott's story in the storybook, then learn how walks into adventures

He's se
and disc
near or ho

dogster
Dogster.com/walk

oves an adventure.

Alcott loves to walk

He's walked all around the world... well, most of it. He's sung opera in Sydney, flown kites in Beijing and even sailed through the Amazon.

...en many things, met many friends
...vered that a walk, no matter how
... far, is always an adventure.

ott afoot

Alcott Afoot
turn your

The Long Ride Home

Emily got up from her desk and stretched. She picked up her glass and walked to the kitchen to get a drink. She poured the water from the carafe into her glass. Emptying a packet of Crystal Lite into the cup, she grabbed a stir stick and mixed the drink as she walked back to her office. She took a long drink and sat down behind her desk.

Within minutes, she began feeling lightheaded. Emily felt as though she was floating; the room spun uncontrollably; she tried to stand. Immediately, she fell to the floor, hitting her head on the edge of her desk.

Emily felt herself being lifted. Unable to resist the need to sleep, the red lights and loud sounds slowly vanished as she drifted off into darkness.

When she woke again, she was in a hospital room, an IV affixed to her left arm. Gram and Kate sat at the side of her bed, eyes swollen and red from crying.

"Where am I? What happened to me?" she asked warily.

Gram asked, "Don't you remember anything, sweetheart?" Emily shook her head.

"You were passed out when I arrived," Kate informed her. "Your clothes were torn and scattered around the room." Tears rolled down her face as she continued. "I called 911 and covered you with your coat." Kate wiped at her tears. "I'm so sorry I had flat tires and it took me so long to get to you! If my tires hadn't been slashed, I would have been there and this would never have happened," she cried.

Gram took hold of Kate's hand. "Darling, it's not your fault. If you were there, you may be dead instead of sitting here next to me."

"How long have I been asleep?" she asked.

"About ten hours," Gram told her.

"Ten hours? How could I sleep ten hours? Why don't I remember anything that happened to me?" Emily cried.

Gently rubbing her head, Gram informed her about the drug in her water. Rohypnol, which had been used to render her unconscious and unable to defend herself against her assailant. The side effects were amnesia, drowsiness, stomach pain, and disorientation.

Emily lay there silently as she tried to grasp what Gram had said. She reached up and felt the bandage on her forehead. "What happened to my head?"

"The best the paramedics could determine was that you hit your head on your desk as you fell to the floor," Kate said.

"Wha...what assailant?" It was as if their words were taking a while to process. "Gram, you said there was an assailant. What did he do?"

Gram looked at Kate, who closed her eyes as if to shut out the vision of what Emily must have endured.

"Honey." Gram slipped her hand into Emily's. She rubbed the back of her hand as she explained, "Evidently you were... raped."

Emily's eyes grew wide with terror. Her body had been violated and she had no memory of the horrible desecration. She didn't know whether it was a blessing or a curse not to know. It didn't matter if she remembered the abuse, she had been assaulted. Tears sprang to her eyes as the realization hit her full force.

She had been raped. But by who? "Who would do such a thing to me?"

"Oh honey!" Gram lowered herself onto the hospital bed and took Emily into her arms where she succumbed to her tears. Her body shuddered with each laborious breath. Gram stroked the back of her head and rocked her back and forth. "It's okay, sweetheart. Everything's going to be okay."

Suddenly, Emily pulled away. "There's no way I could've been raped," Emily denied. "I checked all the doors and windows not ten minutes before I passed out. Everything was locked up." She reached for a tissue from the table beside the bed and wiped her face and nose.

"Well then…" Gram took a deep breath and sighed. Tears began to fall from her eyes as she tried to help Emily understand. "It had to be someone who had access to the building."

Someone with a key. Someone who had a vendetta against her. George! That's it! It was George. George must have made a copy of the key and pretended to turn in his only copy, when he obviously kept one for this purpose and this purpose only. He must have waited for months outside surveilling the building, waiting for the moment he could exact his vengeance on her.

"George did this to me. I know it was him!" She glared at both of them. Emily closed her eyes as tears slowly slipped down her cheeks.

Chapter 2

In the beginning, it was difficult to face her neighbors and friends, and especially her church family.

Emily had pioneered a Wait for Marriage group where individuals who joined vowed to wait until marriage to have sex. After nearly a decade, the group had grown to more than two hundred young people from ages fifteen to thirty. Even if you had had relations with someone, you were still allowed to join the club if you vowed to wait for marriage to become sexually active again. Emily found it difficult to leave out anyone with a sincere heart.

Even though Emily was a victim of rape, a violation in which she was drugged to unconsciousness, she still felt the need to step down as the president. No one had as much said an unkind word to her, even when she found out she was pregnant. Still, she had not been to another meeting since the incident. She couldn't stand the stares and questions. No, it was better she didn't attend.

Today, she was being forced to attend a televised concert of contemporary Christian artists in Woodbridge, Virginia. This event was the talk of the local community and churches. Still, she truly didn't want to attend. Begrudgingly, she pulled back her long, wavy dark hair into a soft French braid. Tiny stray strands framed her porcelain face.

Emily leaned against the post, reached up to her forehead and wiped away the perspiration that was unapparent just minutes before stepping onto the front porch. Realizing her benefactors would not allow her to sit in the house another day, she rolled her eyes, pushed herself from the column, and began her descent down the stairs.

"Honey, you'll have a good time. I just know you will." Gram always had a positive attitude, even when Emily confessed she was with child.

She recalled the day she told the slender, gray-haired woman the news. It was rainy and gloomy just like her spirit. "It's all in God's will, my dear child. Just believe He'll carry you through this, and together we'll make it. All of us." Gram soothingly caressed her granddaughter's cheek to wipe away the falling tears. "God will see you through. I promise. Something good will come of this pregnancy. You'll see.

"Leave it in God's hands," she said. "He knows what he's doing." With a little tap on the cheek, Gram removed her hand and herself from Emily's room to retreat into her own. *To pray*, Emily thought. Gram always prayed.

Emily grasped the handrail with one hand; the other supported her lower back as she staggered down the few steps and over to the sport utility vehicle. She was in no mood to go out tonight. But even Gram wouldn't relent and allow her to remain home. "It'll be fun. You'll see," was all Gram would say.

However much she wanted to stay, her friend Kate and Gram wanted her to go.

"Em, it will be good for you to get out. You haven't been anywhere in weeks. C'mon, like Gram said, you will have fun." Kate urged her on to the red SUV. "I promise."

Kate knew how to push her buttons, and Emily didn't feel like an argument tonight. If it were anyone else at any other time, she would retreat and hide in the sanctuary of her own room, leaving them to fend for themselves. Instead, she looked into the most striking hazel eyes she had ever seen and succumbed to the plea.

"Arrrgggh!" Emily growled. "Kate, if it were anyone else but you, right here, right now, I would not be going anywhere! Sometimes I hate the fact that you have such an influence on me." Emily reached the passenger's side door and gripped the handle but waited a moment before opening it.

"Stop it! I don't want to hear your complaints any longer!" Kate argued. "You are going, and that's that!" Kate slipped her arm around Emily and pushed her aside then proceeded to open the door for her.

"It's just not like you to complain or sulk. I'm gonna blame the pregnancy for these sudden changes in your moodiness." Kate opened the door for Emily to climb in. "I've never known you to withdraw like this before—" She suddenly stopped herself from completing the sentence.

"Before? You mean before the baby, don't you?" Emily's head dropped to her bulging belly. Shame filled her entire being, and for the millionth time she questioned God. *How could this happen to me? How will I ever live this down? I know you have your reasons, Lord, but I just don't understand. Please help me to get through the next five weeks. More so, help me get through tonight!*

Comforting her friend, the green-eyed beauty took in a deep breath and confessed, "We've talked about this so many times over the last six months, Em. You have nothing to be ashamed of." Kate wrapped her arms around her friend in a warm embrace.

She peered into Emily's eyes. "No one is judging you, except yourself. Forget about it for one night, okay? Just one night."

"Forget?" Emily pushed Kate away and pointed to her midsection. "How can I forget this? It goes with me wherever I go! I can't escape it! So tell me, Kate, how do I forget about this?" She pointed to her protruding belly, frustrated that Kate would even suggest she could take a "leave of mental absence" from pregnancy.

Emily took stock of herself and her situation and for a brief moment chuckled. Yes, the baby was part of her; however, the situation was not completely hopeless. She could have a good time in spite of her circumstances. For this one night, she promised she would not think of her scarlet letter.

Startled at Emily's stifled laugh, Kate continued her argument. "Look, we have a large group going from church, and we'll all have a great time, including you! You've always loved getting together and going out. The gang has all been coming over to visit with you, and although we enjoy getting together and playing games and such, it's time we all get out as we used to. Just because you're pregnant doesn't give you the right to manipulate what we do and where we go. It's time you participate outside of your precious refuge." Kate pointed her thumb toward the grand house as she assisted Emily in to the vehicle.

Although she had already stopped quarreling, Emily still wasn't convinced she should go. As she climbed into the vehicle, she regretted getting in and turned to get out when she heard a still, small voice: "Go." *What?* she wondered. *Am I hearing things now?* But again she heard the simple command, "Go."

Chapter 3

After gathering at the church with a modest-sized group of friends and church members to convoy to the concert, it was decided that Kate should not drive but that she and Emily ride in Jordan's truck with him and his younger brother, Caleb.

The black 4x4 truck had a crew cab, luckily. This allowed Kate the legroom she needed to fit somewhat comfortably for the long ride.

Kate, a tall, thin, light brunette, liked her leg room. In fact, she had preferred to drive, but everyone decided it would be best that the Jordan drive since he had a larger vehicle.

Kate sat in the back seat with Caleb. Emily realized what a sacrifice it was for Kate to sit in the crew section of the truck with her long, tanned legs twisted to the side. Kate needed more leg room. It was a good thing the chapel was only little more than an hour away, for as soon as they arrived, Kate would be screaming to get out and stretch her legs.

As the convoy began their journey, Emily sat in quiet reserve, watching the rolling hills covered in autumn splendor, contemplating her life as it once was...

Emily had lived with Gram as long as she could remember. Vague recollections of visits with her father in the mental institution were more like dreams than reality now.

She could still recall the stench of urine in the hallways of the facility and the padded walls for those who were more than just severely depressed, like her father.

After the death of her mother and baby brother during childbirth, her father fell into a deep depression. He attempted to care for his firstborn, but his heart died with the love of his life. He left his precious child in his mother's care and committed himself to an institution where he would be out of their lives and out of touch with the world. He'd go anywhere and do anything to remove himself from the heartrending agony of his loss.

Try as she may, Gram attempted to show her son the unconditional love of a child, his Emmie, by taking her on weekly visits. Still his depression deepened until he was nothing but a shell of the man he once was.

Living with Gram had been the best, most wonderful life Emily could have imagined. She never lacked for love. Life was always an adventure. Gram took her on long walks through the woods that once surrounded her farmland. It was there Emily was allowed to discover the wonders the world had to offer. There she met Kate, who would prove to be her lifelong confidant and best of friends.

The two young girls were like sisters from the beginning. When Kate's family moved onto her grandmother's farm to tend the land, the two girls became inseparable. They planned their lives moment by moment in the sanctuary of their "clubhouse," an abandoned tool shed behind the barn. They planned on becoming movie stars, marrying twin brothers, and buying a big house they could all live in happily ever after.

Although life didn't go as planned, they forged different paths, never once losing the unyielding strength of their friendship.

As a child, Kate had always carried a camera. She snapped photos of everything from foliage to people to the crystal snowflakes in winter. Nothing was safe from her scrutinizing eye. It was only natural for her to become a professional photographer after finishing high school. Shortly after completing her training, she became the most requested photographer in the county.

Saturdays were her busiest and longest days, as most all weddings or parties were scheduled on that day. Today, Friday, held many appointments as well, but Kate had scheduled the concert well in advance and planned her day accordingly: a birthday party at ten, bridal sitting at one, and family portraits at three, so by five o'clock she would be well on her way to the chapel. No one was as organized as Kate. No one, that is, except Emily.

Emily planned her life from the time she entered middle school. She knew she wanted to be an accountant. Accounting took her love for numbers and organization abilities and blended them together into the perfect career. She planned to graduate from high school, attend college, go to grad school, work for several years, meet the man of her dreams, fall in love, get married, have two children, a boy and a girl, and become a full-time mother and wife. Life would be perfect. She had it all worked out. Until the untimely pregnancy.

Now, her world had been altered beyond her wildest dreams. Never would she have imagined being pregnant, unmarried, and unemployed. Reluctantly, but at the insistence of her attorney, she stepped down as lead accountant at her community association immediately after she realized who it was who had drugged and raped her. A lawsuit was in litigation. So much was pending on the birth of this baby—the "proof," as it was referred to by the father's legal team. Humph. She knew it was him. She may have been unconscious through the rape, but she knew what he was capable of, and she knew his terrorization wasn't just threats. She knew one day he would do something. Only, she didn't know what that something was. That's why she had had friends with her at all times. But that proved to be futile.

At the Hylton Memorial Chapel, the convoy pulled into the parking lot. Since Jordan's vehicle was pulling up the rear, he had to circle around for an empty space. There seemed to be an abundant supply in the rear of the building, so he dropped off the girls and Caleb at the front door and then proceeded to the empty parking lot in the back of the structure.

The lines were long on either side of the doors. Emily saw a few others from church at the end of one line and taking her place behind them struck up a conversation. Eventually, the entire group joined them near the back of the line as they arrived. By that time, the line had increased to wrap around the edifice.

An hour earlier than scheduled, the doors opened to allow the audience access to the cooler temperatures indoors. The cool air was like a blast of arctic air to Emily. It was such a vast dissimilarity; it sent chills over her body.

Chapter 4

The Hylton Memorial Chapel opened to a large vestibule decorated in brilliant fall colors. An abundant floral arrangement in dazzling yellows, bright oranges, and radiant reds was accented with majestic purples and deep greens. It sat as a focal point atop a sizeable circular cherry claw-foot table. The table stood on an Oriental carpet in deep reds and shimmering golds.

The vestibule sat outlined in double spherical cherry railed staircases lined with thick amethyst carpet. The walls were layered with rich gold and purple ornate paper. Emily stood in the middle of the atrium so captivated she barely noticed the cramping she felt in her abdomen. It slowly increased to a slight squeeze above her stomach.

More Braxton-Hicks. Emily had been having these cramps for the last several weeks. At her last doctor's visit, she was told she might have them up until the actual day of labor so not to worry…until they became regular and consistently stronger. The nurse gave her relaxation techniques to help diminish the pain. Breathing deeply, she pushed the pain aside, mentally at least. Halted by an unusual pain in her lower back, she reached around and massaged the base of her spine with her fist. Then, once again, she took a deep breath, exhaled slowly, and then joined the others by the curved stairs on the right of the foyer.

She walked toward the staircase. Just ahead of her was a young couple mesmerized by the splendor of the lobby, speaking quietly. Emily overheard the young girl: "I heard they stand a live twenty-foot Christmas tree between the two stairways the first of December. It's decorated after the Victorian era—in gold, rose, plum, and ivory, with lace and real candles. It would be a lovely setting for a wedding. So romantic. Don't you think?"

The smile that stretched across the face of the young man reflected the excitement in his eyes. "Mmm. It does sound romantic. Well, we'll just have to come back during the holidays and see for ourselves." They walked to the stairs and began their ascent, hand in hand.

Emily's heart pulsated rapidly. She knew chances of ever marrying were entirely in God's hands, but in her heart she longed for someone to be a part of her life; only now that special someone would have to accept her baby as well as her. She swept the thought of a beautiful Victorian Christmas wedding far from her mind. The last thing she needed to think about was something that may never happen or, at the very least, ensue in the distant future.

Before entering the auditorium, Kate and Emily excused themselves from the group to locate the restrooms. Inside the ladies' room, Emily confided in Kate what she had overheard the young couple say and her desires for a God-fearing man who would love her as well as her child.

"Wait just one minute!" Kate was shocked at what she had heard. She and Emily had discussed her options so many times over the last several months that she believed the baby would be given up for adoption. At least that was how Emily had left it a few days ago. Now she was confused. "You and your baby? I thought you were giving it up for adoption."

"I was, but…" How could Emily convey to her friend the confusion she felt about giving up her child? How could she explain the peace she felt about keeping the baby and raising it in a loving, Christian home? If she gave the child up for adoption, she would never see her again. She would never know if she was raised to know God. She would never know if the child was happy or sad, loved or estranged. She would never see her first step, first tooth, see her ride the bus on the first day of school, graduate from high school, send her off to college, get married… As tears began to fall, she attempted to impart all this to Kate.

Taking her into a loving embrace, Kate acknowledged she understood. "So, you want to raise this child on your own?"

Emily pulled away and nodded her head.

Grabbing a tissue from the countertop, Kate wiped the tear-stained face of her best friend. "Now look at you. You're a mess!" As she disposed of the tissue, she continued, "I noticed you are calling the baby a girl? Do you know for certain?"

"No, but I feel in my heart that this baby is a girl." Emily turned to see her reflection in the mirror. To her amazement, she realized Kate was just teasing about her being a mess. Opening her purse, she took out her blush to touch up her cheeks and then grabbed her finishing powder and applied another layer over her entire face. Thanks to Kate swabbing her eyes, she didn't have to touch up her mascara or eyeliner. She returned her things to her purse. "Thank you for understanding. Gram said you would."

"You've already told her?" Kate asked. She rolled her eyes. "Of course, you have!" *After all, she's going to need Gram's help with raising the baby.*

Emily nodded her head. "Yes, and she agreed that she would help raise her great-grandchild and love her with all the love she has in her heart. She admitted she had already grown to love her and was feeling a bit disheartened at the prospect of her being adopted. So I'm sure you can imagine how relieved I was when she told me that."

"Well, that's good to hear. And that baby will be loved by everyone, including me! Now that's going to be a lot of love."

"Yep."

"Well then, now we need to schedule some baby showers for you! And…go shopping! Oh, I can't wait to buy little girl things." She bent down and spoke into Emily's stomach, "Auntie Kate will spoil you rotten, little one!" She was truly happy for Emily and wanted to support her in every way possible. The girls laughed as they walked back to the auditorium to find their seats.

As they entered the great room, Emily was awed by its immensity. Pausing at the end of her row, she turned to look at the balcony.

It was also adorned with cherry wood railing to correspond with the stairways. The room had to hold fifteen hundred people or more, she theorized. And it was completely packed. Not an empty seat to be found, barring hers and Kate's.

As they proceeded to settle in, Emily realized she was sitting in the middle of the row. Glad that she had utilized the ladies' room before the show, she prayed she would not have to leave during any performance.

Nestled between Caleb and Kate, with Jordan on the other side of Kate, Emily commented on the seating. "Great seats." She told Kate and the others close enough to hear.

"Yeah, Jordan was able to get us the best seats. Not too close, not too far." Caleb gave his brother a thumbs-up. Jordan simply nodded his head.

Total opposite of his brother, Jordan was a man of few words, which was why Emily had been shocked when he dropped by her home one evening several months ago.

"Hi, Emily!" Jordan stepped out of his old rattletrap of a vehicle and walked up the steps to the front porch. Emily was sitting in the gazebo. It had not been long since she stepped down from her post as president of the Waiting for Marriage club. She was still quite upset and confused.

Wait for marriage was her life-long motto. But now? Well, even though she had no memory of the coital act, she felt it could no longer be her adage. Even though there were others in the group that'd had relations before joining and had taken on the decision to abstain from further sex until they married, Emily felt, under her circumstance, she didn't belong. She had been encouraged by her pastor and many of the members to remain as president or at least a member, but she didn't feel right about it. At least not until she was comfortable with her situation.

Jordan was one of her most fervent allies. He strongly encouraged her to remain as a member. One not to coerce, he understood Emily's decision to step down as president but didn't see the point of her withdrawing her membership. So after a long conversation, which was more like a debate, she agreed to remain in the association but would not attend the meetings until after the baby was born. Jordan was satisfied with that compromise and left her alone after that. Until the day he showed up on her front doorstep.

This spring day, Emily sat in the swing enjoying the light breeze and smell of the Morning Glory blossoms wafting all around her. She reached over and pulled a delicate floret from its vine as she watched Jordan ascend the steps two at a time.

Jordan, dressed in black slacks, green shirt, and tie with his hair still wet from showering, motioned to the rocker across from her.

Pushing the swing slightly, she nodded and he sat down. "What are you doing here? I thought you'd be home relaxing after a long day at work." Jordan was a computer programmer at a large company outside of DC. He had a short commute, but it took more than an hour each way as he traveled with everyone else who lived in the suburbs and worked eastward. Jordan was one who took his work very seriously, like everything else in his life. He prayed about everything long before acting upon it. So coming to visit Emily must have been a serious and long thought-out event; just dropping by was not in his vernacular.

He ran his hand through his dark, wet hair. "I thought I'd come by and talk with you. I've been thinking a lot about your situation and have something to say."

Surprised, Emily sat and waited for his next words.

"Emily, I realize you are in quite a predicament, and I'd like to help."

Shocked at his announcement, Emily didn't quite know what to say. "How do you mean to help me, Jordan?"

He sat back in the rocker, fidgeting with his hands. Taking a deep breath, Jordan carefully thought out his words. "Did you know during our childhood I had a crush on you?"

"No." She shook her head. "I didn't."

"Yeah. Back when we first moved here, I developed this horrible crush on you."

"Horrible?"

"Well, not horrible horrible." He coughed, embarrassed. This wasn't going as he had planned. He continued, "It was horrible for me to not be able to tell you, I mean."

"Oh."

He explained how he had adored her for many years and still felt a deep admiration for her. Nervously he spoke, "What I'm trying to say is I would be honored if you would allow me to be your husband and father to the baby." He waited an awkward moment. "What'dya say, Em? Will you marry me?"

Shocked at his confession of admiration and desire to be a father to her unborn child, Emily simply smiled. *Marry Jordan? He doesn't love me but admires me.* She knew he had to have thought about this for quite some time as he wasn't impulsive like his brother, Caleb. But marriage? No, that was not in the equation. He never said he loved her but admired her. That was not enough to base a marriage upon.

Thinking she may have thought he was jesting, Jordan interrupted her musings. "I'm serious."

"Of course you are, Jordan. I just thought…" She stood and walked over to the railing to look out over the lake. Barely three months into her pregnancy, she still wasn't showing, although her sundress was snug around her waist. A light breeze stirred the material. She gently placed her hand on her tiny abdomen. "I just thought that you'd—"

"You thought I'd never marry, didn't you?"

She turned abruptly. "No, it's not that."

Frustrated, he let out an audible sigh. "Then what is it?"

Emily took a moment to ask God for wisdom. "Jordan, you know I love you. You've been like a brother to me—"

"But you don't love me, not like a husband. Is that it?" Jordan was annoyed. He stood and looked deep into her eyes. "Maybe you haven't had enough time to think about it. How many proposals do you think you'll have now that you're pregnant with someone else's child?" It was out before he knew it. He didn't mean to be so blatant and callous. He didn't want to hurt Emily at all. He just wanted her to realize he would make a good husband and father. He looked away from her, mortified at his offensive remark.

She considered her answer. Here was a man she admired and respected, one who was offering to be both husband and father. Should she turn down the only proposal she could possibly ever have? "I have thought about it. It's wrong, Jordan." Emily went on to explain that if she weren't pregnant, the conversation wouldn't even be taking place. She knew Jordan meant well, but even though they had a mutual respect for one another, respect would not be enough for a lasting marriage.

Jordan slowly returned to the rocker. He leaned his elbows on his knees, clasping his hands together. "But we would be good together. You would grow to love me."

Emily closed the distance between them and sat down in the rocker beside him, placing her hand on his knee. "No, I don't believe I would. And it would be a mistake. I just know it would."

"Please, Emily, don't say that." He took her hand in both of his. "We'd be good together. Don't you see?"

Uncomfortable with the show of affection, she pulled her hand away from his. "How do I explain?" She pondered a moment. "God is not in this proposal. That's how I can say that. You've prayed, but I'm sure God doesn't want us to marry…one another."

Jordan scoffed. "How would you know? I'm the one who prayed and asked God what I should do to help you. And this is what I came up with."

"You see? You just admitted that you came up with the idea." She was incredulous.

He ran one hand roughly through his hair. "Yeah, but I felt it was an idea from God."

Emily reached over and once again placed her hand over Jordan's. Shaking her head, she explained that if it were an answer from God, they would both be in agreement. Since she did not feel the calling, it definitely wasn't of God. She took the time to explain how both should be in agreement if the proposal had been a sign from heaven. Because she wasn't in concurrence with the idea, it couldn't be God sent. It took some convincing, but eventually she got through to him.

A few days later he called to apologize. He realized she was right. Emily had said they would one day laugh at the situation. He hoped so because he felt like a complete idiot.

Chapter 5

As the emcee entered the stage, Emily was surprised to see that he wasn't at all what she had envisioned as the channel 89.1 radio station announcer. He was short, overweight, and balding. His melodic baritone voice didn't fit his image. He stood there in black slacks with a white button-down oxford shirt. His red tie was crooked on his oversized belly.

He positioned the microphone close to his mouth. "Ladies and gentlemen…" With his free hand, he reached for his tie and straightened it. "I'm David Hennesy, morning announcer for channel 89.1, WFTH FM, the 'faith' channel." The crowd erupted in applause. He quickly announced to the audience the show was to be a televised performance broadcasted live to millions of people around the country. Their encouragement to the performers would yield an action-packed concert. The audience supported his pronouncement with whistles and applauses.

The first group was announced as Brothers for Christ. They were four Christian men with a zest for music and God. Dressed in jeans and black shirts, the men entertained them with upbeat music. The audience stood to their feet and clapped to the rhythm.

Immediately Emily noticed the handsome, broad-chested singer. His black hair shimmered in the lights as his bright-blue eyes expressed his love for God and the music. She was mesmerized. She found it difficult to keep her eyes off him.

After their first set, they introduced themselves.

"Hello, Faith listeners!" One of the singers waved his free hand to the crowd as he waited for the applause to subside. "Wow!" He laughed. "You are awesome!" A round of laughter and cheers erupted in the auditorium.

"Although our group name is Brothers for Christ, it doesn't mean we are related. In fact, we aren't!" Laughter resounded throughout the room. He continued. "But we have been singing together for about two years now—"

"Two years, three months, one day, seven hours and...twenty-three minutes," interrupted the man by whom Emily was captivated, the one who appeared to be the eldest of the four. Everyone burst into laughter, including the four singers.

"Okay, well, now that Seth has broken it down into milliseconds..." the first man spoke again.

"No, actually. But I could if you want!" The crowd enjoyed the bantering between the two men.

He waited for the audience to quiet down again. "I know you could, Seth, but let's just leave it at two years, three months for now."

Seth, obviously enjoying the amusement, continued, "Are you sure? I mean it wouldn't take me long..." More laughter exploded.

The man raised his hand as if to stop him, "Um, no. Thanks anyway, Seth."

"It's not a problem, really."

"Seth! I'm trying to introduce the group. Do you mind?"

"No, not at all." Seth reached out his hand toward the guy on his right. "To my right is Logan." Moving to center stage, he motioned to the guy farther out. "Next to him is Zack, and standing over there"—he pointed with his thumb to the one on his left—"with his jaw on the floor, is Heath!" Walking over to Heath, he put a finger under Heath's chin and pushed his mouth closed. The audience roared in laughter as he continued with the introductions. "And, as you know by now, I'm Seth."

Barely maintaining self-control, Heath tried to act aggravated and said, "I said I was going to introduce them!" He placed his hand on his chest.

"Oh, you asked if I minded, so, obviously I thought that you meant you wanted me to do the introductions!" Seth stood there looking as innocent as a boy with his hand caught in the cookie jar. Unable to keep his composure any longer, Heath allowed Seth to take control, something Seth seemed to do with natural ease.

As the audience quieted down, Seth began again. "In all earnestness, as you can see, we are just four guys trying to use our talent for the Lord. We've been touring in our local churches in Fayetteville, North Carolina, and were invited to perform here tonight, for you." He pointed toward the audience. They applauded in approval. "Thank you. It's great to know that we have provided you with entertainment you have enjoyed." As the people stood to their feet to show their appreciation, Seth resumed his speech. He moved to the edge of the stage to look into the eyes of the people standing in ovation. As they began to seat themselves, a figure caught his eye. He leaned forward to get a better view.

It was as if no one else was in the room but her. He could not believe his eyes. She was there. Fifth row, center. She sat just inside the range of lights so that he could only get a faint view of her lovely face. But he knew it was her. She had the dark hair, and although he couldn't see her facial features that clearly, his heart told him it was her. *It's her. I knew I'd meet her, just didn't think it would be here while I'm on stage and her in the audience. God, she is lovely. I know You have brought her here for a reason. Just please, please let us meet tonight. I've got to meet her.*

He didn't know how long he stood there, but a hand on his shoulder brought him back to reality and the task at hand. He picked up on his part of the prepared script on introductions. He just had to keep focused on the audience and avoid looking in the direction of the woman who stepped out of his dreams and into reality.

Heath, confused at his friend's sudden loss for words, took over. "We appreciate your positive reception"—he walked over to Seth and placed a hand on his shoulder, hoping to bring the man back to earth from wherever he had gone—"and hope that we can return for the next Concert for Christ!" More approval rang throughout the theater.

At the touch of Heath's hand, Seth was able to carry on. "What God has placed in our hearts is a love for people who don't know Christ..."

Logan stepped forward and, imitating Heath, placed a hand on Seth's other shoulder. "To lead them to Him through whatever means. If God can utilize our voices-"

"And our music," continued Zack as he walked up to Logan and repeated the gesture by placing his free hand on Logan's shoulder, "to increase His kingdom, then we know that our talents are being used for His glory."

All three men shook their heads in agreement as they turned toward Zack. Seth lowered his head in prayer before speaking again.

Emily noticed that this stature of a man was humbled by his love of God. *Oh, to meet someone half as handsome as Seth who loved the Lord as much as he appears to.* She shook her head to command the thoughts to leave. How could she be thinking such thoughts? *Hormones. It must be the hormones.* She shifted in her seat to ease the continuous lower back pain and then focused on the finelooking man who had caught her eye and made her heart skip a beat when it appeared he looked straight at her. *One day, Lord, I hope to have a husband and more children with a man who loves me. One who puts You first, above all.*

Zack's voice broke into her thoughts. "No matter how we sound or how much we sing, only if we dedicate ourselves and our songs to the glory of God can He achieve His desires for your hearts. 'Seek ye first the kingdom of God...'"

"That's right, Zack," Logan remarked. "Our voices are just instruments to be used by God. As long as He is the center of our lives, we will succeed for His kingdom." He paused momentarily and then walked along the length of the stage. "If there is anyone of you out there tonight who does not know the Lord as your Savior, we invite you to pray this simple prayer with us…"

Heath stepped forward. "Everyone, please bow your heads and repeat after me." The audience reverently obeyed. "Our heavenly Father. I come to You today as a sinner, asking You to forgive all my transgressions. Come into my heart and make me new. I love You, Lord. Thank You for giving your life for me. Amen." After the prayer, the group sang one last song.

Emily sat there, focusing on one man. Seth sang with a fervor that spoke to her heart. It was as if he sang to her alone, as if some invisible bond had connected them. Each time he looked her way, her heart soared and her stomach reeled with excitement.

Chapter 6

That evening, Mary sat on her settee at the foot of her bed and tried to feel the lump on her right breast, to no avail. Ever since her best friend, Pam, had been diagnosed with breast cancer the year before, she performed self-examinations on a monthly basis. Well, not diligently, but at least every six to eight weeks. That was more than most of her friends could say.

She'd had her mammogram earlier in the week. After the initial x-ray, she was asked to wait outside of the room while the radiologist reviewed the pictures to verify they were satisfactory. When she was called back in to take a second set of x-rays, she began to question why. At the end of the second session, the radiologist walked into the room to confirm his original findings.

He stepped behind the screen. "Mrs. Woods." The tall, lean man motioned for her to come behind the protective booth and pointed to a small dot on the screen. "Do you see that?"

She caught a faint whiff of his cologne and smiled. It was the same cologne her husband wore.

Mary shook her head in wonder. Straining her eyes, she gazed at the picture on the screen. "Um, yes," she said timidly, uncertain as to what she was looking at exactly. It appeared to be a small blemish on the film.

"I hate to alarm you, but it's a lump in your right breast," he said matter-of-factly.

Mary's eyes grew large with fear.

"You'll need to see your doctor right away. I suggest you call her the moment you get home. I'll have the results faxed over to her office immediately."

"W-why?"

He continued as if Mary hadn't said a word. "I apologize for causing you to endure the machine a second time, but the lump had appeared on the first set of films, and I wanted to be certain it wasn't a damaged film, which is why I ordered a second set of x-rays."

"Was it in the second set of films?" Mary's voice began quivering.

"The second set is identical to the originals taken."

Mary placed her hand against her chest and gasped.

"I compared this year's films to last year's. The lump wasn't there at your last mammogram. My concern is that if you wait to see your physician, it will spread."

Tears sprang to her eyes. Mary sniffed. The doctor reached over to retrieve a tissue from the table beside him. He handed it to Mary. As she wiped away the flowing tears, the doctor continued.

"I'll leave you now. You may get dressed. On your way out, pick up a digital copy of the mammograms at the front desk. Your doctor will want to see them." He placed his hand on her shoulder and then turned and walked out of the room.

Just like that her life turned upside down. In the small dressing room, she stood at the door wondering what the doctor had said. She tried to recall the words he had spoken so succinctly as she slipped her top over her head. The word *cancer* had played over and over in her head so much so that it appeared to be all she heard. As she donned her lightweight sweater, it came to her. "Call your doctor." That was what he'd said.

After procuring the disc at the front desk, she walked out to her vehicle. The rain pelted her car where she sat, dumbfounded. The words rang in her ears again. She must call her doctor. With trembling fingers, she looked up the number in the contacts section of her cell phone and then pressed send. She dared not wait until she arrived home for fear someone in her family might overhear. For now, she wanted to keep the news to herself, just in case there might be some mistake. As she waited on the line for the nurse to answer, fear began to seep in.

What if she lost her breasts? She recalled how rigorous the treatments were on Pam. Would she be able to withstand the chemotherapy? She reached up to touch her long, silky black hair. She recalled what Pam had gone through during her battle with breast cancer. She'd lost her hair shortly after her chemotherapy treatments commenced. Would she be like Pam and lose her hair, too? Would she suffer the same ill effects? Could she be as strong as her best friend had been during her entire ordeal?

The nurse came online and interrupted her musings. "Hello, Mrs. Woods, this is Louise, Dr. Nelson's nurse. How can I be of assistance to you?"

The sound of the rain pelting her vehicle drummed in her head. "Um...I just had my mammogram this morning, and there seems to be a problem." Her voice was quivering as she spoke. She tried to swallow the lump in her throat. Her mouth went dry.

There was a slight pause as the nurse waited for her to continue. When she didn't, Louise did. "Yes, as a matter of fact, the fax came in just a few minutes ago. Are you calling to make an appointment?"

"Yes...yes, I am." Mary took a deep breath and released it slowly. She fought back the tears threatening to come.

She heard Louise tapping on the computer keys. "Doctor Nelson will want to see you right away. It looks as if we're going to have to fit you on Friday. Can you be here just before we close in the afternoon? Say...four thirty?"

Mary didn't hesitate. "Yes. I'll be there."

"Okay. We'll see you Friday at four thirty then." A moment passed, and then Mary heard Louise say, "Is there anything I can do for you now, Mary?"

She released an audible sigh. "Only if you can take away my anxiety." She tried to sound like she was joking, but it came out as a desperate cry.

"Mary, just remember where your strength comes from. But if you need something to help you relax, I can call in a prescription for you."

Mary thought it over. "No. I think I'll be okay for now. Thanks."

"Rest easy, okay?"

Easier said than done, she thought. "I will. See you Friday afternoon." Friday couldn't come soon enough. How would she endure an entire two days with the uncertainty? Would Chris perceive she was not telling him something? She determined she would just have to do a good job hiding the truth from him and her children.

It was early Thursday morning and she needed to get breakfast ready for her guests. It was part of her bed and breakfast business. Each morning she would make something unique so that her guests, as well as her family, would not get bored with the menu.

This morning it would be fresh cinnamon rolls, eggs, bacon, toast, and fresh-squeezed orange juice. The guests always loved her breakfasts, which was one of the reasons why she had a thriving B&B. That, and her knack for hospitality. Every one of her guests was so warmly welcomed they felt as if they were in their own homes.

It had been a successful business venture. Never mind the difficulty of raising children in a home filled with strangers on a regular basis. As it turned out, many of her guests were repeat customers. Since the military installations were close by, quite a few of her visitors were military or government workers moving to the area. They tended to stay for several nights as they looked for a new home or were on their way out after selling their houses. Some of her guests were on their way to various destinations for vacation. But what kept the B&B going were the military and government employees. It worked for them and gave her some extra money to help her children through college.

Not that the ranch didn't prove to be profitable. It had always been lucrative. Having a stud ranch with the most prestigious bloodlines was key to its success.

Yet the children had needed the extra cash during their college years, just a little something to allow them to focus on their studies instead of working part time to pay for their books or gas for the occasional trips home.

Of course, Seth was the exception. He didn't want to attend graduate school, so she no longer had to assist him. He had a gift—an exceptional gift that he used for the glory of God and entertainment for others. Mary knew he would be famous one day. That day was coming soon; she felt it in her soul.

A man by the name of Cameron had heard Seth and his band at one of the local churches and invited them to join him and several other groups in a benefit concert in northern Virginia.

Seth, her eldest son, was the one who most resembled her with black hair, blue eyes, and dark skin. The Native American resemblance was incredible, with exception of his blue eyes. His grandfather called him his "Black Beauty" since his skin tone was dark, even as a baby. Growing up on the ranch allowed him time in the sun, which only darkened his reddish-brown skin even more. Working with the horses all of his life left him with a rough and rugged body that all the local girls swooned over.

His good looks combined with his strong build won him "Best Looking," "Most Likely to Succeed," and "Homecoming King" his senior year of high school. No one was more surprised than she when he decided not to continue his education any further than college.

Although his undergrad major was science with a minor in music, he pursued a career in singing. It was difficult, financially, but he somehow saved enough money to purchase a beautiful sports car earlier in the year. He didn't want payments, so he waited until he had the full amount set aside; then he went to the dealership, made an exceptional deal, and paid them in cash.

Her Seth. She was so proud of him, as she was all her children, but Seth was her firstborn—and her friend. She knew he, as well as her entire family, would be disappointed if she didn't follow through with the doctor's appointment. But she couldn't find the lump no matter how much she pressed and prodded. She felt the x-ray must have had a defect if she couldn't feel the protuberance.

That night she prayed. Diligently.

On Friday at four thirty sharp, she walked through the doors of the women's clinic. It was on the second floor of a prestigious building. The double doors opened to a spacious waiting room. It housed several cherry stained Queen Ann style chairs and two identical burgundy sofas. She sat in the sofa closest to the door. To help pass the time, she thought she'd read a magazine. She'd read the same paragraph three times and still couldn't recall what it was about. She just couldn't concentrate.

Breast cancer.

She had a lump in her breast, and she was there to see the doctor following a routine mammogram that turned out to be anything but routine.

Chapter 7

"Man, what got into you back there?" Heath tilted his head back toward the stage area. He had never known Seth to lose his place in the rehearsed script. The man had something of a photogenic memory when it came to reading. He could recall anything and everything he'd ever read. That's why he excelled in college. It was a surprise to everyone when he announced he wanted to sing and perform rather than attend graduate school.

Running his hand across his forehead, he shook his head. "I just lost my place, that's all." Knowing Heath wouldn't believe him but needing a minute to gather his wits, he paused before continuing. "It's just that"—he took in a deep breath and exhaled slowly before divulging any more information lest he appear to be out of his mind—"I saw the girl in the audience. Ya know?"

Heath was incredulous. "You mean a girl, right?"

"No, I mean *the* girl." She had been sitting right there in front of him with her ivory skin and long, dark tresses so silky it made him want to reach out and touch them.

"Girl? Man, there are hundreds, maybe a thousand girls in the audience." Heath threw his hands out to the side. With a shrug, he asked, "What are you talking about? What girl?"

At the risk of sounding foolish, Seth wondered if he should continue. Heath was his best friend. He knew eventually he would have to relent as Heath would persist in his inquisition. Rather than chance it, he tilted his head in the direction of the dressing area. Pausing momentarily at the door, he looked around to verify they weren't being followed before opening the door for Heath to pass through.

In the makeshift dressing room, Seth closed the door behind him and then sat in the chair farthest from the door to avoid being overheard.

Sitting across from Seth, Heath, tired of the deliberate caution, huffed a sigh. "Okay, so what are you talking about, Seth?"

Seth paused to consider what he would say. It was difficult enough to believe, he admitted, but it was so true. His mom always knew what she was talking about, and this was no exception.

That's where he would begin, with his mom and her prophesies. "You know how my mom always told us to pray for our future brides?"

"Yeah...?

Seth took a long moment before continuing, uncertain he should convey his feelings to Heath. In the end, he reluctantly announced that when he was just fifteen he began having dreams of a beautiful girl. Heath called it puberty, yet Seth continued.

"There is this girl with dark hair and eyes as blue as the sky on a rainy day."

"Can the sky be blue on a rainy day?"

Seth rolled his eyes and continued. "You know, the color of storm clouds just before the sky turns dark."

"You mean gray?"

"Never mind. Just forget it." He waved his hands in the air. "I don't know why I even thought I could confide this in you anyway." Seth stood to leave the room.

Heath rose to his feet and took hold of Seth's arm as he passed by. "Man, I was just messin' with you. I'm sorry. Please, sit down and tell me about this girl with the stormy eyes." Heath released his arm when he saw the fight leave Seth's eyes.

"This woman...she's beautiful. With long, dark, wavy hair." His expression was one of confusion. "All I remember about her face are her eyes. They're the oddest shade of blue...no not blue, but smoky blue."

He ran his fingers through his hair. "In the dream she has a child in her arms. I feel this strange attachment to her baby. It's as if it's my own child." It was then he announced, "The girl in my dreams"—he let out an audible sigh—"well, she's here."

"Here? As in here…you mean here, in this building?" Heath pointed toward the floor.

"Yep. In the audience." Seth nodded his head and pointed toward the auditorium.

Heath was incredulous. "Where in the audience? How could you have seen her with all the lights in your face?"

It was then he explained how she was just inside of the range of lights—fifth row, center seat.

"So you saw this mystery girl just inside the lights, and it caused you to drop your jaw, so to speak?"

"Why else do you think I lost my place in the script? Senility?"

Heath couldn't believe what he was hearing. How could he truly see this indistinctive woman and know she was his soul mate? "So you saw this anonymous woman just inside the lights?"

Seth nodded his head. "Just look during the finale. You'll see her. I swear."

Heath could hardly wait to see this girl. Was she truly the one for his best friend?

The final song to be performed was as an assembly of all the performing artists. The lead singers were the four Brothers in Christ. Seth found it difficult to keep up with the choreographed steps that took him away from the line of sight of "his girl."

Heath was surprised that he could see the woman yet not be able to distinguish the delicate features of her face. *How can he be so sure this is the woman of his dreams when her face is barely visible? What if her eyes are brown instead of blue? What if they are blue but not "smoky blue" as Seth so vehemently described. Oh, Lord of heaven, please don't let Seth fall for the wrong one.*

After the concert, there was to be an autograph session with the performers in the main lobby. As the audience began filling the entrance hall, Seth scanned their faces hoping to catch a glimpse of the woman of his dreams. But autographs must be signed and pictures taken with their new fans. The selling of their compact discs—though not professionally recorded—pictures, and various paraphernalia was taking place in the front of the building by volunteers from the church sponsors. He saw so many of their CDs pass by that he prayed they would sell out. Time flew by and yet stood still with no sign of her. Of course, there was a long line that rounded the corner. His prayers were that she would be somewhere beyond the bend. *Please, Dear Lord, let her be there. I've just got to meet her.*

Chapter 8

"Hey, Emily, are you as hungry as I am?" Kate asked in the restroom after the concert. She began brushing her hair and reapplying her makeup.

"Actually, I'm really not hungry at all." Emily stood at the sink washing her hands. Standing to a full upright position, she reached for a paper towel when pain shot through her back and blasted around to her abdomen. Unable to conceal her pain, she bent over, holding the edge of the counter.

"Emily? Are you all right? Is it the baby? Please tell me it's not the baby or I'll just freak!" Kate asked anxiously.

Taking a deep breath and blowing it out slowly until the pain subsided, Emily glanced over to Kate and assured her it was false labor pains. She began rubbing her protruding belly with one hand and her lower back with the other. "It's nothing, really. No need for alarm." Emily tried to reassure her friend as well as herself.

"Some of the others from church are going out to eat. Don't you want to come?" Kate knew it was pushing Emily, but she wanted her friend to join in on the fun. She had missed out on so much since the pregnancy. Kate wanted her to continue to enjoy the night.

Avoiding more questioning, Emily admitted she had a good time and was glad she came. All she wanted to do now was to go back home and get in bed. Her back was aching, and her feet were swollen. "No. Thanks anyway. I think I'll just go home and call it a night."

"Come on! Let's make this night go on a while longer." Kate grabbed Emily's hand and opened the door. "Let's go see if the guys are up for a late dinner and dessert. I would love one of Cassidy's hot fudge brownie explosions." Kate had a weakness for chocolate. The hot fudge brownie topped with ice cream drenched in hot fudge was—as far as Kate was concerned—the absolute best in the state.

"I really don't feel up to it, but you guys can go. I'll catch a ride with some of the others from church. I saw a few of the young married class members during intermission. I'm sure someone would give me a ride home."

"You know, I saw Lydia from that class just before heading into the ladies' room. She mentioned that she would like to go to Cassidy's. I'm sure that you could switch places and ride home with her group since they aren't going out. I think she rode with the Smiths." Kate's eyebrows lifted as she made the comment.

"What about her husband? Didn't he come?" Emily asked as she walked through the open doorway into the corridor.

"No. She said Brendan was called into work at the last minute. It must be difficult being an intern. I'm sure they'll be glad when he finishes and opens his own practice. I wonder if he'll be as busy then as he is now though."

Looking around at the crowded hallway, Emily wondered if they would be able to even find the young woman. "Do you think you can find Lydia in this crowd?"

"Yeah, she said she would be at the autograph session. Let's just get in line and wait to see if she finds us."

The two found their way to the end of the autograph line that looped around the hallway on both sides. They saw Lydia across the way. Kate waved her hand above her head to get Lydia's attention. Once she was within hearing range, Kate asked, "Do you still want to go to Cassidy's?"

"You betcha. Brendan will be at the hospital all night, so I'm in no hurry to go home to an empty house," the young woman with curly blond hair declared as she drew closer to the women.

"Bummer," Kate replied.

"Yeah, but only ten more months remaining and we'll be setting up practice! I can see light at the end of the tunnel!"

Lydia's infectious smile spread across her face. "Thank God for small miracles!"

"Do you think Emily can ride in your place and return with your group?" Kate asked.

"You mean the Smiths? Sure." Lydia turned to Emily. "Don't you want to go?"

Emily shook her head. "I'd rather just get home." She had reached around and was rubbing the small of her back with the ball of her fist. "Do you think they'd mind us trading places?"

"Well, I'm sure you can take my place in the Smith's van. They parked on the south side of the building, under the first parking light in the first row." She pointed toward the south. Emily nodded.

"Carter and Lisa Smith are waiting for everyone to get autographs, so you don't have to hurry. As soon as I see someone from our group, I'll let them know we switched places and you are waiting in line for autographs." She turned to Kate. "Where are you parked?"

"Oh, um, we parked in back of the building. Just to the left of the doors as you exit. We rode with Jordan. Have you seen his new wheels?"

"No! You mean he finally put the rust pile to rest?"

"Yep."

"It's about time. What kind of car is it?"

"It's not a car but a black crew cab truck. You can't miss it. It's double-parked on the last row!" Kate laughed. "I thought they would call him out to move it since the parking lot was so full. Come on out whenever you are ready to go. I'll let Jordan know that you are riding with us."

"Great. I'll see you out there." Lydia returned to her spot in the line. She hoped she would find someone in her group before they left.

Lydia ran into several of her friends from work and took time to talk with them. She was unable to find anyone from her ride;

instead, she asked one of the young girls from church to pass on the message when she got out to her car that was parked next to the Smiths' van. With that little task handled, she continued to mingle and talk. When she saw Kate enter the room to get her autographs, she made her way out to Jordan's new truck.

Chapter 9

As she and Kate entered the autograph room, Emily realized she had no concert memorabilia. "Kate, I have nothing for them to sign."

Flashing her program, Kate said, "Just have them sign your program. That's what I'm going to do."

"I can't."

"Why not?"

"Because I didn't get one."

"Oh. Well, they have a booth set up in the lobby with T-shirts and paraphernalia. Do you want me to get you something?" Kate could see her friend was not feeling well. Emily's face had grown pale, and she kept a hand on her back at all times, massaging it constantly.

Emily considered the options. She knew that Jordan had a short fuse when it came to patience, and he'd already been waiting for Kate more than an hour. "Hmm. Tell you what," she said as she dug her fist into her lower back, "I'll go and get something myself. You know how impatient Jordan can be and since Lydia said that Carter and Lisa were waiting for everyone to get autographs. I have more time than you." She rolled her eyes toward the lobby. "I'll just go over, get something, and then get back in line. If you're still here when I return, I'll jump in with you. Does that sound like a deal?"

Nodding, Kate whispered, "I hate to be the cause of Jordan's temper flaring. Thanks, Em." She gave Emily an appreciative hug.

Emily waddled over to the row of booths set up by each performing group. Nothing really appealed to her, so she decided to look for the Brothers for Christ stand. A large crowd gathered at the opposite side of the lobby. Curiously she walked over. Somewhere, through the crowd, she saw a little table with a small selection of T-shirts and compact discs. Unable to get the last few CDs before they were snatched up by the kids in front of her, one particular T-shirt caught her attention. *That's it! That's exactly what I want them to sign.* It was a tan shirt with a photograph of the four men. Seth's jovial face stood out among the group. It was the last shirt, so she quickly laid claim to it. Although a bit large, she figured she could wear it through the remaining weeks of her pregnancy and sleep in it after the baby was born. Pushing her way through to the front of the table, she grabbed the shirt and waited her turn to pay.

Ten minutes later, she stepped away from the table carrying her treasure. Before joining Kate again, she decided to make another stop in the ladies' room.

Eventually, the line dwindled down to where Seth could see a small group of people lurking somewhere beyond the end of the line. Seth's heart sank as he realized the mystery woman was not among them.

Emily withdrew from the ladies' room yet again. Her back had been aching so severely that she thought at times she would throw up, thinking all along that if she had not purchased the shirt, she would just leave. The pain never went away, at least not long enough to make a difference. She walked to the back of the line, passing a group of young people on her way.

The small group joined Emily at the rear of the assembly.

One of the girls introduced herself. "Hi. I'm Diane." The young girl stretched out her hand.

She took her hand and smiled tentatively. "Emily."

"My husband is over there." She thumbed toward the chair where the newly wedded young man sat patiently awaiting his bride. "We just found out I'm pregnant." She beamed a smile that brightened her face. "I'm due at the end of April." Her eyes widened. "When are you due?" Without waiting for a reply, she asked, "Is it a boy or a girl?"

Diane continued, "I don't know if we'll find out the gender or not." She lowered her voice slightly. "But I'm secretly hoping it's a girl. Of course"—she thumbed back toward her groom again—"he wants a boy." She rolled her eyes. "You know how men are."

Emily nodded although she didn't actually know.

She had barely dated in high school, and in college she was far too busy for anything serious. The conception of her baby was an end to a very bad situation, and she hated to even think about it.

Brought back from her thoughts by the endless questions from the young lady, Emily simply told her she was having a girl and that she knew the baby would be perfect because babies were a gift from God.

"I feel the same. But God forbid if the baby is mentally challenged or something awful like that." Diane's lips twisted in disgust. "I just don't think I could handle that."

"You'd be surprised at what you can handle. Once you see your baby, the love will overcome every obstacle."

Diane thought Emily was so wise with what she had said.

The baby started kicking. Emily instinctively rubbed her belly. The young girl asked if she could feel the movements. The group of girls suddenly surrounded her, each wanting a turn. Happily, she consented. This was the part of her pregnancy that she truly adored. Knowing she carried a life within her body, the miracle of it all still awed her.

Seth continued signing T-shirts and CDs, allowing his busyness to overshadow his desire to meet her. Determined not to look up beyond the fan in front of him, he didn't even glance toward the end of the line for some time. When he finally got the chance to search for her again, he saw a young woman with her back toward him. She was surrounded by a small group of people. When the young woman turned slightly, he could see she was great with child. The girls were each taking a turn feeling the baby move within its confined limits.

He couldn't take his eyes off of the mother-to-be. He felt inexplicably drawn to the woman in the small crowd. Then she turned. Wisps of long dark hair framed her delicate, porcelain skin and eyes of smoky blue. She instantly caught him staring at her. Their eyes met, and neither one moved a muscle. They were immediately united in that one moment in time.

Disappointment hit him like a freight train. He couldn't believe God would allow the woman of his dreams to be spoiled. He wanted a woman who had waited for him. Not someone who had given herself to another man.

Unaware she was holding her breath, Emily felt a sudden move in her belly. Jolted back to the reality of her helpless situation, she looked away, ashamed. How could God bring any man into her life now? How would any man be interested in her once he found out the dirty truth?

Chapter 10

Emily reticently smiled and timidly turned her eyes downward. *God, help me! I can't stop staring at him.* She took a deep breath and moved forward. The electricity between the two of them was as strong as an ocean current pulling her adrift. As she finally arrived within conversation distance, a disappointed Seth asked her if she enjoyed the show.

Surprised at the veracity of this tall, dark, and handsome man, she stammered, "Y…yes! It was awesome! You guys are truly blessed." She watched as he signed the compact disc Diane gave him. He wrote his name with an elegance she had rarely seen in a man's handwriting.

Since Seth rarely initiated conversation with fans, Heath looked up from his enthusiast to see with whom Seth was conversing. There she stood. But she was pregnant. *This couldn't be the girl Seth was talking about.*

He had to admit Seth was right. *She is beautiful and simply glows. Must be the pregnancy.* Heath had heard that pregnant women had a glow about them, but her glow had come from within. Only a true Christian carried that kind of radiance.

Her face seemed to reflect the love of God. It was true what Seth had said; she was obviously a Christian, but there was something else, something more. His eyes wandered down to her left hand…no ring. *Hmm, could be a good sign. But why would Seth want to marry an unwed mother? Would God really have this in store for my friend? Is this the baby in Seth's childhood dreams?*

"Excuse me, but would you mind?" The adoring fan in front of him waved a camera, hoping to get a picture with Heath.

"Sure." He posed as she sat on the table and handed the camera off to her friend. Heath stood and put his arm around the girl. The picture was taken, and the girl moved on to the next artist.

Emily stepped up to the table. Logan and Zack spoke casually as they signed their image on the shirt she handed them. When she reached Seth, his eyes darkened and his face became flushed.

"Are you all right?" Emily reached over and touched his hand.

There was fire in her touch. He instantly jerked his hand from underneath hers, but the warmth remained. He realized she must be embarrassed and began to apologize. "I'm sorry. You just startled me." He reached his hand out to invite hers again.

"My name is Seth. Seth Woods."

Emily placed her hand in his. "It's a pleasure to meet you."

Trying to gather his wits about him, he turned to the task at hand and poised his pen over the shirt. "So what's your name?"

Still distracted by the chemistry she felt with the mere touch of his skin to hers, she didn't respond immediately. Waiting for her response, Seth reached out to touch her hand again. The touch sent shivers through her body.

Startled, Emily shook her head. "Oh, I'm sorry. My name? Duh." She rolled her eyes. "Emily. Emily Wilkerson."

Seth bent his head to autograph her T-shirt. He noticed she wore no ring and didn't even have a tan line where one might have been. He thought she might be wearing it on a chain around her neck but saw none. Not that it mattered. Of course, she could be widowed, but not likely. *Lots of young ladies are having children without being married these days, but she just doesn't look the type. But, what does that type look like? Come on, Seth. Get over it...just sign the shirt and let her move on. She's not the girl for you.*

No matter how hard he tried, he couldn't let it go. When he turned his attention back to the T-shirt, he found himself making a special effort to check her right hand. *Maybe she doesn't believe in wearing jewelry.* On her right ring finger she wore a college ring. This negated the thought of her being part of a religion that didn't believe in jewelry.

He autographed his picture on the shirt; then, without knowing why, he included 1 Peter 5:7. He made a mental note to look up the scripture when he returned home.

Not wanting to seem aloof, he attempted a conversation with Emily. "So do you live in the area?" He passed the shirt to Heath and looked into her blue eyes.

"No, actually. I live on a lake about an hour's drive northwest of here. Give or take a few." She couldn't look in his eyes without feeling as though he could read her mind.

"So you live near a lake?"

"Actually, it's in my back yard."

He was surprised that she would live on a lake and not have bronzed skin.

"Really? That close? I wouldn't have guessed." He smiled gently not wanting to reveal his curiosity.

She slowly ran her hand across her abdomen. She looked down at her feet and hands, pale in comparison to most of the inhabitants of Ashburn. She began to blush slightly.

"Oh, you're referring to my lack of a tan, aren't you?" She chuckled slightly.

"Was it that obvious?" His eyes widened in question.

"Well, kind of. It's not good to be out in the sun when you are as large as I am. Someone might mistake you for a beached whale and toss you back into the water."

Seth had to laugh at her jesting. It was good that she had a sense of humor, but he sensed that she was not quite comfortable with her condition.

"When are you due?" Heath asked. There was no one left in line except Emily. In short time, the T-shirt had been passed more than halfway down the stretch of tables.

She turned toward Heath, "Oh, umm, the end of October. I still have a way to go yet."

Seth was surprised that she was due so soon. Comparing her to his memories of his mother when she was pregnant with each of his siblings, this young lady was only half his mom's size. But then, his mother had already given birth to twin boys, and he was still young when his siblings came along. Everything tended to look bigger to little eyes.

"You must be excited," Heath commented.

"Actually, I'm a little apprehensive. I mean, I've never had a baby before. It's a little frightening," Emily confessed. "Though, I know God is in control, as long as I leave it in His hands, everything will be all right. But I'm still nervous."

"You can't go wrong with that frame of mind," Logan included. He initiated the first move to leave by standing. The others followed suit.

Seth stood. "We'll keep you and the baby in our prayers. Do you have someone waiting for you out there?" He nodded his head toward the front doors.

"Yes. I imagine they are waiting rather impatiently now that I have taken more than my fair share of time. Thank you for your concerns and prayers. I appreciate it. One can never have too many prayers go up on one's behalf." Emily looked down to the end of the tables, and there was her T-shirt, signed and neatly folded, waiting for her to take it home. She gathered her shirt and turned to leave the room.

Looking back, she offered good night wishes to everyone and thanked them for a great evening. With a wave, she turned and stepped out of the room.

Chapter 11

When Emily walked out of the concert hall, the humidity took her breath away. It took every bit of energy she had to inhale. She looked around; the parking lots were empty. Slowly she walked around the right of the building, hoping that the Smiths' van would be somewhere…anywhere. Nothing. Then she walked around the left of the structure. Nothing. She wondered what could have happened. The Smiths would never intentionally leave her.

She checked her cell phone. No charge. *Oh God, what am I to do now?* She couldn't call a cab or Kate. And with the increased pains she was experiencing, she couldn't even call 911.

She remembered there were pay phones inside near the restrooms. Once she reached the front of the building again, she pulled on the doors. Locked. *How am I supposed to call anyone?*

She looked around. The area was full of restaurants and fast-food joints, but it appeared too far to walk in her condition.

But walk it she must. Just as she resigned herself to hike the distance to the McDonald's across the street, the cramping began again. This time the intensity was more so than the last. Reaching her hands down to her belly, she bent over as each agonizing throb seared through her body. The spell didn't last long but felt like an eternity. She had to get to a phone. She was in no shape to walk anywhere. All she wanted was her own bed and the soothing voice of Gram.

She knocked on the doors. No answer. Again she knocked. No answer. Out of sheer desperation, she pounded on the thick wooden doors that separated her from the interior of the structure. *This time someone has to hear me.* Still, there was no answer. She turned her back to the doors and leaned her aching body against them.

Another contraction. She lowered herself to the threshold. *This can't be false labor. This is just too intense. I've got to get inside and find a phone!* The pain was just as severe with this contraction, as was the last, yet it felt as if length was increasing. *Breathe, Emily, breathe. Okay, get yourself together. There were cars and buses around the back. Maybe someone will still be there by the time you get around there. Hurry, Emily. Get up and get to the rear of the building. God! Please give me strength. Take away the pain. Just let me get home!*

Just as she gathered herself up from the doorstep, she heard the faint sound of vehicle engines sputter to life. She began to panic. If they left without seeing her, she would be there without hope of ever getting to a phone. She heard the sound of an engine coming closer. She stepped out into the illuminated opening toward the entrance gate. *God, please let them leave through this gate and not another. I really need you to guide them to me.*

Just as she finished her prayer, she saw the headlights of a large vehicle coming toward her. *A bus! It's a bus! Oh God, please let them see me!* She waived her arms and began yelling, "Here! I'm over here! Please stop!"

Emily breathed a sigh of relief as she saw the bus pull to a halt. She carefully approached the window on the driver's side of the vehicle.

Red slid open the glass. "You need some help, ma'am?"

Relieved at his pleasant demeanor, she informed them of her peculiar situation. "Oh, yes, please. I have no way to get home and no way of calling for a cab. I saw a pay phone inside. Do you know how I can get into the building and make a call? I won't be any trouble, really." Emily's eyes pleaded with them.

Red looked up to his boss who was leaning over him, one hand on the driver's seat the other on the steering wheel. "What'd'ya think? Sounds pretty horrible to be out there alone in her situation." Red's thick southern drawl comforted Emily.

"I don't know, Red. We have no key, and the curator left before we did."

"Well, you and I got phones she could use."

"Yeah, sure." Cameron looked through the window at the pregnant woman. "You can use my cell phone. Come on around, and we'll let you inside."

Emily's eyes lit with relief. "Oh! Thank you so much. I'll pay you for your trouble."

"No need," he said as he motioned for her to enter the bus. He watched her slowly cross in front of the vehicle to enter through the doorway.

He handed her his cell phone and explained they would give her a ride home, but it was in the opposite direction. "I've got another show in North Carolina at noon tomorrow. Got to get my beauty sleep, ya know."

"Of course." Emily had not expected him to give her a ride home. The phone would allow her the means to contact Gram and have her call a taxi to come get her in a relatively short time. Not wanting to alarm Gram, she didn't mention her labor pains.

She finished her call and handed him the phone. "Thank you so very much. You are a life saver! Literally!" She rubbed the small of her back, attempting to ward off another contraction. She managed to get through the contraction without alarming the men of her agony.

Cameron reached to retrieve the phone from her small hand. "I'll leave it with you, and you can just mail it to me later if you'd like."

"Although it's been a blessing to have the opportunity to call my gram for help, I think I'll pass on your offer. Besides, you'll need it for your time on the road." Cameron took the phone and set it in its cradle on his belt.

She told them she would wait under the lamppost so they could get on their way. Just as she turned to exit the bus, another contraction hit her…hard. She doubled over in pain.

"Hold on there, little lady." Cameron reached out and grabbed her by the arm. "Now wait one minute."

Emily turned to face this tall, full-bodied man. Although her every instinct told her to get off the bus, she felt a peace rush over her.

Sensing her discomfort, Cameron removed his hand from her arm. "You don't think we are going to just leave you out there alone, do you?"

Slowly Emily rose and timidly smiled at his kind gesture. She explained that she was having false labor and there was no need for the men to stay. There was no telling how long it would take for the taxi to arrive, and she'd be safe under the lamppost. "It's kind of you to offer to stay with me, but you've got a long ride ahead of you, and you need to get on the road."

"Nonsense!" Red exclaimed. "I kin get this man to his destination with time to spare. He'll sleep right back there in dat bed fit for a king while I'm drivin'." He took a deep breath and tossed his head back as he motioned toward the back of the bus. She turned to find a set of large doors separated the rear of the bus from the rest of it. "'Sides, he ain't gonna get no sleep 'til he knows you got a ride home."

Cameron motioned for her to have a seat in the luxuriously spacious confines of the vehicle. "Please, sit down and wait comfortably."

A thankful Emily lowered herself into the plush, tan-colored chair. It was easier to breathe inside the cool space. And getting off her feet just might stop her labor pains.

Just then, a blue sports car pulled up beside the bus. The driver's door opened and out stepped Seth Woods. Emily couldn't believe her eyes as he stepped into the bus.

"You guys all right? Need a jump or something?" He climbed the few steps into the bus and looked around at the inhabitants. He saw Emily making herself comfortable in the chair behind the driver's seat. A slight pang of something he couldn't quite determine hit him like a rock as he wondered why she was inside this vehicle with the notoriously eligible Cameron Hall. Was it jealousy he felt? Or was he just concerned?

"No. We're fine," Cameron assured him. He waved his hand toward Emily as if he were showing off a prize. He explained they were simply waiting for Emily's cab to arrive.

Raising one eyebrow, Seth tilted his head and reminded her, "I thought you said you had a ride waiting in the parking lot." The little tease was immediately replaced with concern. "What happened?"

Emily shrugged her shoulders and explained that no one was waiting for her when she got out and how she walked around the front of the building looking for anyone from her church who could take her home, but no one was there. She sighed, yet was relieved when she saw Seth move closer into the vehicle.

Although she knew all these men were Christians, she still couldn't help but feel vulnerable, especially in light of her condition and only able to speculate how she came to be in the predicament in the first place.

She nodded toward both men. "These kind gentlemen offered me the use of their cell phone so that I could call a cab."

Cameron sat down in the overstuffed tan seat across from Emily. He rotated the chair to face Seth. He had sensed chemistry between the couple. Recalling the conversation between Seth and Emily during the autograph session, he offered for Seth to join them in their wait for the taxi.

"I would, but the guys are in the car, and they are all famished."

Cameron nodded in understanding. Seeing her in the bus with Cameron caused Seth to lose his appetite. "Thought we'd try to hit one of the fast-food joints across the way there on our way out." He pointed his thumb over his shoulder toward the outlet mall parking lot. He looked over to Emily and asked if she would be all right or if she needed money for the cab.

Emily blushed at the offer. "Oh heavens, no, thank you." Here complete strangers were being compassionate and thoughtful when members of her own community ignored and even gossiped about her, speculating how she came to get pregnant. Truth was, only God and the man who did it knew. Tears began to swell up in her eyes before she could stop them from running down her cheeks; she looked down at her purse, hoping no one noticed. She discretely wiped her face dry and then looked up to the man whose presence seemed to filter throughout her entire body.

"That is really sweet of you to offer. But I'll be just fine." Another tear rolled down her cheek. Unable to escape the embarrassment, she turned her face to inspect the scope of the vehicle's interior more acutely. The contractions had become manageable for the moment. *Thank goodness*, she thought. She believed it was because of her state of relaxation. She had been so tense in the parking lot; it must have contributed to the intensity of the labor pains.

Seth saw the tears fill Emily's eyes just before she looked away. To give her some privacy, Seth attracted Cameron's attention by asking if he was heading down to North Carolina or going to a hotel.

"Red's gonna drive all night so that I get there in time. Man, I got to get a new agent," he commented. "This one's got me booked ten out of the next twelve weeks. I don't know when I'll get home to spend some time alone."

Wishing his group had the problem, Seth explained how he had weeks before their next gig. "I'll be glad to finally get the break we need to get a recording contract."

Cameron scratched his head. "You know, I don't get it. You guys are fantastic! This was the second show I've seen you open, and both times you got the audience so fired up all the rest of the performers had to do was show up." He smiled apologetically. "I wish my agent had taken my advice and signed you guys on. Sorry, man."

"Don't worry about it. We're doing okay." Seth explained how he was approached by Arthur Fields, a local agent with high hopes. "Ever heard of him?"

"Can't say that I have. But then again, I'm not from this area," Cameron replied.

Seth described the agent as a brawny man with curly, sandy-blond hair and good looks. He had been immaculately dressed in a starched, button-down, white oxford shirt with black dress slacks and Italian leather loafers. He had introduced himself and said he had known of at least three producers who were looking for a sound like theirs. He had offered his business card to Seth and had said to give him a call on the following Monday.

"Should see some results really soon, God willing. We're optimistic." Seth reached out to Cameron, who took his hand and shook it. "Well, we've got to get out of here. Got to get some eats and head home." Seth moved down a step and turned toward Emily.

"I hope to see you again, Emily. Best wishes with the baby." He wanted to give her his number so she could call when she had the baby but figured she wasn't the type to call a guy. Knowing she wasn't the woman for him, he dared not ask for her number.

She smiled brightly. "That would be nice. Good luck to you and the guys."

Seth's smile was all the thanks she needed. The smile reached his eyes and illuminated his entire face. He couldn't remember when "good luck" had meant so much to him. Then, hesitantly, he turned and left.

As the car drove off into the night, Emily observed it until it was out of sight. Cameron had noticed the way she and Seth had interacted, and although nothing out of the ordinary went on for the typical conversation, he could sense the attraction between them.

Moments later a cab pulled up to the entrance of the parking lot. Red started the bus and pulled out toward it. He stopped at the entrance and opened the door for Emily to disembark. Then Red and Cameron watched as the cab drove off into the distance.

Chapter 12

The door hung from its hinges. The smell of sweat, urine, and animal feces was pungent in the dark, damp room.

The humidity level on this Indian summer evening was most unbearable outside, but in this hellhole of a room, it was more than intolerable. Yet there he sat on a tattered sofa that should have been incinerated long ago.

In front of him was a small table with a spoon, lighter, and cotton ball on it. In his right hand, he unsteadily held a syringe filled with the liquid he had just created; his left arm had a rubber tourniquet around his bicep. Hand shaking, he took a deep breath to calm himself and then slowly injected the needle into his arm and gradually released the liquid into his vein.

A feeling of euphoria came over him almost immediately. He felt invincible, as if he could fly. Somehow, he had to get more heroin. Preferably before this dose vanished. This had been his last fix. He had to get some money or his dealer wouldn't give him so much as a piece of dust-sized heroin.

He'd get the money later, he promised himself. For now, all he wanted to do was relax in the reverie.

A few hours later, the short, lanky, oily blond-haired man slunk out of the worn out sofa. He left the condemned building while attempting to think of a way to get some quick cash. Then it hit him. But first he needed some wheels. As he sauntered down the street toward Crystal City, he began checking car doors. Locked! All of them! As he entered the shopping center parking lot, he came upon a red sports car, a beauty of a ride.

Finding the door unlocked, he hastily jumped into the driver's seat and ducked down. He stripped the wires and then connected them. He heard the engine roar to life. Then he sped out of the parking lot on his way to an out-of-town convenience store.

A half hour later he found himself inside a WaWa store just off of I-95 in Dale City. Far enough away from Crystal City that the cops wouldn't spot the car, yet close enough to get back speedily.

The convenience store was brightly lit as he walked around the interior with his head down, canvassing the aisles. Keeping his face averted from the cameras, he opened a glass door and pulled out a six-pack of Budweiser. As the last customer walked out of the store, he unceremoniously strolled up to the cashier. He pulled down on his cap to prevent his face from being seen by the camera and then set the beer on the counter.

"Is there anything else I can get for you, sir?" the young man asked shakily. He knew something was up with this guy. Earlier, as the man had pulled out the beer from the cooler, the clerk had pressed the silent alarm for the monitoring company to contact 911. The cops hadn't shown, and now it was too late.

"Why, yes…yes, there is!" He pulled out a knife and shoved it toward the cashier's face. "Give me all your money. Now!"

The young man jumped. Trembling hands opened the register drawer and withdrew all the currency. Handing it to the man, he raised his arms and backed into the cigarette display behind him, attempting to get away from the blade of the knife.

The thief stuffed the cash in his pockets, grabbed the beer, and took off out the store.

Back in the vehicle, he was thrilled from the excitement. He spun out of the parking lot onto the side road that would lead him to the interstate.

He heard the sound of sirens in the distance. A glance in the rearview mirror confirmed his suspicions. The clerk had set off the alarm!

Immediately he floored the accelerator. He had to get onto I-95 and evade the cops.

He rounded the corner and turned onto the ramp that would take him onto the interstate. Just before he hit the highway, he

The Long Ride Home

floored the accelerator and lost control of the vehicle. He swerved onto the freeway hitting one car. Then another. He heard cars behind him crashing into one another as they skidded on the pavement, but he still had no control of his vehicle. He swerved into the median strip and bounced off the concrete Jersey barrier, turning the vehicle upside down. The car came to a screeching halt. The sports car was a crumpled and mangled mess. The windshield was busted out, but the driver was nowhere to be seen.

Cars spun out wildly as they attempted to miss the car ahead of them only to hit the one beside them or be smashed from behind.

A pickup spun out as it scarcely missed the red sports car. It came to a screeching halt positioned sideways in the road. The driver looked out his window to see the headlights of an oncoming tractor-trailer heading directly for him. Upon impact, the truck rolled over and over on the tar top, eventually coming to a halt right side up. The driver was momentarily unconscious. There was a deep gash on his forehead; blood dripped from the large wound. His back, nose, and arm were broken.

When he came to, he couldn't feel his legs. In fact, he couldn't feel anything. Try as he may, not one limb moved.

"Here, this one's alive!" he heard someone say.

"Help...me..." he whispered. "Someone...please...help...me." Then, everything went black.

Jordan was driving far enough behind to see the accident as it transpired. It was as if everything was moving in slow motion, yet it was over in mere seconds.

As an emergency medical technician, Caleb always kept his bag with him. As Jordan pulled off to the shoulder, Caleb grabbed his gear from the back seat of the vehicle and began checking the other cars for the wounded.

As he approached the wreckage, he saw some of the other spectators attempt to pull a man out of a pickup.

"Don't move him," Caleb ordered as he ran to the vehicle. As a trained EMT, Caleb had seen his share of accident victims. He briefly examined the driver while asking his name.

"G...George...B...Baxter."

"Okay, George Baxter. Where do you feel pain?"

George didn't feel any pain. Blood ran into his eye, but he couldn't seem to lift his hand to wipe it away. His arm must be broken. From where he was sitting, he could see that his legs were pinned beneath the steering wheel.

He could hardly breathe. "I...can't...breathe!" He was only able to take in shallow breaths. "I...don't...want...to...die!" he exclaimed.

"Just hang in there, George. You'll be all right. Come on. You gotta hang in there." Caleb knew the man had little time to live if the paramedics didn't arrive quickly. He had hoped to keep him alive as long as possible, but wanted to help the man accept Christ just in case.

From Jordan's truck Kate called 911 and reported the accident. As Jordan attempted to assist Caleb, Lydia sat in the back seat in shock.

Once Kate finished the call, she checked on Lydia. "Lydia! Lydia! Snap out of it!" Kate grabbed her arm and shook it. "Lydia!"

Lydia blinked hard and then looked at Kate perplexingly. "Oh my goodness!" Her hands were shaking as she looked from Kate to the wreckage ahead of them. "Kate, how could this have happened? Is everyone okay?"

"I don't know yet. We need to get out and see if we can be of any help!" Able to get Lydia to recover, the two of them climbed out of the truck to see if they could help Caleb and Jordan.

They reached the crumpled up pickup and saw the driver inside, barely conscious. Kate thought she recognized the license plate, FUN4GEO. As she approached the vehicle, she could see the man inside. *Could it be George? Could this truly be Emily's former boss?* She looked closer. *Yes! Yes it is him!*

"Caleb, stop!" she yelled. "Don't help him!"

Caleb continued to wipe the blood from George's eyes. He attempted to bandage the gushing wound. Once finished, he turned to Kate and asked through gritted teeth, "What's the matter with you? Of course I'll help him!" He shook his head incredulously. Of course he would help the man. He deserved every opportunity as all the other victims. Besides, if George didn't know Christ, it was up to them to lead him to Jesus.

"No, Caleb, you don't understand." She stepped closer to him and whispered, "He's Emily's old boss."

Caleb looked at her quizzically. "What do you mean old boss?"

"You know, the one who raped her!" Her voice raised a few decibels higher. "He doesn't deserve to be saved!" She threw up her arms in exasperation.

Caleb turned to Kate again, taking the precious time away from the wounded man to remind her of what was important. "Of course he deserves to be saved, Kate. Everyone deserves to be saved," he replied. "Besides," he said quietly, "I don't think he's going to make it. We need to do everything to help him make it into the kingdom of heaven."

"He doesn't deserve to make it to heaven after what he did to Emily." She paced the short distance between the vehicle and the Jersey barrier.

Witnessing the exchange between the two, Jordan realized it was more important for Caleb to take care of his patient, so he interjected, "Kate, you don't mean that." He took her by the arm and turned her to face him.

She nodded her head. Yes, she did mean it, every word.

"No, you don't," Jordan insisted. "Even Emily wouldn't want him to die without the chance to accept Jesus as his Savior."

Jordan left Kate standing by the Jersey wall. He bent down to the man in the truck. "George, my name is Jordan. I'd like to introduce you to someone."

George turned his eyes toward the man who was treating his wounds. "I'm not going to make it, am I?" he stammered.

Caleb shook his head. "Not if you don't get to a hospital soon. I believe you have internal injuries that are too serious for me to treat, and I don't think the paramedics will get here in time. But I'd like to help you make it to heaven."

"Heaven?" The man took a shallow breath. "I don't…deserve to go…to h…heaven."

Jordan was startled by the injured man's confession. "Sir, no one deserves it. They are granted it. All you have to do is ask for forgiveness of your sins," Jordan said hastily. "Just repeat after me, and I promise you'll make it to heaven, no matter what you've done."

The two brothers helped him say a sinner's prayer. After he was done, the man looked over and replied, "I, uh, heard her… say…Emily. Please…tell…her…I…I'm sorry." He paused to take in another breath. "Tell her…the baby is…" His voice trailed off.

In the distance, the sirens of the rescue vehicles could be heard barreling down the highway.

Chapter 13

Try as she may, Mary was unable to sleep. She tossed and turned. Careful not to wake her husband, Chris, she gingerly clambered out of bed and went downstairs. She made herself a hot cup of chamomile tea, hoping it would calm her. All she could think about was the unexpected lump.

She had yet to tell Chris or her children, which wasn't what Dr. Nelson had recommended. She felt it was best not to distress the family until she had tangible evidence. That would come next week. For now, she had to get through the weekend. Nights would be the most difficult. If she told Chris, she might reduce her apprehension, but then he would become concerned. No, it was best to keep this to herself for now.

Earlier that day, Mary arrived at Dr. Nelson's office with fifteen minutes to spare. She was taken back to the doctor's private office promptly at four thirty. There she sat waiting for an answer.

The room was not the typical sterile look of a medical office; it had a homey feel about it. One wall prominently displayed achievements and awards. Below them was a cherry curio cabinet that held a Thomas Kincaid winter village. The walls behind her and opposite the desk exhibited original Thomas Kincaid prints. The last wall bestowed two large windows draped in brown-, ocean blue-, and cream-striped curtains with a floral valance in coordinating colors. Between the windows was a large bookshelf that held various medical hardbacks.

Dr. Nelson arrived, took a seat behind her desk, and sighed.

She greeted her patient then got straight to the point. "Well, it's definitely a mass," Dr. Nelson said matter-of-factly. "It's Ductal carcinoma in situ."

Mary felt herself go limp, and she was confused.

"It means that you have cancer in the milk duct. It is in situ, meaning the cells have remained within the place of origin and have not spread to the breast tissue or lobule. We need to perform a biopsy to better determine if it has spread," Dr. Nelson continued. She sighed heavily and said, "I'm sorry I don't have better news, Mary."

The room began spinning. Mary heard the word *cancer* and failed to hear anything else Dr. Nelson was saying. "Um, I'm sorry, Dr. Nelson. Would you mind repeating that?"

Dr. Nelson repeated herself and then explained the next steps. Her office would schedule an appointment for the biopsy for Monday of the following week. She would send the sample to the lab for tests and hopefully have the results by Wednesday or Thursday. The results would determine which strategy would be best.

So now Mary had to wait again.

She had promised herself she would delay telling the family until the results of the biopsy were in, but it was getting harder to act as though nothing was wrong. She so desperately wanted to tell her husband and children yet felt there was no need to worry them. Better they not know until it was absolutely necessary. Besides, it was only for a few more days, she promised herself. Once she received the results of the biopsy, then she would tell them.

That evening, she went to bed and prayed for sleep to overtake her. But sleep wouldn't come.

Mary sat at her rocking chair and picked up her Bible. She scanned the pages until she came upon a verse that spoke volumes to her, Matthew 6:34: "Therefore do not worry about tomorrow, for tomorrow will worry about its own things. Sufficient for the day is its own trouble." With that came peace, though she felt the need to pray. Praying, now that was something she could do with fervor. Shortly into her prayer, she felt the need to pray, not for herself but for someone else…Seth's future bride.

Seth had performed at a concert in Northern Virginia that night. She prayed for safety to surround him. As in all his born years, she also prayed for the young lady who would one day be his wife.

She felt it in her heart to continue praying for Seth's future wife. She hadn't felt this need to pray about this young lady so strongly in months. She got down on her knees and earnestly sought the Lord's protection for her daughter-in-law-to-be. She prayed for the Lord to provide the strength to get her through whatever she was currently experiencing, for courage to handle the situation at hand, and for peace to release her circumstances to God.

For several hours, Mary sat in her rocker praying for this woman. Over the years, when she prayed for her children, she prayed for their life companions as well. But this time the prayer was different.

This time there was urgency to her prayer. Hours later, exhausted and at peace, Mary returned to her bed and slept serenely.

Emily tried to relax in the back seat of the yellow cab. The cramping was still painful and the backache continued; it had been barely tolerable during her time with Cameron and Red, although she did her best to hide it during their conversations.

Their brief discussions had been on how Red obtained his name, which, of course, she had already reasoned was because his hair was of the same tone, with quite a bit of gray around the temples. He was from the Deep South—Birmingham, Alabama, to be exact, given his deep southern drawl. Cameron boasted on his driver's abilities and allegiance to God and his employer. It was evident to Emily that the two shared more than just their time on the road. They also shared a camaraderie that could be the envy of all employers and employees.

Cameron sat in the comfortable chair across from Emily and told of his ventures on how he came to be a Christian music artist. His large, muscular form required most of the seat, with his long legs extending beyond the center aisle. His physique was quite opposite his driver's, with the undersized legs and oversized stomach that protruded beyond his waist.

Where Cameron was tall, Red was short. Where Cameron was lean, Red was thick and jolly. But both men had a love of the Lord that was unsurpassable.

They shared a common bond, as do all Christians. Although there was an almost profound relationship between the two, there was no differentiating their employment statuses. Cameron never came across as haughty, and Red obliged to his every need, mentioned or not.

As Emily sat in the cab and reflected on the evening's events, she felt a rush of fluid leak from beneath her. A sudden sharp pain exploded through her abdomen. *Breathe, Emily!* She heard a scream. *Breathe! Oh God, not now!* Another scream. She couldn't determine where the screams were originating, but they wouldn't stop. *Please God, make the screams stop! I can't do this! Not yet! Not now! Not here! Oh, dear God! Help me!*

She felt the cab pull over to the shoulder of the road. The cabbie turned around in his seat and took a good look at the young woman.

He saw her face was pallid and covered with perspiration. Her eyes had become blank and distant. "Miz, arle ju o'righ?" he asked.

He tried to reach her, but the pain she experienced separated her from reality. He radioed in to his dispatcher.

His attempt to speak English to the dispatcher conveying the emergency was futile. After several attempts, he asked for a translator. Several minutes of silence ensued before an Arabic dispatcher materialized on the line. After communicating the urgency in his native tongue, he trusted dispatch would get them help.

Strangely, on this rather busy freeway, few cars traveled this road that night. While waiting for an ambulance, he decided to try to stop someone for help, if anyone would pass by. Incredibly, he noted, even at the late hour, someone was usually on the busy freeway, but not tonight. Not when he needed them most! A single pair of headlights shone in the distance. He got his flashlight out of the glove compartment and walked to the center of the slow lane as he waved the flashlight toward the oncoming vehicle. Desperately he waved. The eighteen-wheeler changed lanes and zoomed past him; the driver pulled the lever for his horn acknowledging his existence in the middle of the road. Quickly, he ran back to check on his passenger.

A few minutes passed with earsplitting screams. As he checked on the mother-to-be in his cab, he decided to break the rare moment of silence. In broken English, he asked her once again, "Miz? Arle ju o'righ?"

Emily's pain had weakened for a diminutive moment. She was vaguely aware of this man's attempt to monitor her. She looked up at him with dark, tear-filled eyes. "Help me…please!" Her whispers were hoarse as the next contraction began.

"I try to get help." He looked beyond the vehicle to see another set of headlights. "Ju juss waid here. I tink someone's comin'." He spotted another set of headlights and ran out into the highway, waving his flashlight and hands frantically overhead.

Chapter 14

"Hey, man! What's that?" Heath asked as he pointed to the windshield of the car. He sat across from Seth, shotgun. He moved closer to peer through the windshield.

Seth tried to focus on the windshield. "Just some bugs. I'll wash the car tomorrow. Too late to do anything about it now." He sighed. "Besides, if I use the wiper fluid, all I'll do is smear the guts across the windshield making it worse."

"No, Seth!" Heath said vehemently. "Not the bugs!" He pointed again. "Look at that. It looks like someone is in the middle of the road!"

Seth saw it in the distance. A light was moving above the tar top. Off to the side of the road, a car was pulled over with its flashers blinking. "I don't know. It's probably someone waving a flare or something." He decelerated, uncertain what he could do to help.

Logan leaned forward from behind Seth. "Bet they have a flat tire and don't have a spare."

"That would be your luck, Logan. Not everyone rides around without a donut in the trunk." Zack snickered.

Heath grew concerned. "The car isn't leaning like it has a flat. And the way the person is waving the light looks a bit ominous."

All the guys agreed it appeared to be crucial and they would stop. Between the four of them, the person or persons in the vehicle would have less of a chance to harm them if malice be the case.

Seth pulled the car onto the shoulder, keeping a few yards distance between the vehicles. "All right, I'll check out the problem," Seth informed them as he turned to look at them. "If you guys see anything suspicious, take off and call for help. Heath, you get out and slide into the driver's seat, just in case. Here's my cell phone." He handed the phone to Logan. "If it looks like there is any, and I mean any, threat of danger, call 911 and"—he looked directly into Heath's eyes—"get outta here! Leave me behind and protect yourselves." Seth placed the phone in Logan's hand as he prepared to get out of the car.

As Heath and Seth exited the vehicle, the cabbie ran toward them. They immediately stopped in their tracks.

"Pleez, pleez, ju mus help! De…de girl…she…she in pain." He stammered as he ran to them, waving his arms toward the vehicle. Instantly there came a vociferous scream from the back of the cab.

Seth and Heath looked at each other then took off into a full sprint toward the car. Logan got out of the back of the car and yelled to them, "What's going on?" Then he ran to the other side of the vehicle and jumped into the driver's seat as Zack climbed in the passenger's side. Uncertain of the dangers, they drove cautiously closer to the taxi.

As Seth and Heath approached the cab, they heard a woman screaming in agony. "Please someone…" they heard, "Help me." The last words were scarcely audible. But Seth heard them as he opened the back door of the car.

Inside he found Emily. She was lying on her side, doubled over in the fetal position. Tears streamed down her face as she inhaled quickly and began grunting. She looked up to see Seth bending over her inside the vehicle. One arm propped on the seat behind her and the other gently rested on her foot.

"It's going to be okay. I'll help you. Just hang in there." Seth turned to Heath and explained that the woman was in labor and he needed to call 911. Heath ran back to the car and retrieved the phone.

The cab driver stood behind the vehicle and began pacing the width of it. Zack and Logan followed Heath to the cab.

Seth's heart hammered in his chest. Emily was in labor, and he had no idea how to comfort her. He prayed there was something, anything, he could do.

Heath dialed the phone as he dashed back to the cab. "Nine-one-one dispatch, what's your emergency?" the operator said. Heath practically screamed at the operator.

"Calm down, sir."

Heath took a deep breath and exhaled quickly. "There's a woman in labor. She's in a taxi. We need an ambulance…now!"

"What is the location of the emergency?" After Heath explained their location, the dispatcher made it clear there had been a multiple car accident with fatalities just a few exits south on the interstate and it was blocking the entire northbound route. All units were dispatched to the accident, and it would take at least fifteen minutes for assistance from another county to arrive on the scene.

Heath repeated what he was told to Seth, who realized it would be a gruesome fifteen minutes, but he was more concerned the baby would come before help could arrive. Seth withdrew from the back of the vehicle. "What should we do guys?" He had turned to see all three standing there anxiously waiting to help.

"What do you mean 'we'?" Logan said.

Seth huffed. "I mean all of us, of course." Then he heard her groan deeply. Bending down into the car again, he returned his hand to her ankle and whispered, "Everything will be all right. We've called 911, and they are sending a rescue squad."

She looked up at him and silently implored him to help her. The pleading in her eyes nearly broke his heart. His stomach twisted in knots. He must do something for her…and fast.

He turned back to the guys. "It's Emily, the girl from the concert. We've gotta do something, guys," he urged. "She's in a lot of pain. What if she has the baby before the ambulance arrives?"

"Then I vote you deliver it," Zack said.

"Me?" Seth asked. Rubbing his hand through his hair, he began pacing.

"Yes, you," Zack replied.

Seth stopped dead in his tracks. "Why is it always me who has to do everything?" Seth was ambivalent. He ran his fingers through his hair and released a heavy sigh.

Zack responded, "Because you're the oldest, and that comes with the territory." He paused. "Besides, you're the only one with medical training."

"Medical training?" Seth's eyebrows arched in question. "What medical training?"

"That First Aid, and what was it?" Zack scratched his head.

Logan interjected, "CPR."

Zack snapped his fingers, "That's it! CPR."

"Just because I took First Aid and CPR doesn't make me qualified to deliver a baby!" Seth said through gritted teeth. But Zack had a point. At least he was capable of saving the mother or baby, if necessary.

Warily, Seth took the phone from Heath and spoke with the dispatcher. "Hi. Jerry, is it? I'm Seth. I don't think we can wait for the ambulance. What do I need to do?"

Jerry began explaining the steps to delivering a baby. "First of all, Seth, you mustn't panic. Remain calm so not to inhibit the mother's labor. Keep her as quiet as possible. Remind her to pant or gently push during the contractions. Do not allow her to bare down—that will cause the baby to deliver too quickly.

Emily let out another scream. "Please, make the pain stop! Help me!" she pleaded with him. Her eyes bore a hole into Seth.

Jerry heard her over the cell phone. "Get someone behind her to lift her upward in the sitting position. That will probably help with pushing, but we'll get to that later. Has the baby's head crowned?"

"Crowned?" Seth asked incredulously.

"Yes. Can you see the head coming out of the vagina?"

The blood drained from Seth's face. The tension returned to his shoulders, and he had to concentrate on exactly what Jerry was stating because all he could hear was that he had to check for the baby's head. It kept repeating inside his head like an old 45 rpm record that had a scratch in the middle and kept returning to the same spot over and over again.

Jerry's voice brought his thoughts to the time at hand. Better to remain concentrated on the present than to wander off to the future when all this would be over. Although, he wished he was already there.

"Uh…I'm not sure. I mean I haven't checked."

"Well, please check for me."

"And just how do you propose I do that?" Seth's voice was incredulous.

Jerry insisted Seth remain calm and have the mother lay back in the seat, knees up, and legs spread. This would give him the best view of the baby's head if it were crowning. If not, then there was time to spare and they could wait for the ambulance.

Seth handed the phone back to Heath. "I've gotta check to see if the head is crowning."

He bent down into the car and placed his hand on Emily's ankle to get her attention. He let out a sigh and explained to her what he needed to do. "Emily? I need to check to see if the baby's head is crowning. Will you let me look?"

Emily lay there in agony yet still embarrassed at what he was asking. *Oh God! Not now! Not this! Not him!* A throbbing pain seeped its way through her abdomen. She knew she wouldn't be able to withstand much more of this, so she nodded her head. "Anything…if you…promise… to take away…the pain." She panted between her words.

Reaching out to him, her eyes pleaded. "Please, don't let the others see." She managed to retain some modicum of modesty.

"I'll do what I can, but you have to remain calm, okay?" Emily nodded her head while she attempted to relax. She turned on her back and lifted her dress above her knees.

She was truly embarrassed at the fact that this man, almost a complete stranger, was going to examine her in the most intimate way that should be left for doctors or her husband. But since she had neither, she had to rely on him to use every bit of prudence. She felt in her heart she could trust him to remain discrete, which was the only way she could relax about the delivery. She knew he would do everything he could to make this delivery as unproblematic as possible. She reminded herself to do exactly as he asked for the baby's sake.

"I need a flashlight!" Seth called. He leaned out of the taxi as to block Emily from view.

The cabbie handed the flashlight to Seth and then resumed pacing.

Seth turned to the others and asked them to give her some privacy. Heath turned his back while the others proceeded to the back of the vehicle and joined the cabbie in his pacing.

Seth reached for the phone. "Yes, I can see the baby's head. What does that mean?"

"It means delivery is imminent." Jerry's voice remained calm as he presented the next assignment. "You need a clean cloth or towel. Do you have anything on hand?"

Seth remembered his gym bag in the trunk of his car. "Yes. Yes, I have a clean towel and T-shirt."

"You'll need them both. Can you get someone to retrieve them?"

Seth turned to Zack. "Zack? Can you go check my gym bag in the trunk of the car? Get my T-shirt and towel out!"

Meanwhile, Logan tried his best to calm down the cabbie, which proved to be more difficult than he imagined.

Upon his return to the cab, Zack, to avoid passing out at the sight of blood, passed the T-shirt and towel to Heath.

Emily lay in the back seat feeling more miserable with each contraction. They were back to back now. She wanted to push something fierce. "Please...I need to push!" she cried.

Seth, taking the clean towel and T-shirt, tried to calm Emily. "It's okay. Everything will be all right. Just hold on another minute." He heard Heath inform Jerry they had the towel and T-shirt.

"Good. Let me talk with the Seth again."

Seth clicked the speaker button on the phone. "I'm here. I've put you on speaker." Seth placed the phone in the floorboard so he could talk with the dispatcher. He was anxious to help Emily. She was in so much pain, imploring him to allow her to push.

"Seth, as the baby's head becomes visible, gently cup your hands to catch it as it comes out. Make sure you have the towel over your hands."

With the next contraction, Emily pleaded, "Help me! Oh dear God, help me!" The words were barely audible.

Just then, Seth remembered the dispatcher advised to have someone hold her from behind to give her support while she pushed.

As he placed the towel over his hands, he asked Logan to help.

"Emily?" Seth asked to get her attention. "Logan is going to open the door and sit behind you to give you some resistance while you push." He waited for Logan to open the other door and assist Emily into a sitting position.

"Another contraction is coming!" she strained to inform him. Logan opened the door and knelt inside the vehicle.

"Okay. Logan, support her as she pushes. Emily?" Seth looked her in her smoky blue eyes. "Push with the next contraction. I can see the head."

Seth could sense Emily had lost all her strength while pushing. "It's okay, Emily. I've got the baby's head, and the shoulders are ready to come out. Push again, Emily. Push!"

"I…I can't." She panted.

"Yes, you can. You have to," said Logan. "I'll help you." He gently lifted her forward. "Now breathe and push."

Emily didn't have it in her to push hard. She bore down with her remaining strength.

"Great job, Emily!" Seth cheered. "You have a girl!" He gently wiped the baby with the towel then wrapped her in his clean T-shirt and followed the final instructions Jerry relayed.

A siren resonated in the distance.

"You need to raise the baby's body slightly higher than her head. She should start breathing. Be sure not to wrench on the umbilical cord," Jerry conveyed.

Seth did as he was told careful not to pull on the umbilical cord. But the baby would not breathe. Seth turned his head toward his phone and quietly said, "She's not breathing!"

"Using your finger, gently remove any mucous from the baby's mouth." Jerry spoke with urgency.

Once again, Seth did as he was told. "Come on, little one, breathe for me." He held the baby close and gently rubbed the baby's back to stimulate breathing.

Nothing.

"What's wrong with my baby?" Emily looked up at Logan, who was still supporting her back.

"I'm not sure, but Seth will handle it, whatever the problem may be. He'll take good care of your baby. I promise." Logan hoped beyond all hope the baby would be all right. He could tell by the alarmed look on Seth's face that there was something seriously wrong.

"Seth?" Emily cried for him to look at her and assure her the baby was okay. "Please tell me what's going on."

Seth, concerned for both the baby and her mother, took a quick moment to inform Emily of the situation. What felt like an eternity was only seconds. He knew the longer the baby went without oxygen, the greater the probability she would have brain damage. He had to get her to breathe.

Emily lay their observing the situation. Helpless. She felt helpless. Her baby was not breathing, and there was nothing she could do. *Oh, dear God, please let my baby live.*

Fear set in. If Seth couldn't get this baby to breathe, he would blame himself. He began to pray. *Dear God, help me get this baby to breathe. Show me what to do.* On instinct, Seth began breathing small gentle puffs into her tiny mouth. At first nothing happened. He checked her airway passage and determined there may be a blockage. He gently placed a finger into the back of her mouth. He pulled out more mucous and began resuscitation once more. After a few short breaths, he lifted his head and implored for God to let this newborn live. Once more he tried to clear her airway. A few more little puffs in her mouth. A moment passed, and she gasped. He stroked her back once more. Immediately the baby began to scream. Seth released the breath he had been holding as the baby began to breathe.

The ambulance pulled to the side of the cab. Paramedics jumped out and grabbed their gear.

He placed the baby on Emily's torso and stepped back as a paramedic took over. The man checked the baby's vital signs, gave Seth a pat on the back, and returned to his task at hand. He placed a clip close to the baby's stomach and then proceeded to cut the umbilical cord. He then handed the baby to her mother.

"Looks like you've done everything just right, sirs," He directed his comment to the men standing on the side of the road. "You should all be proud of yourselves." He turned back to the car. Assisting Emily to the gurney, he commented, "I heard you had a little trouble during the delivery. How are you feeling now?"

"Like I'm floating on air."

"Most women say that once they hold their babies for the first time. We'll see how you feel tomorrow!" With a wink, he covered her with a clean blanket and strapped her in the gurney.

Seth saw the EMT wink at Emily, and something triggered inside. He didn't like it. Not one bit. Only he didn't understand why.

Seth watched powerlessly while the other paramedic assisted in moving Emily and her newborn toward the ambulance.

Just before they lifted the gurney into the back of the vehicle, Seth reached for her hand. "If you don't mind, I'd like to follow you to the hospital." He wasn't quite ready to relinquish the newborn and her mother to the paramedics just yet. He wanted to know the baby would be okay. The only way he felt he could relax was to see the newborn safe in the hospital.

Emily nodded her head in agreement, grateful for this wonderful man and his friends. His touch was warm and electrifying at the same time. This man had delivered and saved her baby's life. She would be forever indebted to him. She looked deep into his striking blue eyes and smiled. She thanked them all for their aid and prayers. She then relaxed on the stretcher, gently holding onto the newborn.

Her smile spoke a multitude of words to Seth. He felt her appreciation deep in his heart. Words would never express what she felt; he knew that, so she spoke them through a heartfelt smile that conveyed her gratitude a thousand times over.

The other paramedic closed up the back of the ambulance, turned to the men, congratulated them on a job well done, and then climbed into the front seat and drove off.

Seth followed close behind. Not familiar with the area, he mentally committed to memory the route the rescue vehicle drove. He had planned on visiting the newborn and her mother again, even before the ambulance pulled onto the freeway.

At the hospital, all four of the men stood outside the nursery window in awe of the beautiful baby they'd just helped deliver.

Chapter 15

When Kate arrived home late that night, she felt the need to call and make sure Emily was okay. But it was far too late, so she decided to wait until morning. She knew Emily was not feeling well before they left for Cassidy's but assumed once Emily was home and in her own bed she would feel much better, so she set her alarm clock, just in case, and quickly fell into a deep sleep.

What seemed like seconds later, Kate awoke to the sound of music playing on her alarm clock. She rolled over to check the time. Six fifteen. She had to call Emily. Although Emily wasn't an early riser, Kate had a dreadful feeling in the pit of her stomach. She picked up her cell and punched out a number on her speed dial. Emily's voicemail answered. She left a quick message, hoping Emily would call her back. She got out of bed and prepared herself a cup of coffee. She needed the jolt of caffeine to get her started after only a few hours of sleep. Still the alarming sensation she felt for Emily wouldn't leave her.

She sat down at the table in her small apartment. One day she'd have a home of her own, a home like the one she grew up in; until then she lived in this small one-bedroom apartment. The rent was low for the area in which she lived, which allowed her to save money toward a home of her own. She looked up at the clock on the microwave. Six forty-five. Hoping she wouldn't awaken Gram, she picked up her cell phone and punched out Emily's house number.

Gram answered on the second ring, her voice still groggy with sleep. "Hello?"

Kate vacillated. "Mrs. Wilkerson?"

"Yes?" She took a moment to clear her throat. "Who's this?"

"It's me. Kate."

"Oh, Kate." Gram sat up in the bed and looked at the clock. "What are you doing calling so early? Is something wrong?"

"Oh no…no. Nothing's wrong." At least she hoped nothing was amiss. "I'm sorry to be calling so early, but I tried Emily's cell and she didn't answer. I'm just concerned, that's all. She was in pain when I left her at the chapel last night, so I wanted to check on her."

Gram sat up in her bed. "Well, I should hope you would be concerned, considering you left her at the concert hall without a ride home," Gram chastised her.

"Left her? Without a ride?" Kate was perplexed at the announcement.

"Yes. Without a ride home." Gram explained Emily's frantic call late in the night needing a cab to get home and how she had been left without a means of transportation.

"Oh my!" Kate was devastated. "I thought she was going to ride home with the Smiths." She could kick herself for not passing the information along to Carter or Lisa herself.

"That's what she thought. I still don't know what happened exactly. All I do know is when she left the building; there was no one in sight. She called me around eleven o'clock to call her a taxi. I suppose I'll find out the entire story when I get back to the hospital."

"Hospital?" Kate couldn't imagine what had happened. Unless…unless… "Gram, what do you mean hospital?"

"Oh my, I guess you don't know yet, do you?"

"Know what?" Kate sat on the edge of her seat, anxiously awaiting the older woman's answer.

Yawning, Emily's grandmother took a moment to compose herself before informing Kate of her granddaughter's plight. "Evidently Emily was in labor during the concert but thought it was false labor. She said she had been having backaches and some cramping during the performance but tried to ignore it. It wasn't until her water broke in the cab that she realized she was in labor. She had the baby…in the taxi…on her way home!"

Kate was horrified. Emily had delivered the baby in the back of a car! In the back seat of a cab of all places! "She had the baby? Is she all right? Is the baby all right? What did she have? Where is she? I mean, what hospital is she in?" Kate had a million questions. How did Emily get left behind when Kate believed everything was arranged prior to leaving? She never would've left Emily without a ride. If Kate had known, she wouldn't have insisted on going to Cassidy's. "Oh, this is all my fault! I shouldn't have left without her."

"There, there. Don't blame yourself. As it turned out, things worked out just as they were supposed to." Gram comforted Kate. "Turns out one of the singers, a man from the concert, helped deliver my great-granddaughter."

She knew there must have been a good reason behind the incident. Somewhere along the way something got misconstrued, and Emily was left. *Thank God for the man who came along when he did. If it weren't for him, the baby might not be alive!*

"How are Emily and the baby?"

"They are just fine. Although it was touch and go with the baby at first. Emily and her baby girl are at Fairfax Hospital down off Route Fifty. I met them there late in the night. I came home for a few hours to get some sleep. I'll be heading back out there later this morning."

After hanging up, Kate tried to digest the information. *In a cab? Emily delivered in a taxicab? What happened to riding home with the Smiths?* She had to get in the shower and dress. She was going to the hospital to visit Emily and her newborn baby girl. But first she had to keep her appointments.

It was well past two before Kate was able to leave for the hospital.

The birth of her first great-grandchild brought Gram inexplicable joy despite the conception. With a spring in her step, she arrived at the door to Emily's hospital room.

The space was a comfortable size, with an oversized single bed in the middle. On one side of the bed was a rocking chair; the other side displayed a large set of windows. Below the windows sat a teal recliner. A bedside table exhibited a large bouquet of pink roses.

Gram walked into the room holding a vase of mixed pink flowers with mylar balloons that read "It's a Girl" and "Congratulations" interspersed with pink and white latex balloons.

Emily sat rocking with the baby in her arms.

Gram quietly walked up to peek at the bundle in her granddaughter's arms.

"She's beautiful," Gram proudly pronounced. She set down the bouquet and balloons beside a vase of flowers. "So who are these from?" Gram reached for the card.

"They're from Jordan and Caleb. Wasn't that sweet of them? I still can't figure out how they knew I was in the hospital."

Gram smiled. "They called to check on you this morning, and I told them you were here."

"Oh." Emily smiled gratefully.

Gram turned her attention to the small bundle in Emily's arms. "Oh, my first great-grandchild." Gram touched the baby's palm; the baby's fingers wrapped gently around hers.

"What will you name her?" Gram asked as she took the baby from her mother. Emily stood to allow her grandmother to sit in the rocking chair.

"Well, I'm not sure yet." Emily confessed as she slowly climbed back into her bed. "I would like to name her after the courageous man who delivered her, but I can't think of a female version of his name."

"Hmm." Gram chuckled. "That does pose a problem." Gram changed the subject. "So, what is his name?"

"Oh." Emily smiled. "Seth. His name is Seth Woods."

Gram patiently listened to Emily's rendition of the night before when she left the building to find no one waiting for her and the excruciating pain she had been feeling. She conveyed while in the back seat of the cab her water broke and with it came the sudden urge to push. "If it weren't for Seth and his friends, I don't know what would've happened."

"I can hardly wait to meet this young man."

Emily shook her head, doubtful it would ever happen, although she would gladly welcome the opportunity. "Well, some day I hope to meet and give him a proper thank you." They sat and talked a while until Emily stifled a yawn.

Gram handed the baby back to Emily. "I must let you get some rest. I've got to go buy some things for the baby to wear before she leaves here. She can't go home in a hospital gown! But I'll return later this evening to show you what I purchased. You can't get rid of me for long!"

"Okay, Gram. I'll see you later," she said as she placed the newborn in the small plastic crib by her bed then lay down once again. It took only seconds for her to fall asleep.

※

Kate had her last photo shoot outside in the warm autumn sun. The higher temperatures continued to surprise her. When she arrived home she felt the need for another shower. This time she pulled her wet hair up in a ponytail. She wore a blue floral skirt, white camisole, and a sheer blue over shirt. She slipped on her sandals and headed out the door to the hospital.

She arrived in time to see Gram walking to her car. She followed, hoping to get a chance to talk with her. Kate rolled down the passenger's side window to talk with Gram. Still elated at the thought of having a great-granddaughter, she informed Kate,

"Emily's in room 204. She's resting, so make sure you knock," Gram warned her.

Kate felt the need to apologize again for leaving her best friend behind. "I called Lisa Smith, and she said they never got the message about Emily riding home with them. If they had, they never would have left her there. Then I called Lydia, who was supposed to tell the Smiths. But she said she told another kid from church to relay the message." She rolled her eyes. "Evidently, the kid failed in her duties!" Kate was sure Lydia would chastise the young girl.

The two women conversed a few minutes more before Kate turned into an empty parking space.

In the hospital hallway, Kate knocked on the door to Emily's room. "Come in," she heard Emily sleepily call out.

"Emily!" she squealed. "Are you okay?" Kate looked over at the tiny infant enclosure as the contented baby jumped at the sound of her voice. She placed her hand over her mouth, apologizing with her eyes. The baby began to cry at the sound of Kate's voice. Emily got up and commenced stroking her tiny head. The baby calmed and fell back into a deep sleep.

"I'm fine," Emily said softly. She took a few minutes to divulge the story of how she was left behind at the concert hall.

"If it weren't for Cameron and Red, I wouldn't have been in the cab when I delivered the baby." Emily explained who Cameron and Red were and how they came to assist her in her time of need.

"Right now, I'm exhausted and need a nap," she admitted while climbing into the bed. "I hope you don't mind. I know you drove a long way to get here and now I'm asking you to leave. Please forgive me."

"Not to worry. I'll come back another time," Kate said as she rose from the chair. "Oh. Before I forget, I have to tell you about the accident we saw last night," Kate said. "You'll never guess who was involved!"

Kate told her about the multiple car pile-up and how her own ex-boss, George Baxter, was injured. She explained how Caleb helped him accept Jesus as his Savior. According to the news reports, the driver of the car that caused the accident was found fifty feet from the wreckage, lifeless.

"I'm not sure if George made it, but I haven't read or heard anything in the news yet today."

A tear rolled down Emily's face; she reached up to wipe it away. "I can't believe it! My prayers have been answered," she whispered to herself.

"You mean you prayed he would die?" Kate asked incredulously. She stood by the hospital bed, arms crossed at her chest.

Emily's eyes grew large at her words. "Of course not! I'd never do that!" she admonished. "I prayed for his soul to be saved. Thank God he is in heaven." Emily meant that with all her heart. Ever since she met the egotistical man, she had prayed for his salvation. Although he had caused her more pain than she could ever describe, he also gave her a beautiful baby girl. She knew in her heart he was the father of her little one, even if he never admitted it to anyone.

"Caleb said you'd want him saved. Even after all he did to you, you'd still want the best for him," Kate said. "You are a wonderful person, Emily. I can't say that I would've wanted anything but revenge. But you," she admitted, "You are a much better person than me."

"No, Kate," Emily responded, "I'm not a better person. I've just moved onto a different level, to forgiveness. You'll feel the same soon." She yawned.

"I'll let you get some sleep. Love you, Em." She bent down and kissed the head of the baby. "Love you too, little one."

"Call me tomorrow, okay?" Emily asked.

"Sure thing," Kate replied as she left the room.

After Kate left, Emily called the nurse to come get her baby so that she could get some rest. Hating to be away from her little one for very long, she promised herself this would be the last time she would let them take her while she napped.

Before she fell asleep, she reached for the Bible supplied by the hospital. It was her first opportunity to look up the scripture Seth had written on her T-shirt. First Peter 5:7 read, "Casting all your cares upon him, for he cares for you." How appropriate that he should lead her to the scripture that spoke volumes to her heart and soul.

Chapter 16

He stood in the doorway with a beautiful assortment of wildflowers in one hand, a small pink stuffed teddy bear in the other. Watching as she slept, he quietly walked into the room to place the toy and vase of flowers onto the table next to her bed. Meaning to walk out, he found himself staring at her as she slept.

The light filtered into the room through the closed window blinds. It cast a beautiful radiance on her face. He felt he could watch her sleep forever. *What am I thinking? I don't even know the girl. How can I have such fierce reactions with just a glimpse of her lovely face?* He slowly reached down to move a hair from across her face when she stirred a little.

Quickly, so as not to disturb her, he turned for the door and tripped over the trash receptacle.

Emily awoke with a start.

Catching himself before he fell, he turned back and saw her awake. "Guess I woke you," he said sheepishly.

Emily raised the head of her bed. Still somewhat embarrassed with the man who delivered her child, she blushed. She pushed back the loose hair from her face as she sat up.

He didn't know why the color seeped into her cheeks, but he could only guess it had to do with the intimacy of the delivery and seeing him just a few hours later. He should have thought about her sensitivity at the sight of him. Maybe he should just turn and go. But something kept his feet planted on the floor. He really didn't want to leave her. He wanted to thank her for allowing him to deliver her baby, but was too self-conscious to say so.

"Not at all." She looked at the clock on the wall. She had been asleep for two hours.

"I need to get up anyway. It's about time for the nurse to bring the baby in for another feeding." She rubbed her eyes, stretched, and then pointed toward the door. "Shouldn't be too long now. Have you seen her yet?"

Seth shook his head. "The nursery was closed."

"Well then, since you've come all this way to visit, why not stay a while and see the wonderful baby you helped bring into the world?" She looked down; satisfied the gown her grandmother had brought from home wasn't too revealing, she pulled the bed covers up to her waist.

"If you don't mind having the Magna cum Laude of Madam LaClutz's School of Grace and Poise in your room, I'd be honored."

With that, they both laughed. Seth took a seat in the recliner next to the window. He looked so handsome in his blue jeans and red button-down shirt. She realized how the color complimented his dark features and blue eyes. Her heart skipped a beat at the sight of him. She shouldn't be feeling this way, not toward the man who, just mere hours ago, delivered her baby—in the backseat of a cab, of all places. That was more intimate than she cared to get with a stranger; yet here he was, sitting in her room as if nothing out of the ordinary had passed between them.

"What've you named her?" Seth asked.

"I'm not quite sure yet." She shrugged her shoulders. "I'm hoping something will come to me." She paused. "Maybe you could help me? Have any suggestions?"

"Me?" He pointed to himself. "No, no suggestions. But something will come to you when you least expect it. Want to know what my parents did when we kids came along?" he asked.

"Sure." Emily pulled her knees to her chest and hugged them slightly.

Seth leaned back in the seat and began his story. When he and his siblings were born, his parents had never been able to agree on any names, so they waited until they saw each baby. Eventually a name would come to them. They knew it was the right name. Because it fit, he told her.

"How many children did they have?" she asked.

"Six."

Emily's gasped. "Ouch! You mean your mom went through labor six times?"

"Five," he stated.

"Five?" she questioned. "I thought you said she had six children."

Seth nodded. "She did. I have a twin brother."

Emily's eyebrows arched. "You're a twin?"

"Identical twin, to be exact," he admitted.

"Hmm. Identical? Do you have a picture of him?"

Seth shook his head. He didn't carry any photos in his wallet. He promised that looking at him was just like looking at his brother, Sean, with the exception of Sean's dark-blue eyes. Sean all but ran the ranch. He spoke of his other siblings, Jeremy, a senior at University of North Carolina, Chapel Hill; Grace, a sophomore at Fayetteville State University; and Melissa and Chad were still in high school.

The nurse appeared with Emily's lunch. After scrutinizing it, Emily pushed it aside as if she wasn't hungry. He must have had a puzzled look on his face because she told him she didn't care for beef stew. She explained how she had arrived too late in the night to choose her menu for the day, so she got whatever they brought her. "Tomorrow will be my choice."

Seth knew she needed her nutrition not only for her strength but for her baby as well.

"Would you…excuse me a minute?" She watched in confusion as he left the room.

At the nurse's station, he stopped to ask where the cafeteria was located.

"First floor. Turn right as you get out of the elevators. It'll be on the left." The nurse gave him a flirtatious smile he chose to overlook. He smiled wryly and thanked her for her assistance.

When he returned, he carried fresh salads and two tuna sandwiches along with two bottles of cold water he'd purchased from the cafeteria. He noticed the blinds had been opened to allow the natural light in.

He set his treasure on the over-bed table and rolled it in front of Emily. "Seth, you shouldn't have."

"You need to eat. If not for you, for the baby. You need to keep up your strength." He sat at the foot of her bed, sharing the over-bed rolling table.

Emily unwrapped her sandwich and took a bite. She closed her eyes. "Mmm. This is heavenly!"

He opened the salad container, "I wasn't sure if you'd like tuna, but there wasn't much of a selection. I took a gamble." He beamed a smile at her that made her heart melt.

"I love tuna salad!" She took another bite of the delicacy and twisted off the top her water bottle. "So before you left, you were about to tell me about your family." Emily licked the tuna from her lips.

At the sight of her tongue sliding across her lips, Seth felt as if the room temperature rose several degrees. He gave her a self-conscious smile as he poured his dressing on the salad. "Oh yeah, I did, didn't I?"

Emily nodded her head in anticipation as she finished half of the delightful sandwich. "Mmmhmm."

He told her of his energetic, vigorous father, Chris, who still worked the ranch when he should have retired years ago. "Dad has given the reins to my twin but hasn't quite cut the apron strings yet. Sean helps runs the ranch now. I was supposed to help out, but I became a singer and left ranching behind."

"Your dad must have been disappointed." Emily wiped her hands on a napkin and drank from her water bottle.

"Oh, he was. But he knows I have a calling on my life and that singing is what I need to do right now." He shrugged. "Who knows? I may return to the ranch after my singing career is over, which may be sooner rather than later if we don't get a recording contract."

"Don't give up yet!" Emily chastised. "You've got a good lead on that agent you talked about last night with Cameron."

He nodded slightly. "Yeah, but I can't call him until Monday." His eyes opened widely. "That's two days away."

She nodded her head. "Feels like an eternity, huh?"

He rolled his eyes and nodded.

"Everything will work out. I just know it will." Emily opened her salad and removed the dressing. "You do, too. Don't you?"

"Yeah, I guess I do. It's just been so long…and I've been turned away by several agents in the past. I'm more precautious is all." He unwrapped half of his sandwich and sunk his teeth in it. He lifted his eyebrows. "Mmm…this is good." He lifted the sandwich up a little.

"Told you." She grinned, stabbed her fork in the salad, and took a big bite.

Warmth ran through his entire being at the sight of her smile. "Okay, you've told me about your dad and Sean. What about your mom…and other siblings?"

When he spoke about his beautiful mom, Mary, his face glowed. Mary was the perfect mother in his eyes. She ran the house with an iron hand. She baked daily for her family and guests at the bed and breakfast he called home. She baked fresh breads, cakes, cookies, brownies—anything that her brood of six kids would eat. She was a goddess among the kitchen. Organized beyond belief. "Cleanliness is next to godliness" was her motto. She kept the house running in tip-top order. No one dared step out of line with her. They never had to. Never even wanted to. Mary was the picture of health and beauty mixed with gentility and grace.

Grace, the oldest of his two sisters, was in her second year of college. She was studying to be a veterinarian. She loved animals, and the position would fit her perfectly. His younger sister was named Melissa.

Melissa was special to him. His eyes lit up when he spoke of her. Even though she was grown by all standards, she was the baby girl of the family and therefore would always be his little sister, his favorite sibling. "She's a senior in high school and loving every minute of it." His smile reached his eyes.

"One day, when I was just a boy, my brothers and I were out for a swim in the pool when my two sisters, Grace and Melissa, just toddlers at the time, played outside at the swing while mom hung the sheets out on the line. Somehow Melissa figured out how to unlatch the gate that surrounded the family in-ground pool. She walked into the pool using the steps in the shallow end."

Emily gasped.

"We boys, all playing in the deep end at the time, didn't notice. When I heard mother screaming Melissa's name I turned to see what was going on, then I heard the smallest little splash in the shallow end of the pool."

"Oh no! Please tell me she didn't drown!" Emily pleaded.

Seth's eyes widened with anticipation but he refused to answer her. Instead he continued, "I turned just in time to see Melissa sinking to the bottom. I swam as quickly as my arms would carry me. I dove down, scooped her up into my arms, and brought her to the surface."

Emily was amazed. "How old were you?"

"I turned twelve the next week. I'll never forget it as long as I live."

He chuckled, "My mother was at the poolside just as I surfaced with Melissa. By then, my baby sister was crying. I'll never know if she cried because she was scared or because she had to get out of the pool. Mom grabbed Melissa, thanking God and me in the very same breath." He popped the last of his sandwich into his mouth.

"I can only imagine how relieved your mom was that you were able to save your sister."

"Yes, I became the family hero that day"—he boasted a huge smile—"and Melissa clung to me for days after the incident. The bond was the beginning of a special friendship between the two of us."

Seth wiped his mouth with his napkin. She noticed he missed a spot. What she wanted to do was kiss the tuna off his face. Shaking that thought as quickly as it came, Emily took her napkin in her hand, and with her forefinger, she wiped away the tuna.

Her touch was soft and sweet. He hesitated at the simple gesture. Their eyes met and time stood still.

He felt the walls of protection he had placed around his heart begin to melt away. *She's just a stranger. A fan and nothing more.* He tried to convince himself that he didn't feel an attraction to the new mother. She's an unwed mother, for goodness sake. This young woman, beautiful though she may be, was not the woman of his dreams. He believed God had a woman of virtue for him, didn't He? But reality was to the contrary, and it kept creeping up to slap him in the face.

Slowly, she lowered her hand. She could see something in his eyes. Uncertain if it was his reaction to her touch, a mutual response to her feelings, or if he didn't want such intimacy between them. She believed the latter and brushed all thoughts aside, hoping she hadn't overstepped her boundaries. *For goodness' sake, Emily, you just gave birth to a little girl. This man delivered her. He isn't her father.* No, he wouldn't do to her baby what George had done. He was a much better man, one that wouldn't give her the time of day under normal circumstances. But she could dream, couldn't she? *Quit with your wild antics and daydreaming and focus, Emily. Focus.*

She broke the silence that had befallen them. "Um, I always wanted brothers and sisters. It must be great during the holidays."

More than willing to accompany her to this new topic, he responded, "Yes, it is. Gifts piled under and surrounding the tree. Everyone talking at once. Never being able to finish a conversation before someone interrupts. You try to hide a slice of your favorite cake only to find it has been consumed by another sibling. And quiet…well, that's something you only hear when you are awake in the middle of the night—that is, assuming everyone else is asleep." He breathed a sigh. "Yes, it is rather wonderful."

A smile crept across her face as she returned from imagining what it would be like to be surrounded by loved ones on Christmas morning. Chaos. Total chaos. And yet, she envisioned happiness and lots of love.

He realized he had painted a picture that wasn't as wonderful as she must have imagined it.

"Actually, it is nice. I just enjoy my quiet time with the Lord. And with so many siblings, it's hard to get a moment's peace much less quality time for devotions." He thought back to his time at home. "I guess that's why Dad had family devotions at the breakfast table."

"Really?"

"Yep. Everyone was still half asleep, so there wasn't as much of a ruckus."

"Every morning?"

"Yep, even the weekends. Even when we had friends stay overnight. Now that was a bit embarrassing."

"What was?"

"After being up half the night talking and goofing around then having your dad get you and your guest up for family devotions, well, let's just say I was a bit uncomfortable with it at the time. But, you know, I appreciate it now. I actually had friends come to know the Lord through our morning devotions. I plan on carrying on the tradition with my family."

He was interrupted by the sound of a knock at the door.

"Someone's hungry!" the nurse almost sung as she spoke.

She handed over the tiny bundle to Emily. Seth turned away and offered to go outside while she fed the baby, but Emily simply covered herself with a blanket and asked him not to leave but to tell her more stories of his childhood. After delivering the baby, what was a little discrete breastfeeding?

As the day wore on, Seth told her story after story.

So many stories of his mother and Melissa and his family were told that by the end of the day, as she looked down at the sweet baby in her arms, it hit her.

Marissa. That's it! She said it out loud. "Marissa." It fit perfectly.

Seth stopped midsentence when he heard the name. "That's beautiful. Is that what you're gonna name her?"

Emily nodded her head and smiled. "Marissa Elizabeth."

A big smile spread across his face, telling her I told you so. Instead of saying it, he simply said, "I knew it would come to you if you waited," he reminded her. "Are you naming her after anyone in particular?" he asked.

"Actually, Seth, I wanted to name her after you since you delivered her for me." Tears welled up in her eyes. "But I couldn't come up with anything feminine sounding from 'Seth.'" They both laughed. Emily put Marissa on her shoulder and rubbed her back to get her to burp.

"No, there is no feminine derivative of my name. My parents said when I was born, I was all boy and Seth seemed to fit. No guessing with me, if you know what I mean." He paused. "As for my twin, Sean…well, he was a bit more demure, hence the name!" They both laughed. "No, not really. It's the Irish version of John. They wanted us to have the same initials since we are twins."

"So what is your full name?"

"Seth Anthony Woods." He smiled. "Sean's middle name is Aaron."

"What nice, masculine names."

Emily smiled down at Marissa. "Actually, I thought of how much you love both your mom and Melissa, and it came to me. A blended name. The first three letters of your mom's name and the last four of your sister's name. Marissa. Elizabeth is my gram's middle name."

His brows furrowed in confusion.

"Oh." She chuckled. "That's my grandmother, Hannah Elizabeth Wilkerson." She paused, thinking. "I guess I could name her Antoinette or Antonia instead of Marissa. That way she'd be named after you."

Seth stood from the lounge chair and walked over to her bedside to peek down at the small bundle in her arms. "I'm honored." He placed his finger against the baby's tiny palm. The tiny little fingers coiled around it. "But I like Marissa. It's a beautiful name, just like she is. And it seems to fit her."

"Would you like to hold her?" she offered.

"Would I?" he asked incredulously. "I thought you'd never ask!"

Seth scooped the baby up in his arms, reveling at the thought that he had helped deliver such a beautiful baby girl. He sat in the rocking chair and hummed a lullaby as Marissa fell fast asleep.

Helen Baxter sat on the veranda of the family mansion. As was her daily routine, she read the daily news after consuming her breakfast. The headline caught her eye, "Woman Delivers Baby in Taxi on I-95." She began to read:

> Last evening, Emily Wilkerson attended the local Concert for Christ in Woodbridge, Virginia. After the concert, she had been inadvertently left behind by her friends, forcing her to take a cab home. Shortly after entering Interstate 95 northbound, she went into labor.
>
> Because of a fatal accident in the northbound lanes a few exits south, the road was oddly deserted. The said accident caused miles of congestion, but for Ms. Wilkerson, no one was around.
>
> Ten minutes into labor she began to give up ever having any assistance, except that of native Arabian, Jamal Kumar. Mr. Kumar attempted to convey the urgency to

his employer's (the Stealth Cab Company) dispatcher. Unfortunately, there was no interpreter at the desk at the time. It took several minutes to locate someone to assist Mr. Kumar during the emergency, only to be told of the accident causing a complete backup. "No emergency vehicles were available as they were all dispatched to the multiple car collision behind them," said Sherriff Elijah Curry. "A Fairfax County Emergency Vehicle was dispatched from Lorton, Virginia, but it would take several minutes to arrive."

But Ms. Wilkerson didn't have the luxury of several minutes. She was ready to give birth. Just in the nick of time, several men happened by. They saw Mr. Kumar waving his flashlight and decided to stop and assess the situation.

Within minutes of their arrival, Ms. Wilkerson gave birth to a baby girl.

The men who assisted Ms. Wilkerson were unavailable to comment.

"Winston?" Helen Baxter called out.

Immediately, the butler appeared at her side, standing erect, hands behind his back. "Yes, Madam?"

"I read here in the paper that Emily Wilkerson, the woman who has accused George of that unspeakable act, gave birth to a baby girl last night. Find out where she is located. And then bring the car. I want to call upon the administrator of the hospital to which she is admitted."

"Yes, Madam." He took the paper from her raised hand and walked through the glass entry into the Baxter manor.

Chapter 17

When Seth arrived that evening clutching a small bunch of balloons, he noticed Emily had several visitors. Uncertain whether he should enter or not, he stood outside the door in the hallway.

An attendant appeared from the nursery carrying Marissa. She looked down at the baby and said, "Say hello to Daddy." Then she handed Marissa to Seth and quickly walked away.

It happened so quickly, Seth didn't get a chance to correct her. He took a moment to look at the tiny bundle in his arms. *Daddy.* The word stuck in his throat. He had thought that he would've been married with several kids by now. At twenty-nine, he had nothing to offer. Nothing to show for his life except a college degree he didn't utilize and a sports car. He longed for a wife and children. He imagined what life would be like if Emily were his wife. He'd have a ready-made family. Was he ready for something like that?

Marissa squirmed in his large muscular arms. His thoughts returned to reality. He quietly hummed a lullaby, and she calmed down. Slowly, he walked into the room.

Kate, Gram, Jordan, and Caleb all looked at him holding Marissa. Everyone but Gram recognized him.

"Hi Seth!" Emily beamed him a beautiful smile. "Seth, meet my grandmother, Hannah Elizabeth Wilkerson." When Gram was presented, he nodded her way. She began to rise from her perch in the rocking chair.

"No need to get up, ma'am." Gram remained seated.

"Gram, Seth is the one who delivered Marissa," Emily confessed.

"You mean this is the young man responsible for delivering our precious bundle of joy?" she asked as she stood and walked over to peek at Marissa, who was looking up at Seth. "Oh, would you look at this?" Gram declared, "Marissa's just as content as can be in his arms." She looked up at Seth. "And you...you are a natural!" She relieved him of the bouquet of balloons and set them in the corner of the room.

Emily disclosed Seth had a twin brother and four younger siblings and that he should be a natural with so many brothers and sisters.

"Emily's told us so much about you, Seth," Gram said. "So are you the oldest or youngest twin?"

Seth walked over to Emily's bedside and reluctantly handed her the baby. "I'm the oldest," he replied.

Gram smiled. "Well, you are good with Marissa. You're a natural!" she complimented again. Gram couldn't get over how content Marissa had been in Seth's arms. He was so tall and handsome. He would make a wonderful father one day. If only he could be Marissa's father, which would be a dream come true. For her and Emily.

Emily's doctor came in. "Well, aren't we the popular one?"

Emily looked up from her baby. "Oh Dr. Curtis, you remember Gram from this morning." It was more of a statement than a question.

Dr. Dwight Curtis nodded Gram's way and then greeted each one of her other visitors as they were introduced. When Emily presented Seth as the man who delivered the baby, the doctor walked across the room and took Seth's hand in his.

"Marvelous job delivering the baby," he complimented. "Not many people can maintain their composure under such circumstances, but you...you performed perfectly."

Still shaking hands with the doctor, Seth replied, "Thank you. But I couldn't have done it without the help of my friends and the 911 operator." He glanced at Emily. "And such a courageous patient!"

"Yes. She is a wonderful patient," Dr. Curtis agreed as he released Seth's hand. "One I hate to discharge, be that as it may, I must release her."

Dr. Curtis looked at Emily. "How does tomorrow morning sound to you, Emily?"

Emily looked around at the smiling faces in her room. "Sounds great to me! Thank you, Dr. Curtis."

"You're welcome. I'll take care of your discharge papers and will check with you in the morning." With that, Dr. Curtis left the room.

A discussion began of who would take Emily and her baby home. Seth asked if it would be okay with everyone if he took Emily and Marissa home.

Emily said, "Why, thank you, Seth. I'd…um, Marissa and I would love that. If that's okay with you all." Emily looked around. Gram caught her eye and gave her a wink of approval.

Jordan felt the electricity between Emily and Seth. Though he wanted to be the one to transport the baby and her mother home, he relented with a nod of his head. They each agreed. Seth, the man who delivered Marissa into the world, would deliver her one more time.

"Mr. Baird," Helen Baxter reached out her hand as she strolled into the hospital administrator's office, "nice to meet you."

The tall, lean man gently grasped her gloved hand and kissed the back of it. "Mrs. Baxter, I am honored that you would visit my hospital." Mr. Baird knew of the Baxter fortune and the accusations behind the last heir to the fortune. He also knew that the said heir, George Baxter, was in the building and figured she was there to see him. Not wanting to appear presumptuous, he spoke. "To what do I owe this pleasure?"

She removed her gloves and sat in the nearest seat as he took the chair facing her. "I am sure you are aware my son is in your institution. But that's not why I'm here." She waved her hand. "I've already arranged to have him transported to the medical facility closer to our home. They should arrive later this afternoon."

"Yes, yes. I believe I heard the report this morning." Spencer Baird sat across from the wealthy woman. Leaning back against the leather wing-back chair, he crossed his ankle over the opposite knee.

Helen Baxter set her purse in her lap and placed her hands upon it. Legs crossed at the ankles, she appeared the elegant, prestigious woman Spencer Baird had imagined. "As you may be aware, there was a scandalous accusation about my son some months back."

Spencer nodded.

"Yes. Well, it appears the reprehensible woman is a patient here in this establishment." She raised her eyebrows and tilted her chin to her chest. "Were you aware of this?"

Spencer shook his head. "No, ma'am, I wasn't aware of any such thing." He ran his fingers through his thick, wavy brown hair. "I'll see to it that she is discharged right away."

Helen raised her hand. "Not necessary." She lowered her hand to her lap once again. "What I'd like is to have a private conversation with the young woman." She paused for the request to penetrate his mind. "And I want the baby's DNA tested to see if, in fact, she is my son's child. Discretely, of course."

"Well, yes, of course. I'll arrange both your requests right away." He stood and walked over to his desk. He raised the handset to the phone and pushed a key. "Mrs. Sutton, would you come in here a minute?"

He waited until the woman closed the door behind her before explaining Helen Baxter's requests. The woman disappeared behind the door as quickly as she arrived.

"I trust you will keep the results of the test private."

"Of course, Mrs. Baxter. Confidentiality is our number one priority." He assured the obtrusive woman.

Mrs. Sutton reappeared. "Arrangements have been made. Ms. Wilkerson's guests have just left, and she is alone with the baby.

The blood work will be done this evening when the baby is in the nursery…away from her mother."

"Good. Good. Absolutely perfect." Helen Baxter gathered her handbag and stood. Spencer Baird walked around his desk and escorted the prominent woman to the door.

"Thank you, Mrs. Sutton." He nodded and turned to Mrs. Baxter. "Shall I escort you to the young lady's room?"

"That won't be necessary. Thank you." She reached out her hand once again for him to place a kiss upon the back of it.

※

Helen stood in the doorway of Emily's room, watching the new mother with her tiny baby. Of course, from the distance she couldn't tell if the baby belonged to her son, but the tests would provide the answer soon enough. It wouldn't be a surprise to her if he were the father. After all, he had been a thorn in her side from the time he was conceived.

Helen gently knocked on the open door.

Emily looked up, surprised to see George's mother. "Mrs. Baxter? What are you doing here?"

Helen walked closer to the bed. "Why, I've come to see you and your baby, of course." She peered at the baby in Emily's arms. "You did claim that she is my son's child in court." The older woman pursed her lips. "I just wanted to see her for myself…after all, if she is as you allege, then she is my granddaughter. The heir to the Baxter fortune. But that's probably what you want, isn't it? The Baxter fortune?"

Emily recoiled at the woman's accusatory words. "She *is* your granddaughter, Mrs. Baxter. Of that I am certain. And, no! I don't want your money!"

Her words made the woman step back.

To reduce the tension building between them, Emily changed the subject. "I understand George was in an accident last night and has been hospitalized here. Is he going to be all right?"

The haughty woman clasped her hands together. "Yes, well, he is only here for the moment. I've arranged to have him transported to the family hospital."

Emily knew the Baxter's had donated large sums of money to a hospital further north and presumed this was where George would be taken. "I understand."

"Yes, well, he'll get the best attention money can buy at our hospital." It wasn't really their hospital. Only one wing had been named after the late Theodore Baxter. Still, Helen behaved as if the entire hospital was Baxter property.

"I'm sure he will." Emily tried to remain civil, but felt disparaged by the woman's attitude.

Helen looked around the room, disgust written on her face. "I didn't come here to discuss my son."

Emily's eyebrows shot upward.

"I came with a proposition." She motioned toward the rocker. Emily nodded. Helen withdrew a tissue from her purse, wiped the seat, then lowered herself into the chair. She continued, "I'd like to take the child in."

Emily's eyebrows furrowed. "What do you mean exactly?"

"Oh for heaven's sake, what is it you don't understand about me taking the child?"

Emily remained silent waiting for an explanation.

Helen lifted her nose slightly to look down at the young woman. "I want to raise the child myself." When Emily didn't react, she continued, "I can provide everything for the child and more. She will attend the best schools. Have the best tutors. Travel to foreign countries, and so much more." Helen paused.

Emily glared at the woman.

"Don't you see? You can forget you ever had the child. Your life can go back to the way it was before the child was born. No one need ever know about your past."

"But I'll know," Emily reminded her.

"Yes, but you can put it behind you and go on with your life. Get married, have other children if you want."

"But what if I want my baby?"

Helen couldn't believe what she was hearing. She closed her eyes and shook her head from side to side. "You don't know what you're saying, child. You don't need to be burdened with a child at your age. You're young…attractive…eligible. A child will weigh you down. No man wants a woman who has had another man's baby. Besides, it will be difficult enough to find someone who will take you after being with another man after all."

Emily flinched. She knew the woman was right. It would be challenging to be accepted by anyone after they learned she had been compromised. But to add a baby in the mix would only serve to complicate matters all the more. If she was to keep the baby, she may have to raise her alone. Never marry. Her heart ached. She knew it would be arduous as a single mother. But in her heart of hearts, she wanted more for herself and her baby.

"If you're concerned about what I'd tell the child about her mother, you needn't worry. I'll simply explain you died while giving birth."

"My mother died that way," she muttered the words. "I won't allow my baby to live without her mother like I was. Not when I am alive and well." She narrowed her eyes at the woman resolutely. "No! You can't have her!"

Helen stood abruptly. "Well! I never!" She peered at the new mother through beady eyes. "I can have her taken from you, you know."

Emily looked the woman in the eyes, "You probably can. But you'll have a fight on your hands. Is that what you really want? You can't even say she's a baby. You just keep saying 'the child' as if she isn't a real person."

Helen stood there gathering her thoughts. The girl was adamant. Emily wasn't willing to relinquish the child to her so she had to try another tactic. "Well, if she is George's as you allege, don't I have a right to see her at least?" Helen reminded her of her vast empire as well as friends in high places.

This troubled Emily. She was certain all Helen Baxter had to do to was make a phone call and she'd get all she wanted. Helen had the money and the resources. Emily couldn't contend with her riches, nor could she even begin to try. Emily conceded to allow Helen visitation. Emily released a loud sigh her voice quivered, "I'm sure she'd love to know her grandmother."

As soon as she was discharged, she would allow Helen to visit. Emily gave her address to the woman. "It's the house next to the empty lot on the right."

Just as Helen turned to leave, the nurse came in to take the child down to the nursery on the pretense of giving Emily some time to rest. Helen bid the girl farewell and exited with the nurse.

On the day Emily and Marissa were discharged from the hospital, Seth was there. Just like every other time he'd visited her, he had a gift for her and Marissa. This time it was a single pink rose for Emily and a beautiful silver bracelet for Marissa.

Over the few days since Seth delivered her baby, Emily had to admit, her attraction had grown toward him. Not only was he charming, tall, and talented, but also attentive and generous, and he was the man that delivered her baby. Her own personal hero.

Emily allowed Seth to latch the car seat into the back seat of his car as she climbed in behind the driver's seat.

She admired his good looks as he crossed in front of the sports car. *God, please give me a husband as wonderful as Seth one day.*

Who was she kidding? Who she really wanted was Seth. He fit the bill. He was everything she ever wanted in a man and then some. She could imagine what life would be like if she were married to him.

They would have daily devotions together; share their dreams over breakfast, lunch, and dinner; laugh and cry together; coach Marissa's softball team; drive her to gymnastics; watch her grow up into a beautiful young lady; and eventually have more children together…

But who was she kidding? He wasn't interested in her, only in Marissa, with whom he had bonded as quickly and as well as any true father would to his own newborn baby.

"So which way should I go?" Seth asked as he climbed into the car and closed the door. Brought back from her musings, Emily gave him the directions as he pulled away from the hospital.

It was a beautiful sunny day. Temperatures had dropped, and the humidity was low. Trees were beginning to turn from green to reds, yellows, and oranges. The drive was lovely and peaceful even with the northern Virginia traffic. They made effortless conversation during the ride.

"So tell me about your grandmother." Seth kept his eyes on the road as he waited for her answer.

"Oh, she's the greatest." Emily explained how she came to live with Gram. She was just a toddler when her father fell into a severe depression after losing her mother and little brother in childbirth. After several years of battling the disease, he had finally checked into an institution and left her with his mother. She visited her dad until his death a few years later. He had been a veteran in the US Army and was buried in one of the local memorial cemeteries in Arlington.

"I've been living with her all my life. She's all the family I had…until now." Emily peeked at her sleeping baby, so peaceful and content. She reached over to caress Marissa's tiny hand.

"You know"—Seth looked into the rearview mirror straight into Emily's eyes—"you never mention Marissa's dad. Is he out of the picture?"

"Yes," she said softly, "he is."

Seth didn't realize he was holding his breath until after she answered. He hadn't seen Marissa's father visit Emily or Marissa during their stay in the hospital, but then he wasn't there all the time either.

When he was there, the conversations were mostly about his childhood, his career, and where God was leading him and the guys in their music. The one piece of information he refused to discuss was that of Arthur Fields and the possibility of a contract. He didn't want to jinx it, so he dared not speak of it to anyone outside of the guys.

"Does he know about the baby?"

Emily softly sighed. "Yes, but he denied she was his."

"Oh." The look on his face reflected his aversion toward irresponsible men. *Typical loser guy thing.* He considered the possibilities. How did he feel about Emily? he wondered. Was she the one for him like he first believed the night of the concert? It wasn't until he saw that she was pregnant that he had doubted she was the girl of his dreams. He always believed God had a girl for him who had waited for marriage.

But then, the more time he spent with her, the more his attraction intensified. He had to control his fascination of this wonton beauty. The more he learned about Emily, the more he wanted to be part of her life, no matter how insignificant. He considered since she wasn't the one for him, then he could be her friend and a father figure for Marissa. After all, didn't she name the baby after his mom and sister?

"He never wanted to have anything to do with Marissa." Emily's voice brought him back to reality. As she looked away, he could sense she had much more to say.

What is it? he wondered. *God, help her to feel comfortable enough with me to share her deepest feelings. I don't need to know the details. Those are for You, Lord. But heal her heart from the pain and sorrow she is obviously experiencing from her unplanned pregnancy.*

The Long Ride Home

"Are you okay with that? I mean, him not being a part of Marissa's life?" Seth wondered if he was pushing too hard. If she didn't answer, then he would drop the subject.

Emily's answer came after a long pause. "I'm okay with it. There's no doubt about that." She sighed loudly. "I just dread the day when she asks why she doesn't have a daddy like the other kids and how she came into the world without one."

"If it were up to me, she'd never know that sorrow." Seth let his thoughts escape his lips. He looked away from her reflection in the rearview mirror. "Uh, sorry about that. I mean, I'm sure you'll know what to say when and if the time comes."

As he exited the interstate onto Route 28 north, he inferred, "Maybe God will give her a daddy while she is too young to know the difference, and as she gets older, she'll love him too much to care. You never know."

Emily let out a sarcastic laugh. "Do you know how difficult it will be for me to marry now that I have a child out of wedlock?"

He hadn't thought of that. There must have been plenty of guys who would have jumped at the chance to marry her, but now...now that there was a baby involved, well... *Let's just say a baby has a way of separating the men from the boys rather quickly.*

"But if it is God's will, you will marry," he added, "and he'll be a great husband, Christian, and father to Marissa. I feel that in my heart." Seth felt as though he was talking about himself. Yes, he was a Christian, and yes, he loved Marissa already. He knew he would be a good husband and father because his own father had been a great role model.

His father brought his children up in a God-fearing home. He never raised his voice to his kids even when he was furious with them. He always allowed the child to speak his own argument before determining the disciplinary action. Sometimes he was lenient on discipline because the child had argued his case admirably. His father showed affection to his mother freely at home but kept public displays of affection to handholding only.

He believed adoration should be something best displayed in the privacy of his home and taught his children they didn't need to illustrate their affection until they were mature enough to handle the temptations that naturally followed. And temptations couldn't be controlled while going through puberty. This was why he didn't allow the children to date until they were juniors in high school.

Emily smiled at him in the mirror. "Thank you. I needed to hear that." She sighed again. "After all I've been through, your words of encouragement mean so much to me."

Seth didn't push the discussion any further. He could sense she didn't want to divulge any more than what she had already, but he was curious. *What kind of man wouldn't want this beautiful woman to be his wife? And to father a child and not have anything to do with her, what a disgrace. A disgrace on him, not Emily.*

No Emily was not "tainted" or "used" but perfect, and any fool could see that he would be a better man if he married this woman. *God, please give her the kind of man she needs. She has a deep desire to marry. I can see that. And Your Word says that You will give us the desires of our hearts. And my desire is that she have what she wants in a man.*

Seth decided he could be a father figure for Marissa…just until Emily found someone with whom to share her life. He was willing to be there for the baby, no matter how long it took. *Yep, that's what I'll do.*

Emily was lost in thought. She didn't want just any man to be a father to Marissa. She wanted Seth. But did she want Seth because he delivered her baby or because he would be a great father to her child? Or was it that she was developing more than just an attraction toward Seth? Even now she was questioning her fascination toward him. Emotions were gripping her heart and turning her stomach upside down. Every thought of Seth had been of him being the dad Marissa would never have. But now, her thoughts were of him as a man—a Christian man whom she would never have. A single tear fell onto her cheek. She wiped it away quickly and bent down to kiss Marissa before Seth had a chance to see her tears. Then she turned all her attention to her little one sitting in the seat next to her. *Better not to think of what she has lost but to dwell on what God has given her.*

"Count your blessings," Gram always told her.

She gladly counted Marissa and Seth among them.

Chapter 18

Seth turned into the circular driveway as Emily told him the story of her home.

She had grown up on the land that surrounded the house and community. In fact, the entire community was built on her great-grandfather's property. It had been passed down from generation to generation until there was only Gram and Emily left to work the land. After Gram received custody of Emily, she didn't have the ability to run the farm on her own. She had hired a foreman, Kate's father, when her son became ill and allowed Kate's dad complete rule of the farm. Eventually, Gram had been approached by a developer back in the late nineties who gave her a reasonable offer, one that she was quick to decline.

Gram didn't want the land to fall to ruin with the developer, who was well known for empty promises. But several years later, another more prominent developer approached her with a much more substantial offer. She gave it careful consideration and prayer before accepting. She had some of her own needs to put on the table before there could be any agreement.

Gram had wanted a brand new home built free of charge. It would be built on one of the largest two lots in the community, one that overlooked the entire hill and homes that were to be built. It was to be completed on one parcel of land, the other to remain for development on a later date at cost only. This lot was deeded to Emily. The small community was to be situated on a man-made lake that sat in the south side of the hill.

She also demanded that she be on the board of developers to ensure she could have input in what would be privy to the community and its development. After the land had been urbanized, she requested to be on the board of directors for the community. She was voted in unanimously.

Seth was impressed at the size of the home. Not too big as to be ostentatious but not so small as to be disregarded. It sat back off the street some fifty yards on an impressive two-acre lot. The yard had been landscaped with trees and flowers indigenous to the area. A stone walkway led up to the wrap-around porch with a corner gazebo.

Seth drove up to the center of the circular drive and parked by the porch steps. He disembarked and shifted the front seat forward to allow Emily easy egression. He opened the passenger's door to remove the car seat and handed it to Emily and then turned to remove some of Emily's belongings from the trunk of the car.

It took several trips to get all the gifts and flowers into the house. Afterward, Emily and Seth sat on the porch swing with a glass of iced tea enjoying the early fall breezes. Conversation was light and easy between them. It was as if they had known each other for years rather than just a few days.

Shortly after their arrival, Gram pulled into the driveway.

"Oh, I was hoping to be home from church before you arrived." Gram closed her car door and walked up the steps.

"That's okay, Gram. We've only been here a few minutes anyway," Emily consoled her. "Marissa is in the living room sleeping. We thought it would be nice to sit out here and enjoy the weather and quiet time before she wakes."

"That's nice, sweetheart. Hello, Seth," Gram said cheerfully.

"Ma'am." Seth stood to help her into the wicker chair just beyond the porch swing. He had turned it to face the swing so that they could visit a while.

"Seth?"

"Yes, ma'am?"

"Would you care to join us for dinner tonight? I'd like to honor you for safely bringing our precious little one into the world." Tears of appreciation welled up in Gram's eyes. "I don't know what would have happened if you hadn't been there." She gently dabbed her eyes with the tips of her fingers.

"Well, since you put it that way, I'd be honored to accompany you for dinner."

"Good, then you can tell me the story about how you came to be on the interstate when Emily went into labor."

Later that evening as they sat around the table drinking coffee and eating dessert, Seth's phone rang. "Excuse me." He stood from the table and walked out of the dining room to allow himself privacy. "Hello, Melissa. What's up?"

"Something's going on with Mom." His little sister sounded distraught. She sighed audibly. "I mean, Mom just isn't herself. Seth, I think whatever it is, it's serious." The way Melissa described his mother's recent habits, or lack thereof, lately, convinced Seth something was definitely out of sorts.

"All right, I understand. Have you noticed if she has been sick or to the doctor recently?" Seth knew that his mother never went to the doctor except for her annual exams. If she had been for anything else, it would justify reason for concern.

"Not to my knowledge. That's just it. If she has been to the doctor, she is going surreptitiously. How do I continue to pretend that everything is normal when she won't eat? I've noticed that she is up during the night, sometimes for hours at a time. And she is always up every day at the crack of dawn acting like everything is as it always has been. She cooks, cleans, and does all her usual daily tasks, just not with the same vigor as usual. Seth, she looks like she has aged years in just the past week."

Seth thought a moment. He had been gone from the ranch only two months. *She might be depressed that I'm gone. No.* He shook his head. *Something else must be wrong.* "Is Mom crying excessively?"

"No. In fact, she hasn't been crying at all," Missy conceded. "I know what you are thinking."

"You do?"

"Yes, I've thought of it myself. But she isn't depressed. You've been gone before, and it didn't affect her like this. I mean, sure she gets a little down at first. But after a few weeks she springs back. She still misses you when you're gone, but it's not like that this time..." Missy's voice trailed off.

"Okay. Look, I'll call tonight and talk to her, to try to nudge her to tell me. If I can't get anything out of her, then I'll..."

"You'll what?" Melissa hoped Seth would say he would come home.

"I don't know. First I need to talk to Mom. All right?"

"Sure. That's fair enough, I guess."

"I know you want me to come home. But I have a lot going on right now. I can't just pick up and leave without good reasons, okay?"

"I understand." Melissa sighed audibly.

Seth could hear the disappointment in her voice.

Then she added, "I love you, Seth."

Seth understood his little sister needed him. But he also knew that she needed to depend on someone bigger, someone who could take away her fears, and could heal the pain she had suffered. Until she realized that she could let it all go by surrendering it to God, she would continue to depend on Seth to make her feel safe. He hated the responsibility of putting her through the torture of separation. But God had let him know long ago that He was in charge and He would take care of his little sister. All Seth had to do was trust Him.

"I love you too, Melissa. I'll call you later to tell you what Mom says."

As he hung up the phone, a weight seemed to settle on his shoulders.

He returned to the dining room and thanked Gram and Emily for the appetizing dinner and lovely evening. He excused himself, explaining he had to get back home. "It's getting rather late, and I have a bit of a drive ahead of me."

"I understand." Emily stood and walked with him to the front door. She noticed the change in his demeanor and asked if the phone call was bad news.

"No. Not really. It was just my sister wanting me to come home." He wasn't really lying, just not telling her the whole truth. He thanked her again for the wonderful evening and hugged her good-bye.

In the car, he retrieved his cell phone from his jacket pocket and dialed his mom, but the call proved futile. Even though Mary wouldn't divulge anything he could tell there was something amiss. Her voice wasn't as cheerful as it should've been. The call ended almost as quickly as it had begun. He felt the burden grow heavier. It was more than he could bear on his own. He knew what he needed to do.

As he pulled into the driveway of the house he was sharing with Heath, Logan, and Zack, he noticed no lights were on inside. He walked through the living room and climbed the stairs to get to the master bedroom. It appeared the guys had gone out. He was relieved as he needed this time alone. He had to make a call—one that didn't require a phone.

As he knelt down by his bed, he poured out his heart to God. He knew God would understand his pain and uncertainty. God had the answers, even if He didn't communicate them to Seth.

Chapter 19

It had seemed like an eternity since the biopsy when the call finally came. Dr. Nelson wanted to see her again.

This can't be good news, God. What'll I do if it's not contained as Dr. Nelson believed? What'll happen to me? How will I tell Chris and the kids? Dear God, what do I do?

The compassion in Dr. Nelson's eyes was evident the minute she walked into the room. As she sat behind her desk, grabbed a folder and opened it. She studied it for just a minute before speaking. She knew Mary was apprehensive yet eager to know the results of her biopsy, so with compassion, she went straight for the jugular. "Mary, it's just as we thought."

"Cancer?"

"Yes. But it's contained within the milk duct." Dr. Nelson looked at her with compassion in her eyes.

"What do I do now?" A million questions permeated her mind. "How long do I have to live? Will I need to have chemotherapy?" Mary took a breath. Whispering to herself, "What am I supposed to do now? How do I tell my family?"

She couldn't have cancer! She didn't want to lose her breasts. When Pam had had her double mastectomy, she'd cried for weeks. She'd said she no longer felt like a woman. Then the chemotherapy claimed all her hair and dignity. It was several months before Pam's insurance agreed to pay for reconstructive surgery. It wasn't until then that Pam felt like herself again.

"One step at a time, Mary," Dr. Nelson interjected. "One step at a time." She closed the file and placed her hands one on top of the other and leaned closer to the desk. "As I mentioned the other day, this cancer is restricted to your milk duct. It is operable, and since it is contained, you may keep your breasts. If I had to choose a breast cancer, it would be this one." She relaxed and leaned back in her chair. Clasping her hands together across her midsection, she shrugged. "I'm not sure how long you have to live. No one knows that. But when you do die, it won't be because of this particular breast cancer."

Relief spread over Mary's entire being like a cool wave on a hot summer day. "You mean I get to keep my breasts?" She released a sigh.

"Yes." Dr. Nelson leaned in again. "With some six to eight radiation treatments, you'll be just fine." She paused for just a moment to allow the news to penetrate Mary's thoughts. "Radiation will be mild and directed to the immediate area affected. You will have a small dimple after the operation, but other than that, you'll have no side effects."

"You mean I won't lose my hair either?" Mary's eyes widened with relief when she realized she wouldn't lose her hair or suffer the horrific side effects of chemotherapy. She realized she was being callous toward the procedure Pam had endured, but she was so relieved to escape Pam's misfortune.

"No." Dr. Nelson released a chuckle. "You won't lose your hair."

"So when do we schedule the surgery?" Mary was so relieved she was practically in a hurry to get the surgery done and over with and get on with her life. "How much will this interrupt my life, Dr. Nelson?" She was relieved beyond words. Knowing what had happened to Pam, she wasn't ready to endure the same treatment as her friend.

"Well, other than taking a few days off after the surgery to rest and allow the wound to heal, you won't be affected at all. You can even schedule the radiation therapy for whenever it is convenient as long as you follow the radiation schedule to a tee."

"Okay, so when can we get started?"

Dr. Nelson leaned forward and let out a sigh of relief with a chuckle. "Not so fast, Mary. You still need to talk with your family. I don't want you going through this alone like you have thus far." She shrugged her shoulders. "I don't know why you chose to walk this path without your husband by your side, but I'm sure you have your reasons. I just can't allow you to have surgery and drive home alone. Someone will have to be there for you."

Mary looked down at her lap. She had been holding a tissue that was now shredded to bits. She looked up. "I've not wanted to worry anyone until I was certain of what it was. Now that I know I'm going to be okay, I'll tell them." She sighed. "I'll tell them all."

They scheduled the surgery for the following week. Mary would have to take some time off and close the B&B, but since this was something she rarely performed, she wasn't opposed to it.

As soon as she stepped out of the office building, she reached inside her purse for her phone.

"Seth, honey. It's Mom."

"Hi, Mom. How are you?"

His concern was overwhelming. He was the first one she was to tell. Even before telling Chris. She didn't want the news to get to Seth by anyone else but her. "I'm all right, I guess."

He sighed audibly. "You guess?" Mary could hear his frustration through the connection. "Mom, I know something has been going on with you for some time now. Melissa called to tell me you've been acting odd. Please tell me what it is." He sat at the kitchen table, one hand holding his cell phone to his ear, the other hand running through his hair.

"If you'll give me a few minutes, I'll share all that I know. Deal?"

"Deal." Seth allowed his mother the time she needed to gather her thoughts. Then with a thick voice, she began telling him of the lump in her breast found during her routine mammogram, the diagnosis, and upcoming surgery. She explained the cancer was contained within the milk duct and fully operable. The doctor expected a completely successful operation. No need for him to worry.

"I'm coming home, Mom," he determined.

"Honey, you don't have to come all this way just for a little surgery. I'll be fine," she reassured him.

"I want to be there," Seth explained. "Besides, I'd like to bring someone. If you're up to it."

"Of course, of course. Bring whomever you like." She rummaged through her purse for a tissue. Wiping her eyes, she paused a moment to collect herself. "Seth, I'd been so scared. Now that it's all been explained to me, I know that I'll be okay."

"Mom, everything will be all right. God has it all under His control. You'll be just fine."

Mary smiled. Her son always knew what to say. "Yes. Yes, He does." Her voice, no longer quivering from the sobs she had be holding at bay, now held a resolute belief. "So who is this you plan on bringing home for the family to meet? Is it a young lady?"

Seth released a chuckle. "Yes, Mom. It is indeed a young lady." He paused a moment to correct himself. "Actually, it's two young ladies."

Seth took advantage of this call to tell his mother about the roadside delivery. He spoke with vivacity and passion when he mentioned how Emily had decided to name the baby after her and his sister, Melissa. Every time he mentioned Marissa or Emily, his heart soared. He wondered if his mother could detect his heart's reaction through his enthusiasm as he spoke. He explained how much he wanted his family to meet them and how they would fall in love with them both as soon as they met.

"Mom, it was the most incredible thing that's ever happened to me! Watching a child come into this earth that way was remarkable! Holding her for the first time, I felt as though I knew her. I loved her at first sight."

Mary couldn't help but laugh. Ah, it felt good to laugh again. "It is an extraordinary phenomenon, to see a child born, but to deliver her yourself…well now, that's an exceptional way to fall in love!"

"That's not all, either."

Mary was taken aback. "What else could there be?" Could he be in love with the mother? An unwed young lady? God, please don't let it be that! Mary felt chastised immediately. In her heart, she knew she shouldn't judge the girl, and if God had other plans for her son, then she would just have to accept them.

He informed her of the baby's inability to breath upon birth. "Mom, I had to perform resuscitation on her. If it weren't for the First Aid class you forced me to take back in high school, I'd never have known how to save that baby's life!"

She could hear the gratitude in his voice. "I never thought you'd have to use it. I just felt it was important for you kids to take the course is all."

"Well, I, for one, appreciate the importance of having such training." He was too. Very grateful indeed.

Helen had stayed by her son's hospital bed since his transfer. Tubes seemed to be coming out of every orifice of his body. George had been intubated and placed on oxygen because his lungs were too weak to breathe on their own.

The doctors determined his internal injuries were not life-threatening, but his other injuries would cause severe pain so they had placed him in a drug-induced coma.

A week later George's vital signs had strengthened significantly enough for his doctors to reduce his medications. He could regain consciousness at any time.

She listened to the pump of the oxygen concentrator as it impelled oxygen into his nose. The heart monitor beat steadily. The rhythmic sounds of the two machines lulled her mind. *Somehow she had to take the child from its mother*, she thought.

She heard a groan in the distance. She remained still and silent. She slowly opened her eyes, realizing she must have dozed off.

The moan grew louder.

Helen stood from the recliner to check on her son.

George lay there, slowly swaying his head from side to side. He sluggishly opened his eyes to find his mother staring down at him. He smiled slightly at her tousled appearance.

He had never seen her disheveled. Throughout his life, she always appeared groomed and impeccably dressed. Today, her makeup was almost non-existent. Her hair stood up like alfalfa sprouts in the back, and her linen suit looked as if she had been sleeping in it. If he wasn't mistaken, she probably had.

He ran his tongue along his dry cracked lips. "Thir...sty." He managed to convey his needs.

He watched as Helen reached for the cup of water on the bedside table. She bent the flexible straw to his mouth. He drank slowly and deliberately, never taking his eyes off of her.

Somehow he had to communicate with her. "W-where... am...I?"

"Well, now, son, can't you see you're in a hospital?" The woman didn't have a comforting bone in her body. Her eyes were as cold and rigid always.

"N-no, mo...ther, I can...not." He tried to remain calm. How could she think he would know where he was? All he could see was his mother, white walls and the light above his head. That certainly was no indication as to where he was at the moment. Rather than becoming agitated, he decided to ask another question.

"W-what h-happened?"

Helen huffed in exasperation. "You were in an accident." She was at a loss for something to do, so she pulled the covers up to his neck then straightened out the wrinkles. "You broke both of your legs and your arm and totaled your truck." She stated deprecatingly.

"H-how long...have I b-been here?" He lifted his good arm to stop her from wiping at the blanket.

Helen was taken back at the gentle touch of his hand. She looked into his eyes. They were full of compassion and understanding, something she had never seen there before. She stammered weakly, "Long enough."

The heavy set nurse sauntered in the room, surprised to find her patient awake. "Well, hello, Mr. Baxter! It's so good to see you awake." She inspected the machines then took his vitals. "I'm Miriam, your day nurse." She patted his good shoulder. "I'll bet you're hungry."

George nodded his head.

The gray-haired woman smiled. "Well then, let me see what I can conjure up for you. The kitchen is preparing lunch right now, so I'll have to see what we have in the fridge to tie you over." She looked over her shoulder as she walked out of the room. "I'll be right back."

He tried to sit up, but was unable to do so on his own. Helen depressed the button to raise the head of the bed and placed several pillows behind him.

Miriam returned with a container of yogurt, cherry Jello, and chocolate ice cream.

"Here we are." She placed them on the utility table and rolled it over to him. "I've called food services and placed an order for your lunch. It'll be here around noon."

George looked at the clock hanging on the wall below the television. It was ten-fifteen. He pointed to the goodies Miriam had brought him. "These should…hold me over…until then. Thank you…Miriam."

"Don't thank me yet. You may not like your lunch. Since you haven't eaten for a while, the doctor ordered you a bland liquid diet." She left him to his snack.

Helen reached for the yogurt, but George stopped her. "No. The ice…cream…first. It…melts." Helen huffed, reluctantly opened the container, and began to feed it to her son.

He couldn't remember when chocolate ice cream had tasted so good. He relished every bite.

After George consumed his snacks, Helen fabricated an implausible excuse about needing to check on her staff after her many days away from the manor house. George understood the real reason for her leaving. Helen despised hospitals. She wanted nothing more than to immerse herself in a hot tub of water and cleanse the detestable hospital germs from her body.

Helen bid her son goodbye, doubtful she would return before his discharge. Relieved, she left the building and her son behind her.

His doctor was pleased to see him alert when he made his afternoon rounds. "Well good day, Mr. Baxter." Dr. Reilly Burke said enthusiastically as he entered George's hospital room. "I'm glad to see you are sitting up in bed." He opened his patient's chart and scanned it.

"The nurses all say you are refusing your pain medication."

George nodded his head. "Yes."

"Mind telling me why?"

George shrugged his shoulders. George wasn't in the mood for visitors. Especially a doctor.

"I see." Dr. Burke placed his chart on the bedside table. "So, how are you feeling?"

"Fine." How did he answer such a question? He felt trapped. Confined like a caged animal.

"Okay. Do you have any questions for me?"

"When can I go home?"

"Well, first you need to be able to do the basic things for yourself."

"Like?"

"Like feed yourself. Wash yourself. You know, that sort of thing."

Dr. Burke wasn't making this easy for him. He wanted out of the hospital. "I've got servants at my mother's house who can do that for me."

The doctor rubbed his chin. "Well, then, there's the rehabilitation you'll need."

"Winston can drive me wherever I need to go."

His patient seemed to have all the answers. "I see you've got it all figured out. Let me give you a quick examination and then we'll talk about releasing you."

He looked over George's broken arm. "This is healing nicely."

"Well that's good news. But I've got a question."

"Go ahead. Ask away." Dr. Burke ceased his examination to focus on his patient.

"Why can't I feel my legs?"

Concerned, Dr. Burke walked to the end of the bed and pulled out a retractable pen from his lab coat.

George watched as the physician ran the instrument against his toes.

"Do you feel this?"

George simply looked at the man.

Dr. Burke moved the pen across the toes on his left foot. "How about this?"

Again, George gritted his teeth but said nothing.

The physician moved up to the top of the cast and ran the pen along George's thigh. "What about this?"

George's eyes could have shot arrows at the doctor. "Can't you tell? I don't feel a thing!" He screamed obscenities at the doctor releasing his frustrations on the innocent man.

Dr. Burke remained calm as he returned the pen to his pocket. From the moment George was transferred to his hospital, Dr. Burke had been concerned that there was more to his injuries than had been diagnosed at the previous medical center. The originating hospital had run tests and performed x-rays, all results were negative. Now he would have to run more tests to determine what was causing George's symptoms.

"George. Before I can give you a proper diagnosis I need to run more extensive tests."

This meant he would be remaining right where he was for the time being. George wasn't happy with the news. All he wanted to do was go home to his mother's. There the staff would care for him. His mother may even hire a private nurse to tend to his needs until he was able to get back on his feet. He wondered if he would ever walk again.

"I realize you want to go home."

"To my mother's home." George corrected through gritted teeth.

"Excuse me. Your mother's home as soon as possible, but I'm afraid your injuries are too severe to release you so soon after your accident." Dr. Burke retrieved the chart and annotated something inside. "Let me determine what is causing your symptoms first. Then we'll talk about releasing you."

Later that day, George was transported to Radiology. He was placed in a large box-like machine with a tunnel in the middle. A portion of the tunnel moved around his midsection.

Shortly after returning from his CAT scan, the hospital minister paid him a visit.

"I understand you're finally awake!" The clergyman exclaimed as he entered George's room.

George turned to see a short, stout, balding man in his mid-sixties walking up to his bed. "Y-yes, sir."

The man's eyes were bright and seemed to illuminate when he smiled. "I'm Reverend Thomas Akers. The hospital clergyman." He offered his hand to George.

George accepted his hand and shook it. "I'm George Baxter."

"Yes. Yes, I know." The jolly man practically laughed when he spoke. "The last time I checked on you, your mother was visiting. Where is she now?"

"Um." George cleared his throat. "Actually, you don't want to know."

The elderly man cocked his head sideways. His eyebrows lifted. "Of course I do. Otherwise, I wouldn't have asked." He leaned closer to the bed and lowered his voice to a near whisper. "I spent quite some time with your mother when I was here last. She's a different sort of woman, isn't she?"

George nodded. "You're stating the obvious, Reverend."

"Please call me Thomas."

"Okay, Thomas. My mother isn't one for hospitals. Once I regained conciousness she left."

"I see."

"Yeah, well…That's my mother." George understood his mother was more concerned with her image than the well being of her son. He also knew Helen would not return to visit him. He was on his own until Winston arrived to retrieve him upon his discharge.

George wasn't quite sure of the man who stood before him, but deep down he felt the need to talk with someone. He had to understand what had happened to him the night of the accident and he felt this man would be just the person to answer his questions.

"Um…Thomas? I, uh, have a question I'd like to ask you."

Thomas tilted his head and gave him a look of compassion. "Well, sure, son." He lowered himself in the tan chair and turned it to face George. "What's on your mind?"

George cleared his throat. With his free hand, he toyed with the string on the blanket. "I really don't know where to begin."

"Well I find the beginning is a good place to start."

"The beginning…" George twisted his lips. No. That was too far back. He wanted to know what had taken place the night of the accident. "Actually, I'd like to know what I'm supposed to do once I've prayed for God to forgive me?"

Thomas laughed joyfully. "Oh, son, that's simple."

George looked at the man with confused eyes.

"Really. It is." Thomas leaned back in the chair, "The first thing you must do is read His Word."

"His word?"

Thomas opened the top drawer of the bedside table and pulled out a book. "This is God's Word." He handed it to George.

George received the book and read the cover. "The Bible?"

Thomas nodded. "It's God's word to us." He pointed to the Bible in George's hand. "That's like a daily guide book on how to live your new life as a Christian."

"Really?" George was skeptical.

"Trust me. I'd suggest you begin reading the first book of John then each of his consecutive books, it'll give you the basics of the life of a Christian. I always recommend a new believer start with these books to get a better understanding of who Christ is and how to be a Christian."

"Okay. But how do I know I've been forgiven?" George thought maybe he needed to do something. A good deed or two. Or maybe he should've felt something, some kind of proof that he was forgiven.

Thomas laughed. "Well son, that comes with faith."

"Faith?"

Thomas nodded. "Yes. Did you ask for God to forgive you of your sins?"

"Well…sort of."

Thomas' eyebrows wrinkled together. "What do you mean 'sort of'?"

George explained how he was in the accident and just before passing out, two men had prayed for his sins to be forgiven. "They said they wanted me to make it to heaven if I died that night."

"Well, you didn't die, obviously, so my question to you is…did you ask God to forgive you when the men prayed?"

George shook his head slightly. "Not really."

"Oh? So what you're saying is that you allowed them to pray for you but you didn't pray yourself?"

"Something like that."

"Well, do you want God to forgive you of your sins and enter into your heart?"

"Will it make me a better person?"

"Well now, that's a possibility. To be honest, it's up to you to change into a better person. No one can do it for you. That's why you need to read the Bible." Thomas pointed to the book in George's lap.

"I'd like to change, only I don't know how."

"Just read the directions in the Bible. Study Jesus and how he lived. Emulate Him and you'll change. Guaranteed."

Thomas took a moment to pray with George and lead him in the sinner's prayer. With great elation, Thomas left George to read of his new faith.

George pondered what the man had said long after he left. He opened the Bible and quickly scanned the contents. He effortlessly found the first book of John and began reading.

He read through the first few verses. Verse eight jumped out at him. "If we claim to be without sin, we deceive ourselves and the truth is not in us." He had lived his life as if there were no consequences. He didn't care who he hurt in the process of reaching his goal. It was his life…what did he care?

As he continued to read he felt an overwhelming pressure. A compelling force to acknowledge the actions of his past. Most importantly, the recent deed…his violation against Emily. An unfathomable desecration of such a kind person.

He thought back on how she had reacted to his constant unsolicited advances. She had caught his attention from the first moment he laid eyes on her. Her lovely face and sweet personality lured him like bait on a hook. He had tried to entice her with dinners, dates, and even employee advancement. But she never showed any interest. Then he began to flirt with her, hoping she would reciprocate. He didn't stop, even when she threatened his job. It wasn't until he was called to meet with the Board of Directors that he realized she wasn't just threatening. He lost his job because of his careless inconsideration of another human being. One in which he had become obsessed.

George had desired her. He was consumed with thoughts of having her. He didn't care what she wanted, his only concern was his own carnal needs. After Emily had him fired, he was obsessed with thoughts of revenge. He wanted the one thing she wouldn't give him…her body. He had planned the assault down to the tiniest detail. Only he never considered getting caught or conceiving a baby.

Now, he had to accept the responsibility of his actions. According to the Bible, he had to live in the light. Somehow, he had to ask Emily to forgive him. This would require admitting his involvement in the rape.

Rape.

Such a devious word. He couldn't believe he had been capable of committing such an act. But he had. George bowed his head in remorse. He had never been a man to succumb to his emotions, but the realization of damaging such a precious soul hit him like a ton of bricks. Tears streamed down his face as he wept shamelessly.

After countless scans and tests, Dr. Burke had given him the devastating news.

A small portion of his spine had been crushed in the accident. It wasn't detected early on because of the massive swelling and internal injuries. Unfortunately, there was nothing that could be done.

"All we can do is wait for the broken bones in your legs to heal, remove the casts and schedule regular physical therapy appointments. Unfortunately, you'll never walk again."

Dr. Burke was surprised at George's response to the news. It was as if George expected to never walk again. He passed the hospital's minister on his way out of George's room.

"Hello, Thomas."

Thomas nodded his head. "Hi there, Dr. Burke. I was just on my way to see George. How is he this fine day?"

Dr. Burke shrugged. "Quite frankly, I'm not sure. I just gave him some devastating news, and he didn't react as I expected."

"No?"

"No. Most every patient with his diagnosis has some sort of breakdown. With George, nothing. No tears, no anger. Nothing."

"Odd. Do you mind me asking what is his diagnosis exactly?"

"How about I let him tell you? Maybe then he'll express some kind of emotion."

"All right then. I'll go ahead in and speak with him."

Dr. Burke wanted to remain outside George's door to hear the conversation for himself. But he had to complete his rounds before his morning appointments, so he strode down the corridor.

Inside the hospital room, Thomas spoke with caution. "Good morning, George."

George sat there, unwilling to acknowledge the minister who had entered his room.

"George? I just spoke with Dr. Burke outside your room. I understand he gave you some rather devastating news."

George glared at the minister. "Devastating? Now that's an understatement if ever I've heard one!"

Thomas sat in the chair by the bed. He felt the need to stay with George a while.

"Mind if I ask what news he gave you?"

George's eyes grew large and menacing. "Sure! Why not! It's going to be public knowledge eventually!"

Thomas cringed at the sinister tone of his voice. Still he waited patiently for George to continue.

"Evidently, my spine is crushed." George turned his head to peer at his visitor. "I'm paralyzed. I'll never walk again!" He picked up the cup of water on the over-bed table and forcefully tossed it across the room. It hit the wall scattering water everywhere.

He covered his eyes with his hand and began to cry.

Thomas allowed George the opportunity to release his frustration and despair. He didn't know how long he sat there before George turned toward him.

"Why? Why would God do this to me? I mean, I finally accept Him as my Savior, and this…" George pointed to his motionless legs.

In a most reassuring voice Thomas replied. "God didn't do this to you. It was the result of a terrible accident, George. Not God. He doesn't work that way."

George flailed his hands. "Then how does He work?"

"He takes those things that happen to us and works them for good. He'll use this paralysis to help others through you."

"But what did I do to deserve this punishment?" The words were out before he realized he already had an answer.

Emily.

George calmed almost immediately. "Thomas?"

"Yes, George?"

"Do you believe a person can commit a sin before they give their heart to God, and then God punishes them for that sin even after they accept Him?"

"I believe God punishes anyone who sins, regardless of when they accept Him. For some, the punishment is immediate. Others, later on in life. Then there are those who will face their retribution in the afterlife.

"Ultimately, God is the adjudicator. He determines the best course of action, whether through the legal system or to hand down the sentence Himself. We don't know why or how He chooses who to punish and who is punished through the legal system. All we know is that when our sins have found us out, we must accept the responsibility as well as the consequences of our actions.

"Do you feel as though you have committed a sin for which God is now punishing you?" Thomas's question was innocent enough. He didn't know what George had done.

George wondered if he should profess his sin to this man of God, instead he replied, "Yes, Thomas, that's exactly what I believe."

Later that day, George asked Miriam if there was a copy of the newspaper containing the article of his accident.

As it so happened, Miriam had set aside all the daily newspapers since his arrival. From her experience as a nurse, she understood the need of her patient to have the opportunity to familiarize himself with the daily events which occurred during his unconsciousness.

George spent the day reading the papers. The accident was depicted on the front page of one paper. He read and re-read the article. He couldn't remember anything of the accident. Except the two men who prayed for him to accept Christ. After the prayer, everything went blank.

He turned the front page of the newspaper. The headline sprung off the page…Woman Delivers Baby in Taxi on I-95. He scanned the article and saw her name. She had delivered the baby, in a cab. Emily had a baby girl.

Chapter 20

The DNA tests came back much earlier than expected. It was positive. Helen's son, George, was the father of Emily's child. Helen wasn't surprised. After all her son had put her and his father through over the years, she wasn't the least bit astonished at the news. George had never been an easy child. One to always get his way, regardless of who he hurt in the process, she had presumed the accusations were true; now she knew; George had assaulted the young girl.

Helen had to have the child. The thought wouldn't leave her alone. In Helen's mind, there was no way Emily would be able to raise the child on her own. She had no experience in child rearing, where Helen did. Helen had all the resources at her fingertips: the best schools, the best social life, and the most influential friends. Why, the child would never be for want. But first she had to get the child.

Emily pondered the conversation she'd had with Mrs. Baxter while in the hospital and realized she had done what was best for Marissa. Even though she would never know her father, the least she could do is allow her to have a relationship with her grandmother. She tried to convince herself this was a good thing. Only, she wasn't persuaded.

Two days ago, Seth had called and asked her to go with him to visit his family's ranch. Naturally he wanted her to bring Marissa as well. He had told her of his mother's scare with breast cancer and her upcoming surgery in a few days.

"I plan on being gone a week," he said. He wanted to be with his mother for the surgery and at least part of her recovery.

Eager at the prospect of spending more time with him, Emily promptly agreed.

As she packed her sweater in the suitcase, the doorbell rang. She quickly glanced at the sleeping baby then left to answer the door. She was surprised to see the postman standing there. She opened the glass door and greeted him. Silently the man gave her a small pink paper to sign then passed her a large manila envelope. He slipped away as she opened it.

Inside were DNA test results. *When was this done? How had this been requested?* It didn't take her long to conclude it must have been at the hands of Mrs. Baxter, George's mother.

Of course she'd have the baby tested. She had every right to know if Marissa was her grandchild. Taking Emily at her word was unthinkable.

She couldn't stop thinking about the DNA results. George had indeed been the man who raped her. She had never doubted it was him.

Although she wasn't completely packed, Emily felt the day was too beautiful to waste inside. Maybe a walk around the lake would quiet her distress. Looking at the clock, she deduced there was time for a quick stroll. Outside, she strapped Marissa in her carrier and attached it to the stroller. Just as she was beginning her walk down the driveway, a strange car pulled up beside her. Inside was Helen Baxter.

Helen's driver stopped the car at the end of the driveway and opened the rear door. As Helen disembarked, Emily questioned her visit. Her eyebrows wrinkled. "I don't remember scheduling a visit for today."

"We didn't. I just purchased a beautiful outfit for Marissa and had to bring it by. I hope you don't mind." Helen motioned for Winston to procure the package from the trunk of the car. She reached in and pulled the clothing out of the bag, "Isn't this just adorable?" she asked, holding up the pink-and-white outfit.

"Yes, it is beautiful. You shouldn't have." Emily warily received it from Helen. "Thank you."

"Nonsense. She's my granddaughter, and if I want to buy her something, I will. After all, who else can I spend my fortune on?" Helen leaned down over the baby in her stroller. "Hello, sweetheart." Helen attempted to soften her voice, to no avail.

At the sound of Helen's presumptuous voice, Marissa began to whimper. Emily looked at her watch and realized it was time for her to eat. Considering the elder woman, she offered her a chance to feed a bottle of formula to the baby. Helen looked at Winston, who was still standing by the open car door. "Yes, yes, I would love to feed her."

With that, Emily excused herself to run inside and make a bottle of formula. Although she was nursing, she would allow this time of bonding for Helen and her grandchild.

As Emily came out the front door, she saw Helen's car speeding down the drive. Emily screamed toward the sedan. "My baby! Bring back my baby!" She turned to the sound of Seth's car pulling into the driveway.

Emily ran to his car yelling frantically and flailing her arms. Seth rolled down the window, "They've got my baby!" she screamed. Please, get my baby from them!"

Seth didn't hesitate one second before he circled the drive and was back on the street chasing the sedan Marissa was in.

He quickly dialed 911 on his cell and explained the abduction, described the car, and gave his coordinates. "There'll be an officer behind you momentarily. Just stay on the line and give turn by turn directions so he can intercept you," the operator said.

"Madam?" Winston said.

Helen looked up at him in the rearview mirror with raised eyebrows.

"There's a blue sports car following us," he informed.

Helen turned to peer through the rear window. To her surprise, there was a vehicle following their every turn. "Well then, Winston"—she turned around and looked at him again—"let's give him something to chase… Floor it!"

Winston did as he was commanded with a lack of enthusiasm. This was not what he was expecting to do that morning when Helen had told him they were going for a ride to see her only grandchild. Although he wasn't shocked at her audacity in taking the baby from her mother. He watched the blue car through the rearview mirror. It made every turn he did. He hoped it wasn't a cop.

Seth was concerned because he was not from the area and didn't know the streets. He was losing time having to slow down to read the street signs. As he turned right onto Waxpool Road, the sheriff's car came into view. Instead of slowing down, Seth accelerated to catch up with the black sedan. The police cruiser closed in behind him, shrieking its siren.

Winston instinctively released his foot from the accelerator pedal. As Helen realized they began to slow, she yelled for Winston to floor it again. Winston did as he was instructed, reluctantly. He knew it was inevitable they would be caught. There was no way they would lose the police cruiser and the sports car behind them. They just didn't have the engine to outrun the two.

A few miles down the road, another deputy's car came on the scene. Winston knew it was useless to continue their quest with the police and the sports cars in hot pursuit. He slowed the car.

"What are you doing?" Helen cried.

"I'm pulling over, Madam."

"No, you're not! You're going to continue driving," she commanded.

"Madam, look ahead…there's a road block and behind us there is a police car and a sports car in hot pursuit. It's futile to continue." Winston pulled the car over to the side of the road.

Slowly he opened the door and disembarked, arms raised over his head.

Seth pulled close behind the sedan. He stepped out of his car and ran over to the black vehicle, the deputy on his heels. He promptly opened the rear door and gingerly pulled out the elderly woman.

"Unhand me, young man!" Helen exclaimed. Seth willingly released her. Brushing her hands on her tailored wool jacket, she stood, back erect, nose slightly upturned, hands woven together.

"Ma'am? Would you mind telling me what you were doing?" The deputy inquired.

"I was just taking my granddaughter for a ride," Helen claimed.

"Then why was this man pursuing you?" the officer asked.

"I'm sure I don't know."

The officer turned to Seth. "As you heard, she claims she was taking her granddaughter for a ride. Perhaps you are mistaken."

Seth couldn't believe what he was hearing. He threw his arms in the air in frustration. "A ride at that speed?" Seth was incredulous. "I'm *not* mistaken. As I pulled into the mother's driveway, she was screaming her child had been taken. I had seen the sedan pull out of the circular drive as I arrived at the child's home and followed it."

"How can you be sure this is the same vehicle?" the officer gave him a look of admonition.

Seth huffed. "I immediately gave chase. Never even let the car out of my sight." He pointed at the deputy, "You saw how close behind I was. You followed *me*, for goodness sake!"

Helen glimpsed at the officer's name tag. "Officer Taylor?"

He turned to the woman. "It's Deputy, ma'am. Deputy Taylor."

"All right then, *Deputy* Taylor, as you can see for yourself"—Helen pointed toward the back seat of her car—"The child is in no harm. She's perfectly content."

Just then Marissa gave a small whimper.

Christa Scott Reide

"Mind you, she's hungry. I was just going to take her back to her mother."

"*I'll* take her back to Emily." Seth stepped closer to the vehicle.

"Hold on there one minute, young man." Deputy Taylor was not about to release the baby to anyone. "I still have a few more questions for the child's grandmother."

Helen gave Seth a knowing look, "Certainly. Go right ahead." She waived her hand. "Ask away."

The deputy cleared his throat, "Um, well, um," he stammered as he continued, "Well, did the mother know you were taking the child for a ride?"

Helen glared at the officer. "Well," she released a loud sigh with the word. "Of course she did."

Seth was appalled. He believed Emily wouldn't have acted so hysterical had she known the woman was taking Marissa for a ride. "Deputy Taylor?"

The deputy turned to the sound of his name. "Yes?"

"Why don't we take Marissa home and you can ask her mother if she was aware of this woman's actions."

"Hmm." Deputy Taylor scratched his chin. "I guess we should all go on down to headquarters." He nodded his head toward Seth. "You can get the baby's mother and meet us there."

Helen grew agitated. She feigned a headache. "Deputy Taylor," her voice was as sweet as butter, "Would you mind if I had Winston take me home, I'm feeling a bit ill at the moment? You can talk to Emily without me, correct?"

The deputy refused. "No ma'am. You'll have to come with me." He waved his hand toward his patrol car. Gently, the deputy took hold of her arm.

"What?" Helen's voice shrilled. "You mean I have to ride in that…that…patrol car?" She was flabbergasted. "Why, I can't be seen in one of those!

"Young man, do you know who I am?" Helen shook her arm loose from the young man's tight grip.

"No, ma'am, and I don't care either. Just get in the car, ma'am."

"Why, you insolent—" Helen was turned around by the officer, who helped her in the car. "When my attorney hears of this, I'll have your job!"

"Good luck, ma'am." The officer wasn't impressed or intimidated. Because of that, Helen was infuriated.

Without delay, Seth climbed into the sedan and unlatched the crying baby from her carrier. He pulled out Marissa and held her close. "Shh…shh." He whispered in her ear, "Everything's going to be all right now. I've got ya." He kissed the side of her head, "I'm gonna take you home, sweet girl."

Marissa immediately calmed at the sound of his voice.

Another deputy arrived at his side. "I don't think I've ever seen a screaming baby calm down so quickly before." He reached for Marissa. Seth's confused look alerted the deputy.

"Oh. Sorry, but I have to take her with me, unless, of course, you're her father."

Seth waved his head from side to side. "No. I'm not her father." He relinquished Marissa to the deputy who promptly latched her in the carrier then transported her to another patrol car.

As Seth pulled into the circular driveway, Emily came running down the porch steps. Gram was right behind her. He climbed out of the car.

Emily anxiously waited for him to give her Marissa. When he didn't, a look of confusion washed over her face. "Where's my baby?" she cried.

"Marissa was taken to child services by a deputy."

Emily and Gram gasped. "What do you mean taken?" Emily was perplexed. Why hadn't he brought Marissa back to her? Why had some stranger taken her baby?

Unable to look into her tear-streaked face, Seth looked down. He knew he had disappointed Emily and Gram by not having Marissa with him, but there was nothing he could do. He explained this to the women. "Since I'm not Marissa's father, they wouldn't let me bring her home to you." He sighed. "They won't release her to anyone but you." He looked at Emily. "I'll take you, if you want."

Emily nodded. She hugged Gram then climbed in the passenger's seat of his car.

Inside the old brick building, Emily stood waiting for the deputy to hang up the phone.

As she replaced the receiver the deputy looked up at Emily. "May I help you?" the young woman had kind, caring eyes.

"Yes." She looked around the small room, "I'm looking for my baby."

"Your baby?"

"Yes. She was taken from me and I've come to take her home."

The look of concern on the deputy's face was mixed with bewilderment.

Seth read the deputy's name tag and cleared his throat, "Um...Deputy Ward, what she means is her baby was abducted from her home by her grandmother a short while ago. The grandmother has been apprehended and the baby was taken to child services." He glanced at Emily who gave him a grateful smile. "This is the baby's mother, Emily Wilkerson, and she's come to take her baby, Marissa Wilkerson, home."

"Oh! Of course! You're the man who called a while back!" She leaned forward, "I took your call. I'd know your smooth melodic voice anywhere." She batted her eyelashes flirtatiously.

Emily gritted her teeth at the woman's brazenness and was relieved to see Seth appeared to disapprove as well.

Seth felt uncomfortable with the woman's shameless advances. "Yes, well, um...what do we need to do to claim the baby?"

Deputy Ward tilted her head slightly, "The baby?" she'd had a momentary lapse of memory, "Ah, yes, the baby that came in with the old lady and the stuffed shirt." She described the butler with disdain. "He talks like a snob. And the old lady? Well she's worse."

Seth and Emily looked at each other, then back at the deputy. "The baby?" Seth reminded her.

"Oh. I'm sorry." She placed her hand on her chest, "I keep rambling on and on. Sherriff Curry has a few questions for you first." She looked at Emily. "Have a seat. I'll let him know you're here."

They waited a while before Sherriff Curry asked Emily to join him in his office. He motioned for her to have a seat across from his desk. He sat down behind the large metal frame in a squeaky vinyl desk chair. He leaned on the table, hands steepled beneath his chin. "So you're the mother of the baby we have in protective services?"

Emily nodded.

"I realize you've been waiting a while, but I was interrogating Mrs. Baxter and her butler, Montgomery Winston." He leaned back in his chair folding his long arms across his broad chest. The man was every bit as intimidating as a person could imagine. Standing well over six feet and built like a lean bear, he had short dark hair, chocolate brown eyes and a thick dark mustache accentuated his strong jaw line. He scratched his head and proceeded. "I'd like to ask you a few questions."

Emily sat in the worn out, burgundy vinyl chair, quivering. She felt as if she had been the one to commit a crime. She nodded her acquiescence, her fear tightening her throat. How would she ever answer this man's questions as terrified as she was just sitting in his office? *Oh how I wish Seth could be with me.*

"First off, when was the baby born?"

"September twenty-third."

The Sherriff removed a small black notebook from his shirt pocket and annotated her response. "What hospital was she born in?"

"She wasn't born in a hospital."

His eyes grew large at her implausible answer. "Was she born at home?"

"No, sir."

He wrote something in his notebook.

"Okay, so you've got me intrigued. Where was she born, *exactly*?"

Emily hung her head timidly, "In a cab on I95."

"North or southbound?"

She couldn't believe his line of questioning. She wanted her baby, now! "What kind of inquiry is this? I want my baby!" Emily exclaimed.

"Just answer the question," Sherriff Curry demanded.

She answered his question quickly and succinctly. "Northbound."

The brawny man leaned back in his chair deep in thought.

"September twenty-third you say?"

"Yes, sir."

"At night?"

"Yes, sir."

"Wasn't that the night of the multi-car pile-up down in the Dale City area?"

Emily nodded her head.

"That was also the accident in which George Baxter, Helen Baxter's son was severely injured."

"What does that have to do with my baby?"

Sherriff Curry smiled wryly. "Nothing. I'm just putting the pieces of the puzzle together." Then his face lit up in recognition. "You're the young lady who has alleged George Baxter assaulted you, aren't you?"

Emily was beyond frustration by now. This man was interrogating her with questions irrelevant to the situation and she was not going to continue to allow him to intimidate her any longer. With her hands clinched she asked nicely but compellingly, "Sherriff Curry, I thought I was here to get my baby back. What does this line of questioning have to do with that?"

He cleared his throat audibly, "Yes, well, like I said, I was putting the pieces of the puzzle together." He stood and walked around to the front of his desk and sat on the corner closest to her. His facial expression changed to one of compassion.

"Young lady, I understand you've been through a lot in your young lifetime. If, and I do mean if, George Baxter raped you, he will be held accountable. If Mrs. Baxter abducted your daughter, she will answer to the authorities as well." He paused momentarily to gather his thoughts. "Why don't you tell me what happened earlier today?"

Emily divulged her side of the story. Sherriff Curry nodded his head in acceptance. "So what you're telling me is that you had no idea she was taking the baby for a ride."

"Correct. I was inside my home preparing a bottle for Mrs. Baxter to feed to Marissa, and when I returned Mrs. Baxter's car was speeding out of my driveway, and my baby was gone!"

"I see." He made note of her comments. "Well, Miss Wilkerson, I believe I have all the answers I need. You may have a seat in the waiting area, and I'll have your baby brought to you."

Seth stood as soon as he saw Emily enter the waiting area. He could see by the look on her face she was distraught. He opened his arms to comfort her. She welcomed the gesture.

His caress was like sunshine after a prolonged rain. She relished the contentment she felt in his embrace. It was like nothing she had ever experienced before. Safety, security, and reassurance.

There was something about holding her in his arms that felt so…right. He couldn't describe it any other way. Although she was not to be his life companion, he knew she could be his friend. He gently kissed the top of her head.

"Here she is." Deputy Ward's lilting voice interrupted their intimate moment.

Emily turned to see Marissa in the deputy's arms. Her heart soared at the sight of her baby girl. Without hesitation, she received Marissa from the deputy.

"Thank you so much!" she offered a warm smile to the deputy.

"She was changed and given a bottle of formula when she arrived."

Emily was pleased to know her baby had been well cared for. "I can't thank you enough."

"Yeah. Well, the guys wouldn't allow her to fall asleep. Everyone wanted to hold her so they took turns. She should be worn out, but look at her!" The deputy wiggled one of the baby's feet. In her lilting voice she spoke directly to Marissa, "You know who's got you, don't you little lady?"

Emily smiled at the deputy. "I think she does."

"Well, I hate to break up this little party, but we need to be going." Seth placed his hand on the small of Emily's back to lead her to the door.

"Um, okay. Bring the baby back sometime. We'd all love to see her again." Deputy Ward reluctantly waved goodbye as the small group left the building.

Gram was waiting on the porch. When she saw the car turn in the drive she practically ran down the steps. "Seth, we owe you another debt of gratitude. How can we ever thank you?" Gram allowed him to exit the car then hugged him tightly as Emily climbed out of the back seat with Marissa.

"I'm so relieved." Emily kissed Marissa's little head. She transferred one arm around Seth and kissed his cheek. "You're our hero!"

The simple gesture left Seth wondering what it would be like to press his lips against hers in a real kiss. He chastised himself for the thought. "I was just doing what needed to be done. I'm really no hero."

"You are to us! And that's what matters." Gram pulled him into another embrace and then led him up the porch steps and through the front door behind Emily.

Emily turned to Seth. "I think I'll take Marissa upstairs to bed. It's been a long day for her. I'll be right back." She thought of inviting him to join her and quickly asked, "Would you like to see her room?"

Seth's eyes lit up with excitement. "I'd love to see it!" He followed Emily with Marissa up the circular staircase.

As Gram turned to lock the storm door, a delivery truck pulled into the driveway. She stood there and watched as the man walked around to the back of the vehicle. He opened the door and disappeared from her sight for a moment. In his hands he carried a large bouquet of pink roses with congratulatory balloons attached. *Who in the world ordered those?*

She accepted the delivery, allowing the man to set them on the table by the stairs. Curiously, she read the card…

I understand you had a baby girl. Congratulations. George.

Emily and Seth descended the stairs. Emily saw the beautiful bouquet and balloons and gasped. "Wow!" her eyes grew large, "Who are they from?" She tilted her head to read the card.

Her heart dropped to her feet. George. She lifted the vase and marched to the kitchen, Seth and Gram followed on her heels. "Of all the nerve!" She mumbled loudly, "I cannot believe he had the audacity to send these to me!"

She stepped on the pedal of the metal trash can. The lid opened. Then with grand display, she dropped them inside. To her dismay the balloons floated freely above the waste receptacle. She walked a few steps around the island, opened a long drawer, and withdrew an ice pick.

She stabbed each balloon, releasing her anger and frustration with every strike.

"How dare he!"

Pop!

"Of all the blatant-!"

Pop! Pop!

"If he thinks...!"

Pop!

"I'll let him get away with this...!"

Pop!

"He's got...!

Pop!

"Another thing coming!"

Pop! Pop!

Gram glanced at Seth who stood in the kitchen doorway amused. She leaned in and quietly spoke, "I take it Emily hasn't told you about George."

Seth shrugged his shoulders, "No, she hasn't. Who is this George?"

"George is Marissa's father." She instantly covered her mouth with her hand, eyes bulging. She couldn't believe she had blurted that out so easily.

Seth's jaw clinched like a vice. His hands balled into fists at his sides. Gram saw a myriad of emotions traverse his eyes.

She placed her hands on his upper arms and turned him toward her. "It wasn't my place to tell you. I should have left that to Emily. Please don't let her know I told you." Gram saw his jaw relax and his eyes soften. At the change of his demeanor, Gram released her hands and walked out of the room.

Seth wondered what kind of man would conceive a child and send congratulatory flowers then callously sign the card without acknowledging the baby as his.

Emily finished stuffing the strips of balloons in the trash. She looked up to see Seth watching her, his expression calm and amused. She smiled self-consciously smoothing her hair and imaginary wrinkles from her clothing. She sighed when she realized how she must have looked through his eyes.

"I'm so sorry you had to see me act like that."

"What? Like a crazy woman?" He smiled brightly.

She laughed and nodded. "Yeah, I guess I did look a little crazy."

"Little?" He was incredulous.

"Well, okay, a lot." Emily smiled, relieved that he was teasing and not criticizing her tirade.

"I've got to go home and pack." Seth shrugged one shoulder. "We've got an early morning and long day ahead of us."

Emily escorted him to the front door. "Yeah, I have a few more things to do and I'll be ready." She paused, "I had no idea how much stuff I needed to pack. Gram helped me by preparing a list." She laughed timidly. "I hope you have a large trunk."

"Oh, don't worry about that. My trunk's plenty big." He stepped through the front doorway onto the porch. Emily followed close behind.

"I'd like to thank you again, for all you've done. Especially today." She fidgeted with her fingers.

He gave her a reassuring hug. "It was nothing, really."

She watched as he descended the steps, climbed into his car, and drove out of sight.

Although she needed to finish up her packing and be ready for Seth by six o'clock the next morning for the ride to North Carolina, Emily took some time to sit on the sofa in the family room. After the day's events, all she wanted to do was hold her little one close and never let her go.

Chapter 21

The drive to Seth's ranch home took over six hours. At the halfway mark of the trip, Seth had stopped to allow Marissa to nurse. He had stepped out of the car and walked around to the back to allow Emily some privacy. She had climbed in the back seat to avoid onlookers. After changing and feeding Marissa, they were back on the road. By the time they arrived, it was time to nurse Marissa again.

Introductions were brief as Emily was led into the house. Seth explained Marissa had to be nursed. He would take Emily and Marissa up to their room. While the baby nursed, Seth would have time to catch up with his family.

"Don't worry about it," Mary said. She placed her hand on Marissa's head and stroked it gently. "There'll be plenty of time to get to know each other after your precious darling has had her fill and is down for her nap. I've taken the liberty to bring down Seth's basinet from the attic. I had Sean put it in your room earlier."

"Thank you very much, Mrs. Woods."

"Please, call me Mary. Now go on upstairs and feed this darling baby. We'll see you in a bit."

Seth escorted Emily and Marissa to the largest of the guest rooms. It was also the most elegant.

Decorated in white and dark blues, the contrast was enchanting. A navy-and-white rug was placed in the center of the room. The walls were a soft blue with accent décor in a sparkling yellow. The curtains were of white Belgium lace with delicate navy stripes hung over large floor-to-ceiling windows.

The honey oak crown molding gave the room an opulent ambiance. A fireplace stood in the far corner opposite the bed.

A luxurious bathroom decorated in the same blues, whites, and yellows was positioned just before the fireplace.

Seth put down her suitcases atop the table next to the dresser. "Well, I know you need to nurse Marissa, so I'll give you your privacy." With a long look deep into Emily's blue eyes, Seth noticed how tired she was and offered to take Marissa once she was done eating to allow her some time alone. He would be waiting across the hall in the Americana room.

Emily was thankful of his consideration and accepted his offer, saying she would love to take a luxurious bath in the Jacuzzi tub.

As soon as Marissa was fed and happy, Emily took her out to Seth. Seth scooped the happy bundle into his arms like a pro. Then kissed Emily on the cheek and said, "Enjoy your bath." And off he went down the stairway.

"Oh, would you look at this precious child?" The women of the household couldn't resist a baby. They each took a turn holding the contented baby. Mary took her turn last and walked to the family room to sit in her rocker.

"Come, Seth, tell me about this Emily and her bundle of joy."

Seth had previously told her about the miraculous birth but failed mention how close he had become with both the baby and her mother.

"It's really just a friendship, Mom." He tried to explain, but Mary knew her son better than he knew himself.

"Sure, sweetheart," she stated. "You may think Emily is just a friend, but I saw something between the two of you that is much more meaningful than an unpretentious friendship." Looking down at the now sleeping darling, she quietly admitted, "You may think you are in love with this beloved baby, but it is her mother you love."

Seth was taken back with his mother's straightforwardness. She'd never been one to mince words, but this was more than which he had prepared himself. He stood up and took the baby from his mother's caress. He walked over to the sofa and sat down. Never acknowledging his mother's comment, he simply said, "I think I'll take a nap with Marissa now." He lay down, placing Marissa on his chest, and promptly closed his eyes.

He pondered his mother's pronouncement. Was he in love with Emily? Sure, he was attracted to the lovely dark-haired beauty, but was it love? He had always believed he would fall in love with a virtuous woman. How could he feel something more than friendship toward Emily? This was more than he was ready to contend with as tired as he was. Just a few minutes rest and he would be able to see things with a new prospective.

Emily felt refreshed and renewed after her lavish bubble bath. She hated leaving Seth with the baby for such a long time, but she had inadvertently fallen asleep while lingering in the tub. Before she knew it, more than an hour had passed. Emily jumped to her feet and hurriedly dried and dressed herself. She ran a brush through her hair and left the room.

As she quietly walked down the L-shaped staircase, she admired the beautiful entryway of the large homestead. There were several passageways in which she could choose. One would lead her to the formal living room, another to the formal dining room. Each one was very large and tastefully decorated as if to say "welcome home" to anyone who sauntered in. Several other doorways led to various rooms decorated immensely different, although maintaining the French country décor throughout the home. Emily found her way to the sun-filled kitchen modestly decorated in wallpaper of fruits and baskets and then enhanced with dried flowers, baskets, and needlework.

She walked through the family breakfast area and noticed an archway to another room. She could hear the soft sounds of wood hissing in the fireplace and Pachelbel playing on the stereo. She stopped in the archway of the family room, captivated by what she saw before her.

Seth was lying on the overstuffed sofa in front of the fireplace with Marissa nestled on his arms. Both were sleeping soundly to the gentle crackle of the fire. Emily thought it strange to have a fire in the middle of the afternoon, but the unusual chill in the fall air necessitated one. Seth had mentioned that he thought Marissa would nap if she were warm and cozy. And she did look cozy snuggled up on Seth's chest.

Emily imagined how nice it would feel if she were the one he was holding. She longed to feel his strong arms around her, comforting her as she slept.

Mary sat across the room engrossed in her cross-stitch. The window seat allowed the afternoon sunlight to illuminate her craft without use of a lamp. She sensed someone else in the room before she saw Emily standing there. Mary placed the needlework on her lap and observed Emily as she, in turn, studied the two sleeping on the sofa.

Unaware she was being watched, Emily leaned her shoulder into the wall of the archway, placing one hand across her midsection and the other hand gently resting below her chin. The casual black sundress adorned with a bold red sweater hung gently over every curve. Her midsection was still a little plump, and her small but full breasts revealed that she nursed the baby. Mary could understand why Seth was attracted to this young lady. Though she wasn't quite sure this was a girl in whom her son should be interested, Mary wouldn't make any decisions until she knew this stranger better. Although she didn't know how Emily felt about her son, the look in her eyes was enough to warrant suspicion.

"Seth wouldn't let her sleep anywhere else."

Caught by surprise, Emily scanned the room from where the whispered voice came. Recognizing Mary's silhouette in the sunlight, she nodded her understanding.

Mary paused, searching for just the right words and hoped her bias wouldn't be too apparent. "Can't say that I blame her for sleeping so soundly."

Emily smiled shyly, attempting not to reveal her thoughts were quite the same.

"Penny for your thoughts?" Mary quietly stated.

Emily looked over the back of the sofa to the corner of the room. Afraid to speak for fear of awakening the two slumberers, she slowly stepped toward the figure in the window seat.

Mary shifted to one side and patted the cushion inviting Emily to sit next to her. She placed the needle carefully in the cloth and set her project aside. Emily sat down where the older woman had indicated and looked out through the window at the breathtaking view of the foothills of North Carolina. "It's beautiful here."

"Yes, it is." Mary beamed a smile. "This house and the property have been in my family for seven generations. It dates back to 1808.

"This is a picture of my grandfather, John Henry Jacobs." Mary retrieved the vintage photograph from the antique library table and handed it to Emily.

Emily studied the photo. "Wow! Seth looks exactly like him." She returned the picture to Mary.

"Yes, he does. Even down to the color of his eyes." Mary commented. "Granddad and I had a very special relationship. I was thankful he lived long enough to see his first great-grandsons born. He bonded with Seth immediately." Mary studied the photo a minute before replacing it on the table. "Seth has a lot of granddad's characteristics. I think that's why he and I are so close. Next to Chris, Seth's my closest friend."

"So won't you tell me about you and Marissa?" Mary asked.

"There's really not much to tell." Emily felt a little reticent to divulge her recent past, let alone the family history.

"Oh, quite the contrary," Mary interjected. "You've got a bit of history yourself, believe it or not. What about your parents?"

"They're both dead." Emily hung her head low.

"I'm so sorry."

Emily appreciated Mary's thoughtfulness. She looked at Seth's mom. "My mom and my little brother died during childbirth. I was just a toddler. My dad died a few years later. The doctors said he died of a massive heart attack. I believe he died from a broken heart." She shrugged. "No matter what the cause, all I know is that I never really got a chance to know either of my parents.

"One of the few things I remember was my father calling me Emmie. As a child I thought it was the letters M and E, so when I learned to write, I wrote my name as M-E!" She gave a shy chuckle.

Mary smiled thoughtfully. "So who raised you?"

"My grandmother…Dad's mom, Hannah Wilkerson. Everyone calls her Gram."

"And what about Marissa? Does her daddy get to see her any?" Mary questioned innocently.

Emily looked down at her hands. She fidgeted with the hem of her sundress, "No, no he doesn't see her at all."

"Oh, I see. How do you feel about that?"

"To be honest, I'm okay with it." Mary was surprised at Emily's admission. "I mean, I didn't…he, um…" Emily wasn't ready to disclose her abhorrence for George to Seth's mother so she simplified the truth a little. "Let's just say Marissa doesn't need a man like him in her life."

"I see." Taken back by her retort, Mary believed something disparaging occurred between Marissa's parents that Emily wasn't ready to reveal. Mary could think of a number of things that could've ensued, but from past experience, she knew it was best to allow Emily the opportunity to open her heart whenever she was ready.

Concerned that Mary might think her callous, Emily attempted to explain her attitude toward Marissa's father. "I'm sorry. I didn't mean to sound so spiteful. George, Marissa's father, and I, well…how do I put it?" She sighed audibly. "We have some animosity between us. I thought I had forgiven him when I believed he had died in a car accident the night Marissa was born. But a few days after I returned home from the hospital, some flowers and balloons were delivered to me with a congratulatory card attached.

"They were from George. Anger reared its ugly head as if it had never departed. I felt all the resentment and rage come rushing back like a flood. I lost all sense of control.

"I tossed the flowers in the trash and popped the balloons with an ice pick. All my pent up emotions discharged full force with every stab of the pick. The worst part was that Seth witnessed it all.

"Though he took it in stride. He joked about it saying I acted like a crazy woman." Emily chuckled. "I was relieved he was so nice about it. I was afraid he might think less of me for my outburst."

"Seth has had his moments, like the rest of us," Mary comforted. "So, have you been working on forgiving George?"

Emily looked away. She had been praying for help in the forgiveness department, but was coming up short. When she thought about all she had lost because of his selfish transgression she realized forgiveness was more difficult than she had expected. "It's harder than I had anticipated."

"You know, Emily, I find it easier to forgive on a daily basis than to forgive and try to forget."

"Really? How do you do that?"

"It's simple, really." Mary explained that when someone offends her, she forgives the offense every time it comes to mind.

"Eventually, I think about it less and less until one day I realize I haven't thought about it at all."

"Interesting." Emily wondered if she could try such a tactic. "It's worth giving it a try."

Mary smiled and patted Emily's hand. "That's all God requires."

"Does George's family acknowledge the baby?"

Mary's inquisition was harmless enough, but Emily was careful with her answers for fear of revealing too much.

"Mr. Baxter died a while back. Mrs. Baxter—that's George's mother—came to visit me in the hospital. She had requested a DNA test completed without my knowledge or consent. She's one of the most affluent women in the area and has enough money to request such a thing be done surreptitiously. I had no idea of the testing until the results arrived at my home just a few days ago. I knew he was the father and the test proved it. Mrs. Baxter had said if I gave Marissa to her to raise, she would see to it that Marissa have the best of everything."

Emily shook her head. "When I denied giving her my baby, Mrs. Baxter accused me of wanting more of the Baxter fortune. I don't want anything from the Baxter's." The threat to take Marissa away still lingered. For all she cared, they could deny her baby and she and Marissa could live their lives the way she wanted without interference from Mrs. Baxter or George. But then, after she thought about it, she couldn't deny Marissa the opportunity to know her grandmother even though Marissa would hopefully never know her father. Now she might never know her grandmother because of the attempted abduction.

They heard movement from the direction of the sofa where Seth and Marissa slept. Mary changed the subject. "How did you end up delivering Marissa in the back of a taxi?"

"Ah, well," she chuckled. "My friends thought I should get out of the house and they convinced me to go to the concert. I knew I shouldn't, but they insisted that I needed some entertainment to get my mind off things, and since I still had a few weeks in my term, I conceded. We had a rather large group of people going from our church that night." She shrugged her shoulders then continued, "I'm sure you know the rest." Emily took another deep breath and gave a weak smile to Mary.

"Actually, no, I don't know the rest," Mary replied. "If you went with friends, how did you end up in a cab?"

"Oh, that. Well, the group I rode with wanted to go out for a bite to eat after the concert. I wasn't feeling up to it, so I switched places with a young lady in my church. At least I thought I'd switched places with her. She was supposed to tell the people she rode with that I was returning with them. Instead, she told someone else who evidently failed to pass along the information, best I can figure."

Emily quickly summarized how Cameron had allowed her to use his phone to call her grandmother who, in turn, called a cab.

"Oh, I see. You poor thing, being left all alone like that."

Emily shrugged. "Now that I think about it, it wasn't so bad after all." She looked in Seth's direction.

Mary could sense Emily's growing attraction toward her oldest son. Although she had observed chemistry between the two, she didn't want to encourage it.

Thus far, she had determined Emily was a sweet young lady and loving mother. But she wasn't convinced she was the girl for her Seth.

Chapter 22

After Marissa woke, Seth decided to help his brothers in the barn.

He had been gone for only a short time when Mary asked Emily if she felt like helping in the kitchen. Marissa was cooing contentedly on the blanket on the floor. Emily scooped up the baby and carried her into the large kitchen. Mary took Marissa from Emily's arms so she could lay the blanket and toys on the floor. It took some time for Mary to eventually deposit the baby onto the soft, furry blanket and set about cooking.

"Hello, stranger!"

Seth looked up from grooming his horse, Midnight Run, to see Amy, his old high school flame, walking toward him.

"Hi, yourself." He felt genuinely happy to see her. Depositing the brush down on the stack of hay next to him, he opened his arms to embrace her.

"So what have you been up to?" Amy unreservedly fell into his embrace. After a quick hug, which ended all too soon for Amy, she shared her most recent activities. She had graduated from UNC Chapel Hill's accelerated nursing program and then went on to become a nurse practitioner. She loved her job with one of the most prominent family practices in the Greensboro area.

"I'm down visiting my parents and heard you were in town. Thought I'd stop by and say hello." She smiled sweetly.

"I'm glad you did. So how are you doing? Do you enjoy your job in Greensboro?"

"I truly love what I'm doing and the patients I see." She leaned her head to his. "Some I see on a regular basis, if you know what I mean." She chuckled. "Actually, I'm here for an interview with Dr. Russell's office."

When Seth didn't respond, she continued. "He's the new doctor in town. Just out of med school." She brushed back a loose strand of blonde hair. "He's opening a new practice and needs a nurse practitioner. I'm hoping to move back home."

"I'm happy for you." Seth replied. Returning home would be a good thing for her. Maybe then she could settle down. Maybe, just maybe, they could date whenever he was in town. He smiled to himself.

Seth told her about delivering Marissa, the intense moments of struggling to get her to breathe, and the bond that had been created between them.

"That's amazing!" Amy was awed at his capabilities to maintain his cool while delivering a newborn into the world without a bit of medical training.

"If it weren't for the 911 operator and the guys," he threw in, "I'd never have been able to do it."

Amy laughed hysterically. "The guys? You mean Zack helped?" She caught her breath. "What on earth did Mr. 'I faint at the sight of blood' do exactly?"

Seth chuckled. "He rummaged through my gym bag to get a clean T-shirt and towel." He realized how ridiculous that sounded and laughed. "He didn't do much, but I'm thankful he was there to help regardless of how menial the job."

Amy looked down at her shoes and scraped them in the dirt. She wasn't sure how to tell him but decided the truth was best. She looked into his beautiful blue eyes and confessed, "I've missed you."

Her eyes glistened with unshed tears. Amy had dated several men during college and even recently, but she never forgot her first love. She had regretted her decision to break it off with Seth when the guy she had dumped him for turned around and dumped her for another girl. She had attempted to date other men but always compared them to her high school sweetheart. Needless to say, none could compare. All she could hope for was

The Long Ride Home

his return to the area and a chance to see him and tell him how much of a mistake she'd made when she broke up with him.

"Seth? I…well…I know I hurt you when we broke up. And, I want to say I'm sorry."

Seth shook his head. "No need to apologize." He stroked her soft, blonde hair. All the fond memories returned. "It took a while, I'll admit, but I got over it."

"Oh." Amy was disappointed. In a way, she still wanted him to pine for her. If he got over it, then does that mean he no longer loved her? "Seth? I've never gotten over you."

There, she'd said it. She waited for him to declare his undying love to her.

Seth was taken aback with her declaration. He looked into her ebony eyes and felt only sorrow. He no longer felt the love and longing he once had for her. Although he didn't believe Emily was for him, he still felt uncomfortable telling Amy about his relationship with her, so he decided not mentioning it was best at this juncture.

When he didn't declare his undying love, Amy hung her head.

"Well…I guess I'd better get back to Mom and Dad's." She said her farewell with a hug and laid a kiss upon his lips, hoping to rekindle any spark there might be in his heart .

Seth glanced at the kitchen window where he'd seen Emily standing not long ago. Relieved she was no longer there, he turned to Amy. "You know, maybe, once you move back home and all…" Seth shrugged his shoulders. "I dunno, but maybe when I'm in town we could go out some."

Amy's heart jumped with joy. Her eyes sparkled when she smiled. "I'd like that." She said her farewell, climbed into her car and drove away.

Seth smiled to himself as he watched her car until it disappeared.

In the barn, his twin brother, Sean stood outside Buttercup's stall watching Seth and Amy. Anger rose within his chest at the sight of them kissing. For far too long, he'd taken a back seat to his twin brother. And now it seemed he would continue to remain there—when it came to Amy—overlooked and unwanted by the one woman who truly held his heart. Only he was much too shy to approach her and profess his love. So, he stood there, leaning on a pitchfork, seething at the thought of the two of them in each other's arms.

At the window, Emily stood watching Seth embrace and kiss the attractive woman. Quickly, so not to be seen, she turned to Mary and offered to make stuffing from scratch. Mary happily complied. She'd resulted to making stuffing from the box for the last several years because it was so much more convenient.

Emily set about her task once Mary had helped her obtain the ingredients. She vigorously chopped the onions and celery while recalling Seth kissing the blond woman. Emily had hoped that he was attracted to her but it was apparent Seth didn't think of her in that way. She wanted something more than friendship. The way he looked at her even encouraged her that his emotions were stronger. Obviously, after seeing him with this other woman, his feelings for Emily were less than they appeared or was she simply imagining he had a fondness in the first place? Granted, he didn't appear too enthused about the kiss; it was more or less a friendly gesture, Emily hoped. But still, she and Seth had never kissed, so how could she know if he was indifferent toward the young blond woman's display of affection?

Disgusted with her thoughts, Emily turned her attention to the task at hand. She dumped the onion and celery in a pot of water and put them on to boil.

Seth finished mucking stalls, bailing hay, and feeding the horses. By the time he was done, it was almost time for dinner. He knew he had to shower and change in order to be allowed at the table, a rule his mother had imposed since he had been a child, so he high-tailed it inside to clean up.

In the shower, he couldn't escape thoughts of Amy and seeing her whenever he was in the area. Although he knew it wasn't completely fair to expect her to wait for his visits, he considered she could visit him on occasion as well. The possibility of reestablishing a relationship with Amy would help him keep his perspective with his friendship with Emily. Only, in his heart, he knew he was eventually going to hurt Emily.

In the dining room, decorated in the same French Country style as her bedroom, elegant whites and chic yellows accentuated the mahogany wood stained table and chairs. An entire wall displayed floor-to-ceiling windows with flowing yellow drapes. In the center of the windows was a set of glass French doors that lead to a covered deck. The square table exhibited a large cornucopia overflowing with gourds, *Indian corn,* and miniature *Jack Be Little* pumpkins in white, yellow, and orange. Green ivy garnishments intertwined throughout the ornamental pieces.

Emily, Mary, Grace, and Melissa had cooked all afternoon. Set before them was a fine example of a traditional Thanksgiving feast. There was roasted turkey with stuffing, mashed potatoes, sweet potato fluff, green beans, collards, and homemade rolls. For dessert there was pumpkin pie and German chocolate cake. Everything was made from scratch.

The stuffing was a success. Everyone loved having homemade stuffing for a change, but Emily's stuffing was beyond delicious. It was succulent. It had the right amount of moisture and just enough sage to make it savory.

Seth beamed with pride when he was told Emily had prepared the stuffing, especially after he sampled it himself. He thought she must be an excellent cook if this was just a sample of what she could do in the kitchen.

Emily explained how she and her grandmother always prepared holiday dinners for the single military personnel in their church. Stuffing was her responsibility from the time she was old enough to hold a knife safely. She could recall the names of many of the soldiers from over the years because they had kept in touch with holiday cards. Many of them said the meal they had with the Wilkerson's was the highlight of their holiday.

Around the table, his brothers and sisters teased Seth by letting him know Emily was a keeper. They weren't telling him anything he didn't already know. Only he didn't believe she was for him.

"If you don't hurry up and marry her, I will," confessed Chad, his youngest brother. "Any gal who can cook as well as Emily deserves a good man." His eyebrows jiggling hinted to Emily that he was the man.

Everyone laughed at his proclamation. "Don't you think you're a bit too young, Chad?" his father asked.

"I'm almost a senior in school, Dad." He emphasized the senior part.

"Almost?" Seth asked. "High school just started a few weeks ago, and you're just a junior!" A round of laughter rang throughout the room.

"I hear that Amy is in town this weekend," Sean announced. Changing the subject to Amy was not a good idea. The room became deathly silent. He, on the other hand, was still riled at the thought of his brother kissing Amy earlier that afternoon. Somehow, he wanted to let it be known of his brother's ill-fated kiss with someone other than the woman who was sitting at their table. Only he didn't know how to broach the subject without giving away his true feelings for Amy.

Mary gave Sean a stern look.

"What?" Sean looked innocently at his mother. "Did I say something wrong, Mother?" He said through gritted teeth.

"Actually, she stopped by this afternoon while I was outside mucking the stalls." Seth nodded his head and explained to Emily that Amy had been his high-school sweetheart. After high school, Amy went off to the University of North Carolina Chapel Hill while Seth went to the local university so he could still help out at home. Then Amy went on to become a nurse practitioner while he sought out his singing career. They had separated as friends, though he had not kept in touch since she left for college.

"Until today," Sean interjected. "Seems like you picked up right where you left off."

Seth gave Sean an angry scowl. Had Sean seen Amy kiss him? Of course he did! He was just inside the barn mucking stalls, so he must've seen them together or he wouldn't have made the comment. *But why is he so enraged? It was nothing but a simple kiss.*

Emily's heart plummeted when she realized Amy was the beautiful blond who had kissed Seth earlier in the day. *Could he still be interested in Amy? So? What if he was?* She, on the other hand, was just another unwed mother. *How can I expect more from him?* she asked herself. Here she was a defiled woman and he, well…he was handsome, intelligent, savvy, and witty. Not to mention talented. Oh, how she longed for his heart to belong to her and her alone.

"Emily?" Seth asked. "Are you okay?" He looked at her from across the table.

She shook her head a trifle, lifted her eyes to his. "Um, yes, just lost in thought, that's all." She smiled tentatively at him. Playing with her food, she realized just how deeply she had come to care for him. *Could this be love? God help me! He's not interested in me. He only has an extraordinary attachment to Marissa. To him I'm just her mother. Oh how I long to be more.* She continued to shift her food around on her plate.

Seth noticed Emily's despondent guise. What if she had seen the kiss? *She couldn't have seen it. She hasn't mentioned it to me. But then, why should she? She only thinks of me as a friend—the man who delivered her baby, nothing more.* Seth didn't know whether he should discuss the kiss with her or leave it alone. Releasing a sigh, he decided not to broach the subject.

Mary had cooked a turkey with all the trimmings. She said she might as well celebrate Thanksgiving with the majority of her family together, as she didn't know when would be the next time they would be under the same roof again.

Seth felt a little guilty with her confession. He knew that it was because of his move to northern Virginia to get a better chance of finding an agent, knowing it was his best chance of getting signed onto a record company.

Things were looking good in that category. He had disclosed the recent events to his family at the dinner table. Meeting with an agent was the first step. And Art promised they would soon be recording with a record label of their choice. Once Art got the sample recording out to agencies, he said there would be many offers from which to choose.

The family was ecstatic at the news. Of course, Emily's heart swelled with pride. She couldn't believe he didn't tell her before. She reasoned that he probably wanted to tell his family first, and she was blessed to be there when he told them.

Seth's brother, Chad, congratulated him on his accomplishment. "Not so fast," Seth said. "We've got to get an offer first!"

"But you will," Chad professed. "You guys are the best group this old town has ever heard. And that says a lot since our church hosts many of the well-known artists in the industry."

"Thanks Chad. While it's true our church hosts beloved artists," Seth affirmed, "Don't you think this 'old town' is just a little biased?" He looked over at Emily and winked.

Butterflies fluttered in Emily's stomach with the minute gesture. He was so handsome in his flannel shirt and jeans; she could hardly keep her eyes off him. It didn't help that she sat directly across from him at the table.

"Oh, and we're going to rename the group to something more contemporary. Hopefully Art will be able to help us." Everyone was ecstatic at the sound of the band getting a new name. The current name was so mundane.

After dinner, the family gathered in the large family room for a game of cards. Emily was unfamiliar with the game they played, so she sat between Melissa and Seth and watched while the others played. Once she got the hang of it, she joined in. They played for hours, laughing and telling stories of Seth's childhood, all the while including Emily as if she were one of the family.

George sat in the wheelchair, anxious to leave the hospital. He was going back to live with his mother. Dr. Burke had discharged him with explicit instructions for his mother's staff to follow.

He still had a few weeks with the casts on his arm and legs. He was scheduled for his first appointment the following week where Dr. Burke mentioned a possibility of his arm cast being removed. The earliest his legs would be liberated from the casts would be the next week, and then Winston would take him to physical therapy twice a week.

He looked forward to his freedom. His heart soared now that he was no longer held in bondage to the hospital and the world. He had utilized his time in the institution wisely. He felt like a new man inside. His heart belonged to God now. His future was in God's hands.

At breakfast the next morning, Seth announced he and Emily were going for a ride to the lake. Emily thought he meant they would ride in the car, but his definition of a "ride" was on horseback. Although she grew up on a farm, she had never been on a horse, so she was a bit hesitant. Seth encouraged her, saying she would catch on easily. It turns out she was a natural.

The day was cloudy and cool. Emily wore her heavy blue sweater, a long-sleeve lavender T-shirt, jeans, and hiking boots. She walked onto the back porch to find Seth and his mother sitting on the porch swing talking.

"Mary?" Although Emily was a bit hesitant to leave her baby, she knew she could trust Mary. After all, she had raised six children of her own. "Would you mind watching Marissa for me while we go on a picnic?" Emily stood there, hands in her back pockets.

Mary's eyes softened. "Of course I'll watch her. Seth had asked me this morning, so I've been looking forward to some quality time alone with her. It's been so long since I've had a baby to spoil." Her smile reached her eyes.

It was heartwarming to know that Marissa would be in such capable hands. "I've just fed her, and she's sleeping in the basinet Seth brought down to the kitchen this morning. It's great that you have kept your baby things. And they look practically new," she complimented. The basinet had been given to Mary when she had brought home both Seth and Sean. Luckily, they were small enough to fit in it together at first. Later, when they were bigger, she'd purchased a playpen in order to keep them together. They were like two peas in a pod, one never wanting to be without the other. They remained that way until college.

As Emily entered the massive building, she was awed at the size of it. There had to be at least twenty horse stalls on each side. Most of the horses were out to pasture, so the stalls were empty. Emily saw a nose peek out from a stall in the farthest corner on the left. The horse must have smelled her scent because it wasn't but a few seconds later that she saw the entire head protrude from the half Dutch doorway to the closed stall.

The head was larger than she'd ever imagined. It had the most colossal brown eyes that appeared to speak to her. She stopped in front of the huge animal and observed him inspect her. The horse tossed his head back and snorted as if to say hello. She reached up her hand and touched high up on his nose. "Well, hello to you too."

The hair on the animal was stiff and colorful. She was surprised at the feel of it. "So what do you think"—she looked down at the half door to read its name—"uh, Buttercup? You like what you see?"

"As a matter of fact, I do!" A familiar voice resonated from the other side of the doorway. Seth was crouched down rubbing Buttercup's front leg. He looked up at the startled face and laughed. "Did I startle you?"

"Um, yeah, you could say that." She stifled a laugh. "I thought the horse could talk there for a minute." She smiled down at him, and his world seemed to grow brighter at the sight of her smile.

Her hair fell softly below her shoulders. He longed to touch the soft, thick locks. He stood from his examination of the horse's leg to look in her eyes. She looked up to his six-foot-three frame and sighed.

"What was that for?"

"What was what for?"

"That sigh you just gave."

"I sighed?" She lied. She knew she had sighed. The sight of him made her legs go weak. He looked so handsome in his plaid shirt, jeans, and cowboy boots.

"Yes. You sighed." He tried to pry it out of her but could see she wasn't going to give. He prayed she wasn't disappointed at the sight of him. He looked down at his boots that were way beyond grungy. And his jeans and shirt…well he wouldn't go there, but he knew he looked unkempt.

"So this is the barn?"

He opened the stall door and stepped out. She moved aside as he exited the doorway. "Yep. This is the barn." He swept one hand out as if showing off a display.

"It's huge." She looked around again. There she went putting her foot in her mouth. Of course the barn was huge; it was the heart of the ranch. "I mean, I wasn't expecting something this vast." She chewed on her lower lip.

"I guess it is rather large." He reached in the bucket hanging next to Buttercup's stall and grabbed an apple. "Here, feed this to

Buttercup. She'll be your best friend forever." He showed her how to feed it to the horse palm open. Shivers ran down her spine at the touch of his hand against hers. The sensation of the horse's mouth against her palm made her giggle.

"Feels neat, huh?"

She nodded her head then reached up and patted the horse on the nose once again. Buttercup nudged her nose against Emily's shoulder.

"See, she likes you already," Seth commented. He looked at his watch. Noticing there was time, he offered, "Would you like a tour of the barn?"

Emily nodded.

Seth told her of the birthing rooms and their importance when a mare was delivering. They passed another stall where an impressive horse stood. "That's Midnight Run. He's my horse." Seth was so proud of his black-and-white stallion. He had sired over thirty Painted foals in his lifetime, and was still in his prime.

He explained how the Painted horse came to America by Spanish explorer Hernando Cortes in 1519. In the 1800s, the West was full of wild Painted horses. They soon became the Native American preference because of the camouflage look. In the 1960s, the American Paint Horse Association was formed, and his horse, along with the other Painted horses on the ranch, was registered with the association.

Midnight Run was a Tobiano. Seth explained how both dark flanks and white legs defined the animal as a Tobiano. He pointed out the black oval spots on the neck and chest were just a few of the features of the Tobiano. But the most striking feature was the solid black head. Midnight Run was a beautiful sight to behold. Not only was he spectacular in appearance but striking in stature.

Midnight Run was no gentle horse. He was powerful and stood at sixteen hands, the tallest of the Painted horse range. Only Seth was able to control him completely, and he looked forward to a chance to ride him once again. It seemed like such a long time had passed since his last ride with his stallion. He longed to be on the back of his animal and feel the earth move beneath him. He was itching to take his horse out for their ride together; even though he wouldn't be able to allow the beast to gallop at full speed, he did intend on taking him for a nice run once in the open field. However, Buttercup was not one to gallop for long, so he would take it easy with Midnight Run for this time out. Later he would take him for a sprint across the ranch acreage. Just for a mile or so, he promised the horse.

They walked back to Buttercup's stall, and he opened the gate. He tugged gently on Buttercup's reins. The animal followed him out into the middle of the barn. "Buttercup is our gentlest mare. She's old but can take you to our destination without a hitch."

In fact, Buttercup had been the horse chosen by all the new riders. She was named for her dun coloring. The yellowish spots of her back and face had a calming effect on her riders. Seth grabbed another apple from the bucket and gave it to Emily. She fed it to the animal as she stroked her white-streaked nose. Buttercup had foaled many beautiful Paints and the foals had been sold at the time of conception or shortly after birth.

Seth saddled the two horses, explaining each step to Emily as he performed it. He hoped Emily would catch on quickly because he wanted to bring her down with him every chance he could. Being with her was as natural as being with his horse.

Emily pulled her hair up in a ponytail and then allowed Seth to help her sit atop the gentle mare. She led the horse out of the barn behind Seth and Midnight Run. The horse followed at Midnight Run's pace. Seth kept it slow at first and then brought them to a slow trot as they ambled down the winding trail.

The trees were bright with colors of yellow, red, and orange. Mixed with the evergreen trees, it was a sight to behold. Emily could scarcely take it all in. She withdrew her camera from her sweater pocket and began taking pictures. Kate would love to see this for herself, but a picture would have to do. It was difficult to lead the horse and focus the camera. Eventually, she had to stop Buttercup in order to snap a photo. She did so often and eventually lost sight of Seth. Fear crept in as she allowed the horse to walk along the path at its own pace.

Slowly they traveled to the middle of what seemed like nowhere. She could hear the rustling of the wind in the trees, the sound of animals scurrying across the ground. She traveled for a long time before Seth and Midnight Run appeared through the brush. Her heart soared at the sight of him. She was so thankful to see him she almost toppled off Buttercup.

"What happened to you?" Seth asked. He had become anxious when he realized Emily wasn't behind him.

"I'm so sorry, Seth. I wanted to get pictures of the countryside but had to stop Buttercup in order to take the photos. You got ahead of me, and I lost sight of you. I'm so sorry."

The look of contrition on her face made her all the more adorable. How could he be mad at her? All she did was stop and take some pictures of the landscape. It was beautiful, and he was ecstatic that she took notice of his homestead and appreciated it. Seth simply tossed his head to the side and said, "Come on. No harm done. Let's go have our picnic."

Within the hour, or longer so it seemed to Emily, they came upon a rushing stream. Seth dismounted his stallion and helped Emily down from the mare. She stretched her long, shaking legs. Barely able to stand, Seth took her hand and helped her to the fallen tree just a few feet in front of them that ran into the stream. She sat cautiously on the old tree trunk while Seth returned to his horse.

"You'll get the hang of it," he told her. Then he acquired the picnic basket attached to his saddle. He set it on the ground next to Emily's feet, opened it, and took out the checkered tablecloth. He shook open the cloth and spread it on the ground. Then he helped Emily over to sit on it while he took out the ingredients of the basket.

He lowered himself to his knees next to Emily.

Emily looked on in wonder as he began explaining the contents.

"Turkey salad sandwiches." He held them up for her inspection. She closed her eyes as she smelled the delicious aroma. Seth set them down, reached in the basket again, and brought out a plastic container.

"Macaroni and cheese." He opened both containers one for each of them. Her mouth was salivating at the enticing aroma.

He set the tubs on the blanket. "Fruit salad." He reached in the basket to pull out two rectangular plastic tubs.

"Mmm." Emily smiled. "I'm starving!" She didn't even realize she was hungry until he began teasing her with the contents of the basket.

Seth held up one hand, index finger pointing upward. "Wait… there's more." Her eyes grew wide. He took out two slices of pumpkin pie.

Emily's eyes sparkled with anticipation. The pumpkin pie from last night's dinner was to die for! She thought of eating dessert first, but uncertain what Seth would think, she changed her mind. She ran her tongue along her lips. "This all looks delish! When did you have time to prepare all this?"

The simple gesture of her tongue running across her lips was enough to drive him crazy. He attempted to make it look as if he meant to drop down on his butt but failed miserably. "I couldn't sleep last night," was all he admitted. Sleep had escaped him. All he could think about was Emily in the room across the hall from him. He realized his attraction to her was growing stronger. He attempted to brush aside his longing with thoughts of kissing Amy which only resulted in contemplation of what it would be like to kiss Emily. He became so confused he wasn't able to sleep. He went down to the kitchen to get a snack of cake and milk. It was then it hit him. A picnic would be a nice way to get Emily alone, away from the house and Marissa. Somehow he had to determine if his love for her child was why he was attracted to Emily or if he was developing feelings for Emily.

They talked amicably while consuming their food. At one point, Seth reached over with his fork and attempted to stab at her piece of pie. Quickly she jerked it away and slapped at his hand.

"Don't even think about it!" She laughed.

After eating their lunch, they sat on the log by the stream. Emily had her shoes off and her feet dangling in the cool water. Seth rolled up his jeans and sat next to her.

"You know, you never talk about George."

At the mention of his name, she cringed. How could she tell Seth what this man had done to her?

Seth saw her flinch when he said George's name. "I didn't mean to offend you. I'd like to know why you became so enraged when he sent you the flowers. I mean I have an ex-girlfriend, but I've never experienced such strong negative emotions toward her as you do toward your ex."

"He's not my ex."

"Oh. Sorry. I just thought you had dated since he's Marissa's father."

Emily was incredulous. "How did you know that?"

Seth yanked off a piece of bark from the tree stump and tossed it in the water. "Um…Gram accidentally told me."

Emily hung her head. "I can't believe she would do such a thing. I mean, I—"

"She didn't mean to tell me. In fact, it was when you were acting like a lunatic tossing the flowers in the trash and popping the balloons that she inadvertently blurted out 'George is Marissa's father'!"

"But there's a reason behind my intense outburst." She inhaled audibly before divulging her rationale behind her rage.

Seth sensed she was on the verge of unveiling her innermost secret. He patiently waited for her to continue.

Emily exhaled slowly, "The truth of the matter is…" she paused, uncertain how to say it. Then she decided to just come right out with the ugly truth. "George and I didn't date or even have a relationship other than a working relationship." She turned to look into Seth's eyes. "He was my boss."

Seth tried to read her expression but she hid her feelings behind cold eyes. "I see."

"No, you can't see. Because, George…well…he harassed me…sexually." To avoid witnessing his reaction, she turned back to watch her feet gently sway in the water. "I warned him to stop, but he didn't. So I turned him in." She picked at a loose piece of bark on the tree. It came free and she tossed it in the water. "You see, George was a vindictive man and he swore he would retaliate. One night while I was working alone in the building, he managed to get inside with a key he had. He drugged the water in the kitchen decanter. When I became thirsty, I filled my glass with the drugged water. It wasn't long before I was passed out on the floor in my office. The next thing I remember is waking in a hospital several hours later."

Seth listened intently. "So he drugged you?"

"He did more than that. While I was unconscious…he…" She hung her head ashamed to say the words. "He…raped me." Tears flowed from her eyes as she turned to see Seth's reaction.

Seth's eyes reflected a myriad of emotions. Anger flashed through them. His jaw tensed. He wondered how anyone could violate this beautiful woman. He considered what she must've experienced: the confusion, the defilement, the reality. Eventually, as he processed her words, his expression moved to compassion.

Without a word, Seth took her into his arms. He allowed her to release all her pent up anguish. He gently stroked her hair, whispering reassurances.

She didn't know how much time had passed during her lamenting interlude. Slowly she pushed away from his embrace.

"I'm s-so s-sorry I l-lost control of my emotions." She looked down, afraid to look in his eyes.

Seth crooked his finger under her chin and lifted her face. He gazed deeply into her tear-streaked face. With his other hand, he wiped the tears from her cheek.

He was tempted to kiss her. He could almost feel her soft supple lips beneath his. He leaned toward her. Emily tilted her head slightly welcoming the upcoming display of affection. He took her face in his hand and leaned in closer. Just before his lips reached hers, his cell phone rang.

Marissa had been asleep since before her mother left. Mary who relished the opportunity to play "grandma," for what it was worth was slightly disappointed. She had thought it odd that the child would sleep so long, but considering the long ride she'd had the previous day and Emily trying to get her on a schedule, Mary wasn't too concerned.

A knock sounded at the back door. Mary wondered who could be visiting. She had closed the B&B for the week and wasn't expecting anyone to stop by. Peering through the window over the kitchen sink, she was unable to see anyone. She opened the smoked glass door, and there before her stood Amy.

"Why, Amy…won't you come in?" Mary opened the screen door, truly pleased to see her visitor.

Amy entered the kitchen, thankful for the hospitable smile Mary displayed. It had been several years since she'd visited. With college then grad school and her job in Greensboro, Amy hadn't had much time to come for visits.

In high school, Amy visited with Mary while waiting for Seth as he carried out his daily chores. She would assist Mary with dinner preparation or baking her famous desserts, sharing in a way a true mother and daughter would. Mary had become a second mother to her. Amy always thought she would one day marry Seth and call Mary her mother-in-law. But she had put an end to their dating and the ability to regard Mary as anything other than friend. Now, after Seth's comments the previous day, she had hope. It may not be too late after all.

Amy stood inside the doorway, uncertainty upon her face. "Um, hi, Mary," she stammered. "Is…Seth home? I thought he might like to take the horses out for a ride." She lifted up the basket she held in her hand. "I thought we could go for a picnic down by the stream."

Mary led Amy to the kitchen table explaining that Seth and Emily had already done so. "They're out riding as we speak."

Disappointment shrouded Amy's face. Her eyebrows scrunched together. "Emily? Who's Emily?"

"She's Seth friend. He delivered her baby a few weeks back."

Amy was confused. Seth had told her about delivering a baby just the day before. He never mentioned the mother or that she was with him while visiting his parents. "Oh. I didn't realize she was here."

"Didn't he tell you?"

Amy shrugged. "Tell me what?"

"He brought both Emily and Marissa to meet the family." She pointed to the basinet in the corner of the room, and motioned for Amy to take a look.

Amy loved babies. "Aww. Isn't she adorable?" She reached down to gently rub Marissa's head. Concerned, she turned and asked, "Mary? How long has she been asleep?"

"Uh…I don't quite know. She was asleep before Emily and Seth left, and they've been gone for at least two hours now." Mary saw the distress in Amy's eyes. She stood from the table where she sat and walked over to the basinet. "I just thought she was tired from her trip. Why? Is there something wrong?"

"She's burning up with fever."

Mary reached down and gently rubbed the baby's head. "Oh my goodness! She is burning up!" Mary removed the blanket from over the sleeping infant, knowing it was best to keep her cool to reduce the fever.

"Is there any acetaminophen in the diaper bag?"

"I'm not sure. It's upstairs in their room." Mary ran up to the room and quietly entered. It felt strange to be in her guest's room without her knowledge. She had to rummage through the entire bag before she found some Tylenol in one of the inside pockets. Swiftly she returned to the kitchen and handed it to Amy. "I found this in the diaper bag as well." She set down the baby's pacifier on the table next to the basinet.

Mary picked up the infant so Amy could administer the fever reducer. Then Amy rushed out to her car to retrieve her medicine bag. Back inside, she took out her thermometer and pressed it gently into Marissa's ear. "One hundred point four." She looked at Mary. "Maybe you should call Seth and get them back here. Something is causing this fever. I'd like to examine her, but I need her mother's permission."

Mary dialed Seth's cell number. He picked up on the second ring.

"Seth, honey, I'm sorry to interrupt your picnic, but I think you should come home. Little Marissa has a fever."

"We'll be there as soon as possible." Seth quickly responded, then disconnected the call.

"They're on the way."

Mary held Marissa close while she and Amy waited.

Emily bounded into the room as Seth took the horses into the barn. She gently took Marissa from Mary. "What's wrong with her?" She kissed the baby's forehead. It was hot to her lips.

"I'm not sure," Amy said, "but I'd like to examine her, if you don't mind."

Emily nodded her head and sighed. Here was the woman whom Seth had kissed just the day before. She had seen them together with her own eyes, and now Amy was here in this house examining her baby girl. Emily didn't know if she should be apprehensive or appreciative.

As soon as Seth walked into the house, he saw Amy. He stopped in his tracks. He looked at Amy then Emily, not knowing what to think. *Why is Amy here?* he wondered. He walked over to the table where Emily was sitting. He placed his hand on her shoulder, "So what's going on?" He was truly anxious. He reached down and rubbed Marissa's head. "She's burning up! What's wrong with her?" He looked over at Amy as he stood next to Emily at the table.

"That's what I'm trying to figure out, Seth." She wasn't trying to be terse, but it came out that way.

Shock flickered in his eyes. Seth was surprised at her response. He kept his mouth shut for the rest of the examination.

Amy listened to the baby's heart and lungs through her stethoscope. "Her lungs are clear, and her heart sounds fine. Let me take a look at her ears."

When Emily shifted the baby for Amy to look into Marissa's ears, Seth pulled out the chair next to Emily and sat down. He placed one hand on the back of Emily's chair, and the other he placed on her elbow.

Amy longed to feel his touch again. After his comments yesterday, she had believed he felt something for her. She would give just about anything to have him hold her and tell her he loved her one more time. Amy had a hard time focusing on the task at hand when she noticed Seth began stroking Emily's arm. Amy glanced up at him and could see it in his face. His look told her he had lost his heart to Emily. A look he had once had for her.

Amy closed her eyes to shut out the image. She inhaled deeply, then exhaled. She looked at Emily. "There's fluid in her left ear." She sighed. "She has an ear infection."

Emily was relieved to hear Marissa only had an ear infection. Not that it wasn't serious, only she had imagined the worst; emergency room, hospitalization, IV's, needles, the works. She was grateful for Amy's astute awareness. If it hadn't been for her, she didn't know what she would have done. She thanked her profusely and complimented her abilities.

As a nurse practitioner, Amy had the ability to write prescriptions. She wrote out one for antibiotics and suggested they continue to use the acetaminophen to reduce the fever. But for her own broken heart, she had no remedy.

She handed Seth the prescription, avoiding his eyes. She held the tears at bay but knew if she looked at him she would lose her composure. She said her farewells and prayed she'd make it to the car before the tears fell. She had lost him. She had lost him years ago when she went away to college. This time she lost him to another woman. The pain was no less difficult to endure than it was the first time.

Sean bumped into Amy as she walked down the back steps. "H-hi Amy." He stammered. He looked into her eyes to see them glowing with tears.

In an attempt to hide her tears, Amy looked down when she greeted Sean. "Hi."

Sean struggled with his inner turmoil. He knew his brother was responsible for her anguish. On one hand, he wanted nothing more than to finally put Seth in his place. He could—no should—go inside and give him a taste of his own medicine. On the other hand, he wanted to comfort Amy. Eventually he succumbed to his concerns for the woman he loved. Sean placed his hands on her arms, not knowing anything else to do for her, pulled her close. He felt the tension leave her body as she molded her form against his. For several moments she cried.

To Sean it felt so right to hold her in his arms. So good to feel her body against his. Finally, he had a chance to hold the woman he loved. His heart elated at the thought of her in his embrace. And yet anguished at the reason she was there. Somehow, he had to convey to Amy how right they were together. *But how?* he wondered. How could he convince her that his feelings were genuine and sincere? A myriad of possibilities ran through his head. Unfortunately, none reached his mouth. As he caressed the beautiful blond, he ran a hand up her back stopping at her head. He entangled his fingers in the softness of her blond tresses then bent his head down and placed gentle kisses on top of her head.

Infinitely aware of his presence and his tender kisses, Amy finally stopped weeping. Countless emotions racked her body and soul. Her thoughts rambled on in a heap of uncertainty. Who was this gentle man kissing her? Why was his touch sending an incredible sensation throughout her body like an electric charge? A consciousness she had never realized with anyone before?

She looked up into his blue eyes and saw a different man. One she never knew existed. This gentle, caring man—Seth's twin, the "quiet one" as he was known—studied her intensely and she felt something stir within. For an instant time stood still.

He placed the crook of his finger under her chin and angled it upward. Slowly he lowered his lips to hers. His hand tenderly ran down her arm and stopped at her waist.

His lips felt warm against hers. A chill ran through her body from the force of his kiss. Had she not been in his arms, she would've dropped to her knees at the unexpected passion she felt swirling within her.

As the kiss ended, she looked into those deep blue eyes and her heart moved. What she saw startled her. The look of longing in his eyes, pleaded with her to see him for who he was—not Seth's twin. But a man. A man deeply in love.

His eyes sparkled with emotions she had never experienced before. She watched as they turned dark and smoldering. This man…this breathtaking, magnificent man, forced her world to tilt on its axis.

No longer was he Seth's brother, but a man she now longed to hold in her heart and arms forever.

As Seth stood in the doorway watching the scene unfold before him, he felt no sorrow at the thought of Amy with his brother. Inexplicably his heart rejoiced at the sight of their kiss. Now he understood the animosity his brother expressed at the dinner table the night before. His brother was in love with Amy. And from the looks of it, she was falling in love with Sean.

By evening, Marissa's fever was down and she was nursing again. Amy had advised them to keep the baby cool and comfortable. Seth had the prescription filled and within an hour was home to administer it. By the time Seth had returned, his siblings had heard the news and were taking turns holding the crying infant, attempting to calm her. Seth gently took her in his arms and began singing to her. Within seconds, Marissa was quiet her eyelids heavy with sleep. From that moment on, Seth was the one who comforted the baby.

Chapter 23

Mary woke to the sound of Chris humming as he dressed. "Good morning, my love." He bent down and kissed her lips.

She stretched. "Mmm. Morning, honey." She sat up and placed her feet on the floor. The clock read 5:05. "You're up late this morning. I thought you'd get started earlier with all you have to do today."

He brushed a tendril of hair away from her lovely face. This woman had been the love of his life. The woman to whom he had been married for over thirty years, now confronted with the worst and most devastating challenge of her life.

"I'm taking the day off." He sat down on the bed next to his wife. "I'm here for you today. All day. Seth is here and can take on a few of my chores. Besides, it's not every day my wife has to have surgery."

She sat up and leaned against him. Tears sprang to her eyes. Quickly she wiped them away. "Thank you." She kissed his cheek. "That means so much to me."

He took her hand in his and kissed it. "I wouldn't have it any other way."

She patted his leg and then proceeded into their walk-in closet to get dressed. She searched through her clothes and chose a light blue, long-sleeve T-shirt and matching sweat pants. *No sense dressing up; may as well be comfortable.*

"Are you nervous?" he asked as he donned his socks.

"No. I guess I'm still in shock. It still hasn't sunk in yet." Mary walked in the bathroom and squeezed toothpaste on her toothbrush.

"I am," he admitted.

Mary brushed her teeth then rinsed her mouth with water. "Why are you nervous? It's a simple procedure."

He stood from the bed and walked to the bathroom doorway. He leaned on the frame and crossed his arms. "Because it's cancer." What would he do if the cancer wasn't actually contained and had spread? He couldn't go on without her. She was the center of his world, his universe.

"Yeah, but Dr. Nelson has said it was contained in the milk duct. We really don't have to worry." She slipped on her shoes. "Besides, there's nothing we can do about it anyway." She planted a gentle kiss upon his cheek. "We have to trust God will take care of everything." She reached up and took his face in her hands. "We must have faith." Then she kissed him soundly on the lips.

As Mary lay on the hospital bed Dr. Nelson walked in to see her. She went over the procedure with the entire family at Mary's bedside. "After your surgery, you'll be taken to the recovery room. No one will be allowed in until you've awakened, and then it'll be limited to only two visitors at a time. I don't want you overdoing it before you leave the hospital." Dr. Nelson canvassed her family members faces and advised them, "Do not allow her to do anything, and I mean anything, for the remainder of the day. Once she is home, she is to rest. Do I make myself clear?"

Everyone nodded in agreement. They would have this opportunity to spoil their mother for a change.

In the waiting room, Mary's family sat and anxiously waited for the surgeon. Instead, a nurse appeared and informed them the surgery went well and Mary would be in the recovery room within the hour. Another hour to wait.

Seth took Emily and Marissa down to the cafeteria and purchased two bottles of water. As Seth looked on, Marissa slept peacefully in her mother's arms. They sat across from each other in a booth in the back away from the commotion of the cafeteria.

"You doing okay?" Emily shifted the baby to her other arm.

Seth reached out to her. "Here. Let me take her." Emily situated the sleeping babe in to his arms. With one hand, he held Marissa; with the other, he held Emily's hand, his thumb stroking her thumb and forefinger. The gesture drove Emily wild with longing. She had never dated anyone who touched her the way Seth did. Even the simple contact of holding hands sent her heart all aquiver.

Seth looked into her smoky blue eyes. "I'm worried about my mom. What if this is more than what the doctor says? I mean, what if this cancer isn't contained as the doctor claims?" He contorted his mouth as if he had eaten something strange. "I can't even say the word without my stomach lurching. Anyway, what if it is in her kidneys or liver or somewhere else in her body?"

Emily patted his arm. "As my Gram always says, 'Don't go borrowing trouble.' Didn't they give your mom the full gamut of tests? I mean, didn't she have an MRI and a CAT scan?"

"Yes."

"And did they come back clear?"

"Yes."

"Then don't worry. She'll be okay. God will make sure of that. You just have to trust Him."

He shook his head. "My heart knows that, but my head keeps telling me something else may be wrong. I mean this is my mom we're talking about."

"I realize that, but you need to quit listening to your head and trust your heart. Your mom would tell you the same thing."

Seth nodded. Of course his mom was okay. All the tests had come back negative. The least he could do was believe his mother was going to be all right. *God please take care of my mom. Guide the surgeon's hands so she removes all the disease from her body...and help me trust you, dear Lord.*

At home, Mary rested while the family waited on her hand and foot. Anything she needed was granted. She lay on the sofa in front of a roaring fire, teacup in hand. Outside, the day was sunny with a cool breeze. She could see some of the deciduous trees releasing their leaves to fly with the wind.

"This is delicious tea, Emily. I don't recall having anything this delightful in my stash of teas. Wherever did you find it?"

Emily blushed at the compliment. "I picked some herbs from your garden out back and added them to your favorite tea."

"But how did you know my favorite tea?"

"Seth told me you liked English Breakfast Tea best."

Mary's face lit up with awareness. "Of course. Seth would be the only one in this family to know my favorite tea. Seems no one else is truly interested in hot tea except me. Occasionally, Seth will join me. He is sort of a connoisseur of teas and coffees." She took a sip from her cup. "I'll bet you didn't know that about him."

"No. I sure didn't," Emily confessed. There was a lot she didn't know about him. She sat in the chair across from Mary. "Please tell me more about Seth. There's so much I want to learn."

There was a great deal to learn. Although they had spent the last few weeks together and had the six-hour drive to his homestead, there was still so much to discover about this man with whom she had fallen in love.

Love... It was still a mystery to her. She had never been in love. Oh, she had dated some but had never really fallen so deeply in love with anyone as she had with Seth. Seth made her weak in the knees. Every time he looked at her, her stomach fluttered and her world spun out of control. Just the touch of his hand sent shivers up and down her spine. Some might say it was physical attraction, but to her, it was so much more. Yes, she was attracted to him. This she could not deny. But it was so much more than fascination that she felt. She couldn't stop thinking about him. She couldn't imagine her life without him in it. Still, she wondered if he felt the same way about her. *No, he couldn't. I'm not worthy of him. I'm damaged goods and unsuitable for such a Godly man.*

"Tell me…what has he told you?" Mary asked curiously.

"Nothing much about himself. Just stories of his childhood and such."

"That sounds like him." Seth wasn't one to speak of himself. He was the modest type, one who would rather ask questions than give answers.

Chapter 24

"Seth is a lot like his dad. Chris is sharp-witted and a joy to be around. He brings laughter to every room he enters. To this day, if one of the kids is sad or down, Chris is quick to turn the woes to glee," Mary recalled. "He distracts them enough to get him or her to disclose the reason for their melancholy. Usually it's just a misunderstanding between friends, and Chris encourages his child to call the friend and resolve their differences. Afterward, the friendship is restored and they're forever grateful to their dad for his wisdom and understanding.

"Like Chris, Seth has always been around for his younger siblings. They all look up to him, even Sean, although he'd never admit it. Too proud, that one." She paused a moment. "Seth was the lead singer in the youth choir."

"That doesn't surprise me." Emily smiled.

"He was also one of the youth leaders once he became too old to be in the group. The younger kids always flocked to him for advice and to take him on in a game of one-on-one or cards. Rarely did they mistake Sean for Seth. Although they are identical twins, the kids always knew the difference."

"You know, it's really not that difficult to tell them apart."

This was news to Mary. None of the girls they dated were able to tell them apart. They used to play tricks on their dates and switch places, pretending to be the other brother. The girls never knew the difference. The fact that Emily could distinguish who was who was enough to surprise Mary beyond words.

Mary told her of Seth's graduating at the top of his class in high school and with highest honors in college. Seth volunteered at the fire department all throughout his teens and early twenties. He saved many lives during his tenure there, as well as several family pets. He was honored as a hero after a severe fire in an apartment building where he had saved an entire family with the exception of the grandfather.

"He took the loss harder than the man's family, I think." She surprised Emily when she admitted Seth had quit the department, vowing never to return. "He said if he couldn't save everyone, there was no reason to continue. It didn't matter that the elder man had suffered a long battle of emphysema and asthma. Turns out the smoke was just too much for his ailing lungs." She sighed. "He died from smoke inhalation."

"Oh, how sad." Emily could understand why Seth would take it so severely. "I can't imagine his pain."

Mary shook her head. "No one could understand why he blamed himself. If the poor man hadn't have been so sickly, he still would've succumbed to the smoke. He was just too old. There was nothing anyone could've done. But Seth felt he should have been able to save the man, regardless of the circumstances."

"Did you know he was a decorated hero?"

Emily's eyebrows lifted. She sipped her cooling beverage.

Mary waved her hand. "Of course you didn't. He was commended for his bravery during that fire. For a while we all thought that he would become a firefighter... until that fateful day. Instead he attended college to study animals and their DNA for breeding. Then, well, his love for God and music became his passion." Mary slowly lifted the cup to her mouth. She closed her eyes and drank the warm mixture.

"Was there a choir at the university?"

Mary lowered her cup and nodded. "He sang in the university choir. On many occasions he had solos as well as a part in the Barbershop Quartet. He was sought out by the North Carolina Chamber Choir but politely declined. He was much too busy with school and the ranch to travel and perform throughout the state.

"Seth is a giver. If he sees someone in need, he will give them the shirt off his back." It wasn't unusual for him to give his allowance to one of his classmates because they didn't have money for lunch.

"In addition to all his chores here at the ranch, he worked part time delivering newspapers on the weekends and volunteered at the church pantry for needy families."

Wow! All this in one man! And a Christian to boot! Oh dear God, If only I were good enough for him. Please, God, I know I don't deserve Seth, but if You will, please give me a man half as good.

"He is an incredible man. I don't know what to say. I had no idea. I mean, he never said a word." Emily was awed at the thought of such a man existing, much more at the fact that it was Seth, the man she had grown to love more now than ever.

"Like I said, Seth isn't one to talk about himself."

George sat on the sofa in his mother's media room. The television was on but he wasn't watching it. Instead he thought about all he had done to Emily. Somehow he had to ask for her forgiveness. He attempted to call her home number, but Mrs. Wilkerson, Emily's grandmother, answered.

"Hello?"

"Uh...is Emily available?"

"May I ask who's calling?"

This was the moment George dreaded. "Um...this...this is George Baxter. Emily and I used to work together."

Gram grimaced. "Oh, I know who you are. Why are you calling here? Haven't you done enough damage to my granddaughter?" She wanted to slam the phone down on its cradle but something kept her from doing so.

"Yes ma'am." George had to get through to Emily somehow, so he had to convince her grandmother he was calling for a good reason. "That's why I'm calling." He hesitated slightly. "I'd like to...apologize to her...and to you."

Gram couldn't believe her ears. "You want to apologize?"

"Yes ma'am. I know an apology will never erase the damage. But somehow I've got to make amends to Emily…and you."

Gram remained silent.

"I realize this may be a shock to you, but I've recently had a change in my life in more ways than one." George wasn't sure he should enlighten the woman but continued anyway. "You see, I've accepted Christ as my Savior."

Gram's reserve yielded slightly. "Well that's wonderful news." Although she was happy to know he had given his heart to the Lord, she remained adamant. After all, the man had raped her granddaughter.

"Thank you, ma'am." George heard the slight softening in her voice. "That's why I'm calling. I…uh…I've been reading the Bible and realize my sins have sought me out. I need to apologize to Emily for…" His attorney had advised against him confessing his guilt to anyone. He chose his words carefully. "Well, for my actions."

Gram realized he didn't admit he had raped Emily. Instead he beat around the bush. "Well George, Emily isn't here at the moment and until you are willing to own up to raping her, there is no need for you to call again." Gram disconnected the call.

George recoiled when she said the word rape. It was such an offensive word, but that was what he had done. He had seriously violated Emily. The thought made him sick. For the first time, he realized the severity of the crime he'd committed. He understood he must accept the punishment for his transgressions. He would call his attorney and change his plea.

Somehow, he had to convey his remorse to Emily. He couldn't go on without her forgiveness. He reached in the drawer of the end table, withdrew the family stationery and began to write.

While Mary napped on the sofa by the fire, Emily took the time to wander out to the stable. Melissa was grooming her horse.

Dressed in jeans and flannel shirt, Melissa's dark brown hair was pulled back in a long thick braid. Emily was astonished at the family resemblance. She figured this was a good time to get to know Seth's favorite sibling, and made her way down the steps toward the girl.

She looked up at the cloudless sky, "Beautiful day, huh?" The autumn air was crisp and cool that afternoon. The sunbeams illuminated the autumn colors of the trees.

Melissa stopped brushing her horse and looked up. "Yes, it is." She smiled sweetly.

"Going riding?" Emily inquired.

Melissa shook her head. "Nope. Just got back." Emily followed as Melissa led the horse to her stall and checked her water bucket and filled it. Then she filled the feed tub with grain and closed the lower half of the stall door.

Emily glanced at the name plate outside the stall. *Windfire*. She reached up and rubbed the horse's long nose.

Windfire whinnied as Melissa moved toward another stall.

"I've got to groom Transporter II. Wanna help?"

Emily nodded her head. "Sure I'd love to help!"

The two women walked the animal outside. Melissa handed her a grooming brush and showed her how to brush the horse with long strokes from the withers to the hindquarters, brushing in the direction of the hair growth. "Has Seth told you much about the family?"

"Oh, sort of. Mostly childhood stories though." She made one long stroke across the horse's back and then worked her way down his side. "He told me about the pool incident where he pulled you out of the water."

"Yeah, I think that's his favorite story. I don't remember it that much, but what I do remember is the attachment I had on him afterward." She blushed. "Still do. Has he told you anything else about me?"

Emily thought a moment and then shook her head. "No, not that I can think of. Why?"

"Well, he was my childhood hero as well as my adult hero."

"Oh?" Emily's eyes grew wide with surprise.

Melissa nodded as she moved the brush along the back of Transporter II. "He never mentioned how he rescued me last summer?"

"Not that I can think of."

So he has *kept it a secret.*

"Do you mind telling me how he came to save you a second time?" As soon as the words were off her tongue, Emily could sense Melissa's reticence. "No. That's okay. I understand if you prefer not to."

Emily understood what the young girl must be feeling. She, too, had skeleton's in her closet. She also believed it was best to discuss what occurred than to keep it bottled up inside wreaking havoc on one's self-esteem. Maybe she should disclose her own personal story to Melissa. It might help the teen realize she's not the only person to experience a devastating, life-altering event.

Emily convinced herself she could confide in the girl. Only she preferred not to see her pity. She avoided looking at Melissa as she ran the brush down the horse's hindquarter.

"I understand how you must feel." Emily sighed audibly, gathered her thoughts and continued cautiously. "Some people in my own church and community shunned me when I became pregnant. It didn't matter how I got that way. To them all that mattered was I had become an unmarried harlot. I became an outcast. They could care less that I'd been a respectable pillar of the church youth up to the night of the incident. All that those people could focus on was my pregnancy and not the circumstances that lead to it."

Melissa stopped grooming the animal to listen to Emily. She too had believed Emily had been promiscuous and her indiscriminate behavior had led to her pregnancy. Now she questioned her original theory and chastised herself for judging her brother's friend.

"Do you mind me asking what happened to you?" Melissa wasn't convinced Emily would divulge her secret. She bit her lip and held her breath, praying Emily would feel comfortable enough to share.

"I've never had a serious relationship with a guy."

Melissa looked at her, confused. "Not even with Marissa's father?"

"No! Of course not!" This wasn't going the way Emily had planned. "I…uh," Emily took a deep breath and exhaled audibly. "The essence of the story is that I was drugged and violated."

Melissa gasped. She couldn't believe someone would do such a horrendous thing. "But how—?"

"It's a very long story. One I've tried to comprehend myself." Emily inhaled deeply contemplating her next words. "Have you ever heard of Rohypnol?"

Melissa nodded. "Yeah, on the street it's called the date rape drug."

"Right. Well, I ingested it though a glass of water one evening while working alone. I passed out. The next thing I remember was waking up in the hospital." Emily paused in the act of grooming momentarily. She looked directly in Melissa's eyes. "There's no easy way to put it…while unconscious, I was…raped." There she'd said it.

Melissa gasped. "I'm so sorry, Emily. It never occurred to me that someone would do such a thing. I mean, some of the kids in my school are sexually active, so I automatically presumed you were too."

Emily had considered Seth's family would think that way. Everyone else had. "Actually, I was saving myself for marriage. It was important to me to follow God's commands and remain a virtuous woman. In fact, I was the president of a club in church that promoted abstinence."

"You were?" Melissa was astonished to meet an adult who considered virginity as a desirable quality. With the kids in her high school experimenting with sex, her cluster of friends had dwindled dramatically over recent years. Melissa was feeling ostracized by those she used to call her friends. Now she realized she was among the elite few who desired morality over popularity.

Emily nodded. "I stepped down as president from the organization when I discovered I was pregnant. I feel it is important to be a role model when in such a position, and in my condition, I was no example to follow, regardless how I came to be with child.

"Although Marissa was conceived against my will, I love her with all my heart. I can never change what happened, but what I can do is raise my daughter with all the love and affection any other child receives. She deserves everything I have in my heart and more. Although I'm no longer worthy of marriage, I'll do my utmost to be both mother and father to Marissa."

"Oh, but you are worthy, Emily! Kids these days are having sex with multiple partners and still find love. I'm sure God has someone special for you and Marissa."

Emily shrugged her shoulders. She understood the girl was consoling her and appreciated her efforts. But deep down she knew there was only one man she would ever love and she would never be worthy enough for him.

Melissa put the body brush aside and took up the horse's reigns. Together the women returned the animal to his stall, fed, and watered him.

"Your assault makes my problem pale in comparison."

"I seriously doubt that, Melissa. Each problem is unique and the damage is irrefutable." Emily helped Melissa lead Buttercup out for her grooming.

"My parents wouldn't allow us kids to start dating until we turned seventeen. Last year the church youth pastor, Blake Harrelson asked me out. We hit it off immediately. It was a beautiful match, even though Blake was seven years older than me."

"Wow! That's quite an age difference."

"I know, but we were like kindred spirits. Blake graduated from college a few years ago. He was new to the area and most of the older girls in church swooned over him, but I was the one he chose." Marissa beamed a timid smile at Emily. "Because of his position in the church, my parents felt it was okay for us to date even with the age difference.

"We were a match made in heaven. At least that's what I thought at the time. Blake asked me to marry him a month after our first date. He wanted me to attend college so that I could have the college experience, but as soon as I graduated, we planned to marry."

"Wow! You were that serious?" Emily stopped brushing the horse to look at the young girl.

Melissa nodded. Then her face went dark. "I don't know when it happened, but looking back I believe it was somewhere between the sixth and seventh month we were dating when Blake began to change." She shivered at the recollection.

"Change? How so?"

Melissa resumed her task before answering. "He became more temperamental. His attitude at church seemed to remain calm and serene, but with me, he was unstable. The smallest thing would set him off on a rampage. If I was even a minute late, he would yell at me and demand to know where I had been.

"If I didn't answer my cell phone each time he called, he would accuse me of being with another guy." Melissa stopped grooming the horse. "Most of the time he called I was in classes or out in the barn working and couldn't get to the phone. Blake didn't seem to understand our way of life here on the ranch. And, he seemed to forget that cell phones weren't allowed in class at school. He would leave malicious voicemails accusing me of going out behind his back. His thoughts of me with another guy consumed him."

"He sounds like a real charmer," Emily said wryly.

"He really was a great guy, at first," Melissa agreed. She sighed audibly. "Then, one day, I returned home from a date with Blake with a bruise on my upper arm."

"You mean he hit you?"

Ashamed, Melissa hung her head. "It had been an unusually hot day, so we went to the stream."

"The one Seth took me to?"

Melissa nodded. "Blake was in a foul mood almost from the moment we left the house. We rode horseback to the sight. I tried to make light conversation by talking about my day at school and the ranch, but it only made his mood worsen. So we rode the remainder of the way in tense silence.

"Once we dismounted, we walked among the rocks in the stream. Blake grabbed me by the arm and twisted me around."

Emily was appalled.

"I cried out in pain. 'Blake, you're squeezing my arm and it hurts!'"

"He said he didn't care. 'Where were you all day?' he said. 'Why didn't you answer any of my calls or call me back as soon as you got any one of my multiple messages?'

"I begged him to let me go. But his grip tightened, and I could feel the blood drain from my hand. I reminded him my phone had died, and I couldn't call until I got home."

Emily shrugged one shoulder. "That seems logical."

"I know, right? But when I arrived home, Mom had me run to the store to get some items for the B&B. So you see, I couldn't call. Not until I had returned home from the store, and that's exactly what I did. Nothing more, nothing less. I told him I called as soon as I could." Her voice cracked as she choked back tears. "My arm hurt unbearably. I continued to plead with him to release me, but he wouldn't."

"When did he let go of your arm?"

"A few minutes later. When he saw the immediate bruising on my arm, he felt like a fool." She shook her head at the memory. "I didn't know what had gotten into him."

Was he really a crazy lunatic? Why would he hurt this young woman if he truly loved her? Emily wanted to cease the horse grooming, but felt it less confrontational than looking Melissa in the eye. "So what happened?"

Melissa released a deep breath. "He began apologizing profusely."

"Well at least he apologized."

"Yeah. He said, 'I'm so sorry, Melissa. I never meant to hurt you. It's just that I love you so much I can't bear the thought of you with another guy. Do you understand?'

"My first mistake was believing him." Melissa shook her head. "I told him I believed he didn't mean to hurt me. Then I acted as if it was no big deal."

"He was too ashamed to admit his loss of control to my family and left it up to me to present to them a plausible excuse."

"I can't believe a man would do such a thing and then expect you to supply an explanation for his ghastly behavior!" Emily felt an odd sense of affinity with Melissa. Although Melissa's abuse had been executed by her boyfriend, Emily felt as though they were both offended by the deplorable acts of pathetic men. "So what excuse did you give your family?"

"I told them I lost my balance and Blake caught me just as I was falling.

"Although Seth was the first to notice the bruise, he said nothing. No one questioned my excuse except Seth. His thoughts were more sinister and right on target. Little did he know how precise they were."

"Did Seth give you a hard time about your explanation?"

Melissa shrugged her shoulders. "No, not really. It was more like a cynical expression. I couldn't look him in the eyes for days after that."

"Did he question you later, after Blake left?"

"No. I avoided him at all costs. Until a few weeks later."

"What happened then?"

"Blake called my parents to meet us at the hospital." Melissa rubbed her wrist absentmindedly. Blake lost his temper and broke my wrist."

"Oh my!" Emily couldn't believe a man would do such a thing to such a sweet girl. "What was your excuse this time?"

"I said I had fallen down the stairs at Blake's apartment." Melissa led the groomed horse to her stall.

"That wasn't the worst of it."

"There's more?"

The two women fed and watered Buttercup.

"Seth became a bit concerned. He noticed I never seemed to limp or act as though I was sore from the fall. Then, several weeks passed by, and I came home with a black eye. This time, though, I said I had walked into the corner of the cabinet door."

Melissa brushed her hands on her thighs as they walked out of the barn and proceeded up the steps to the house. The two women sat on the top step facing the barn.

"A few days later, Seth commented on how I had become accident-prone only since dating Blake. He became more and more suspicious of the injuries and followed me to Blake's apartment one evening in June."

"He did?"

Melissa nodded. "He remained outside in his car watching the windows to Blake's apartment. Everything appeared to be fine from Seth's vantage point. From what he observed, Blake doted on me. We kissed time and time again. After about an hour of watching us, Seth decided to leave.

"Blake had spent the day studying for the upcoming youth group Friday night meeting. He had become less suspicious of me with school out for the summer. The calls were less often, and his demeanor was more placid. I began to relax when around him. He was more like the man I fell in love with."

"That seems harmless enough." Emily noticed Melissa had begun fidgeting with the inside seam of her jeans.

"I wasn't sure if I should mention that my neighbor, Randy Suter, had stopped by the ranch while I was out grooming the horses earlier that day." Melissa looked out toward the barn. "You see, Randy is my childhood sweetheart and remains a good friend of the family even though things didn't work out between us.

"So I decided to tell Blake Randy stopped by the ranch that day. I knew if I didn't tell him myself, he would find out eventually, and God only knew how he would handle himself when he did find out.

"Blake shot up from the sofa where the two of us had been snuggling. Accusations flew from his mouth. 'Did he try to win you back? Did you kiss him?' Things like that."

"What did you tell him?"

"I simply told him the truth. I didn't kiss Randy. I'd broken his heart when I broke up with him to date Blake. Why would I kiss him? I was dating Blake."

Emily shrugged.

"But he accused me of wanting to kiss Randy and wouldn't believe otherwise. Blake raised his hand, I cowered and prepared to take the blow.

"Seth had witnessed the exchange from his car. He saw Blake raise his hand and slap me across the face. Seth wasted no time in coming to my rescue. He didn't even knock on the door but busted it in."

Emily sat there paralyzed at the thought of Seth angry enough to break down a door.

"I had my head down in anticipation of the next blow. When it didn't come, I looked up to see Blake standing there, frozen in time, one hand raised, eyes as big as a deer's in headlights. I turned to find Seth crossing the large room in a few rigid strides.

Blake's hand lowered as Seth reached up and grabbed his collar and pushed him against the nearest wall.

"I've never seen Seth lose control like this before. I mean, sure he and my brothers fought, but never like this."

Seth was infuriated with this man who hit women, but was more enraged that he raised his hand against his little sister. Never before had Seth experience such loss of control.

"I stood there and watched as Seth's fists slammed against Blake's face time and time again. When he didn't stop, I knew I had to do something. I grabbed Seth's arm before he could cast another blow.

"I never said a word to Seth. One look at me and he stopped. He turned to Blake, his words were simple and direct. 'How does it feel to be punched in the face? Huh?' Seth didn't give him time to answer. 'Don't you ever touch my sister again. Do you understand?' It was the first time I had seen Blake speechless. Blake nodded his head. Seth told him to pack his belongings and resign from church, effective immediately. Seth made it clear that if Blake didn't resign he would make sure I pressed charges and promised Blake would never work in a church again.

"All Blake could do was nod his head. He seemed relieved to not be on the receiving end of more of Seth's punches." Melissa giggled. "Blake rubbed his jaw. He said his teeth had loosened. I'm surprised he didn't lose them altogether with the wallops Seth delivered.

"Oh, and Seth made him promise to seek help with anger management as well.

"Before Seth released Blake, he thrust him against the wall just a bit harder...just because, I guess."

Emily could imagine how Melissa must've appeared in Seth's eyes. She had just been physically abused right in front of him and he had come to her rescue.

"When Blake attempted to deny he had ever hit me before, Seth turned to him and spoke with the angriest voice I'd ever heard come from his mouth. 'Don't you even suggest that it wasn't you who caused all her injuries! Do you understand?' It was then I realized I had only been fooling myself. That my—our secret—hadn't been a secret after all.

"Blake shut his mouth quickly. He had intended on explaining exactly what Seth had suggested. But he *was* the reason behind all I had been through. He didn't know what had caused him to abuse me. He had been brought up in a loving, Christian home. Never once had he witnessed his own father beat his mother, but here he was hitting an innocent girl. I guess he was suddenly sick to his stomach at the realization that he abused me because he ran to the bathroom and began vomiting violently.

"Seth gently coaxed me out of the apartment. My cheek was red from the strike Blake doled out. I didn't know how I was ever going to explain this to my parents. Seth seemed to read my mind and told me not to worry. He took me to get a cup of coffee, and promised by the time we arrived home the swelling and redness would have disappeared. I cried the entire time we sat with our coffees. I was so embarrassed. Yet Seth never once said a word. He held me close and allowed me to cry. When I finally calmed enough to voice my fears, I confessed I thought it was all my fault.

"Can you believe I actually thought it was my fault? Then, when I really considered all Blake had done, I realized it wasn't my fault at all, but a sickness in him. Seth told me Blake needed help, and I pray he seeks it before he harms anyone else. I actually considered filing charges anyway, but Seth believed Blake had seen the light, so to speak, and felt he would follow through with anger management assistance. Besides, I loved him too much to hurt him like that." Love. Was it really love? Looking back on it now, several months later, Melissa realized it wasn't really love as much as her desire to be loved by who she thought was a remarkable Godly man.

"Seth never mentioned a word of it to my family. It's something the two of us—now three of us—share. So you see. He's not just my childhood hero but my true hero in every sense of the word."

Emily sat there, stunned. "I had no idea, Melissa. I simply had no idea you had been through so much in your young life."

"It's in the past now. I've let it go and forgiven Blake. Though I'm not as naïve as I was back then. No one will ever do that to me again. I promised Seth I would be stronger, and I am. I don't date much. I'm more particular with whom I spend my time. Even my girlfriends have noticed and don't call as much. I miss them, you know?" She bowed her head. "I miss Randy, too. He has moved on to date other women in college. I heard recently he was dating someone seriously. I hate thinking of the pain I caused him." She shrugged her shoulders. "He's a better man than I deserve anyway."

"You should never think that way. No one is better than you deserve." Who was she kidding? Emily felt exactly that way about Seth, although she prayed he was the one for her. In her heart she didn't feel worthy of him.

Chapter 25

Meeting Seth's family proved to be an enlightening experience for Emily. Every one of them welcomed her with open arms and hearts. She was eternally grateful to Seth for taking her to meet them.

Mary's recovery was better than expected. She was only down for one day and had only a small dimple where the cancer had been, a little reminder of how gracious God was to her. The biopsy results confirmed the original diagnosis and revealed the doctor had indeed removed it all. For the next six weeks, she would undergo radiation therapy. After that, she would have another mammogram then not see the doctor for another year, providing the x-ray gave her a clean bill of health. Such good news.

Upon their arrival home, Gram was delighted to see Emily and Marissa. She could scarcely believe how much Marissa had grown in just a week. Gram took the baby in her arms and said, "Come here, you little darling, you." Gram gave her a kiss as she told the baby how much she had missed her and, of course, her mommy.

The day had been a beautiful fall day. The farther north they traveled the cooler the temperature became. She breathed in the cool crisp autumn air. From the porch, Emily could see the mountains to the west. One day, she hoped to take Seth there to see the majestic colors. It would have to be soon, as pique season was already passed and soon the leaves would fall from the trees. She held the door as Gram and Seth crossed over the threshold.

"Seth…" Gram turned to see Seth deposit the suitcases at the bottom of the staircase.

Looking up, he said, "Yes, ma'am?"

Gram stretched out her hand toward Seth. "Thank you for taking such good care of my cherished Emily and Marissa. They are all I have left in this world."

Seth took her hand in his. "Yes, ma'am. I was delighted to have them join me on my excursion home. My family loved them both," Seth replied. He looked at his watch then over to Emily. "Well, it's getting kind of late. I guess I'd better get back to the guys."

Emily and Gram watched as he kissed Marissa good-bye and then turned to leave.

"It was nice of you to take Marissa and me to meet your family," Emily said as she walked him to his car.

As they arrived at his car, he turned to say goodbye. The words stuck in his throat. He reached up with one hand to wipe loose tendrils of hair from her face. She was so close to him he could feel her breath on his neck. With a measured movement of his hands, he caressed her face. His heart hammered in his chest. For a long moment he gazed longingly into her eyes. Slowly he lowered his head and gently pressed his lips to hers.

Electricity exploded throughout his entire being. He felt Emily shiver upon the touch of their lips. He lowered his hands around her shoulders down the length of her back. She tenderly placed her hands around his neck, enticing him to continue. He pulled her against him to deepen the kiss as she opened her mouth to his. He could sense the passion rise within her as the kiss grew deeper. Then, just as gently as it began, the kiss came to an end.

Their eyes locked together. With arms embraced, it appeared to Emily as though Seth would kiss her again, but he withdrew his arms and took a step back. "I...I'm sorry." He hung his head. "I shouldn't have done that."

He was ashamed to have kissed her. Oh, but the kiss seemed so fervent and loving to Emily. It must have been her imagination that made her believe he wanted the kiss as much as she, but now she was second-guessing herself. Emily had begun to believe he felt something for her. After all, he did take her to meet his family. Something he rarely did, or so his mother said.

Emily was speechless. She didn't know what to say. He didn't care for her like she had hoped. She cringed at the thought. She turned and quickly ran up the steps into the house. Not once did she look back to see him standing there, befuddled.

Seth had watched as her eyes reflected confusion and then dejection. Sorry wasn't what he meant to say. Seth had wanted to kiss her—oh, how he wanted to taste her sweet supple lips. He wished the kiss never had to end.

With Emily, he believed things were different. Had she wanted the kiss as much as he? Was it his imagination that she nearly fell into his arms when their lips met? No, it wasn't his imagination. She kissed with as much intensity as he. There was fire in that kiss. And it caught them both by surprise.

Seth stood by his car and watched as she ran into her house. What could he say? What should he do? He was so confused. After all, didn't he only want to be friends with Emily? Another minute passed before he entered his car and slowly drove away.

Emily stood in her bedroom just beyond the window, looking down at the car as Seth drove away. Tears streamed down her face. She wrapped her arms around her waist and stared out of the window.

Emily heard a gentle knock on her door. "Come in," she said quietly.

Gram entered her room. "The baby is down for a nap. The trip must have really drained her." Emily shook her head as she surreptitiously wiped the tears from her face.

Gram walked over to Emily who still stood in front of the window with her arms wrapped around her waist. "Em, is everything okay?"

A small grunt escaped her lips as she attempted to stop the tears. "Okay? Okay, you ask?" Emily was indignant. She threw up her arms. "I have no idea! First, he takes me to meet his family, who, by the way admitted that Seth rarely takes anyone to meet them, so I must be 'special'! Then, he kisses me…" She paused. "No, not just any kiss. A passionate kiss—one with an eagerness that would rival the most passionate kiss ever! Oh, Gram!" Emily fell into her grandmother's arms and cried. "I thought he was beginning to care for me!"

Gram was confused. If he had kissed her—passionately, as she put it—then why was she crying? These weren't tears of joy but tears of agony.

"Honey child, if it was such a passionate kiss," she asked, "then why are you crying as if you lost your best friend?"

Emily sniffed. Gram handed her a tissue from the box on the table by the window. "Because…" she began as she wiped away the tears, "because after such an ardent kiss, he…he…he…" She hiccupped then took a deep breath. "He apologized!" She threw herself onto her bed and set out into a fit of crying again.

"Oh, Gram! What am I going to…" She gasped for breath a few times before continuing. "What am I going to do?" Emily stood again and paced the floor.

"What do you mean, 'What am I going to do'?" Gram asked. Gram walked up behind Emily and placed her hands on her shoulders. She turned the weeping girl around and lifted her chin so they could see eye to eye. "Child, what do you want to do?"

Emily looked at her, confused. Then all the emotion she was feeling turned to anger. "I never want to see him again. That's what!"

"Dear child." Gram sighed. "How can you not see him?"

"What do you mean?" Emily asked.

"He's already claimed your heart," she exclaimed. "You must see him again and ask him how he feels."

"Isn't that as clear to you as it is to me?" Emily's voice rose a few decibels louder. "He doesn't feel anything for me! All he wants is time with Marissa. It's Marissa he loves, not me!" She wept tears of deep sorrow at the realization. "If it weren't for Marissa,

I would have never heard from Seth after the concert. Instead, he delivered my sweet baby and became so attached to Marissa that he must have thought he had feelings for me." Then it dawned on her. "He must be so confused." She wept into her hands.

"Darling child, he loves you as much as he loves Marissa," Gram exclaimed. "He just doesn't know it yet." Emily looked at her, puzzled. "Give him time to sort through his feelings. He'll be back," she guaranteed.

Emily sat on her bed, flabbergasted. "Do you really think he loves me?" She sniffled, a glimmer of hope rising in her heart.

"Yes, I do."

She flailed her arms. "Then, why did he say he was sorry for kissing me?" Emily asked.

Gram sat down beside her. "I don't know, Emmie. I don't believe Seth even knows why he apologized. Only God knows, honey." She brushed aside the loose hair from Emily's face. "Just pray about it. Everything will work out in the end. Of that I am certain. Now...why don't you tell me about your visit with Seth's family?" Gram changed the subject, hoping to ease some of the wretched emotions with which her granddaughter was struggling.

"Gram, they are the sweetest, kindest, and most thoughtful people I have met in a long time." She went on to tell her of the warm welcome they exhibited to both her and Marissa. Mary had taken a liking to the baby from the first moment she laid eyes on her. It was like she became a surrogate grandmother. Being with Seth's family was a fulfillment of her own desires. She had wondered what it would be like to have a big family. Many times over in her life, she had asked Gram why her father had to die so young. He never truly had a chance to live. But his broken heart just couldn't handle the pain of losing both his child and wife on the same day. It was more than he could bear, so he gave up on life and on her.

Emily talked of the horses and the colts as if she had been there all her life instead of just a week. She had enjoyed her time immensely, and she told Gram just how much fun she had had. She talked about the picnic, and even meeting Seth's ex-girlfriend had been enlightening.

"If it weren't for Amy stopping by unexpectedly, I don't know how long it would have taken me to realize Marissa was sick."

Come to think of it, she never knew why Amy had stopped by in the first place. Had she come to visit with Seth again? Had she wanted to rekindle their relationship? Maybe this was why Seth apologized. Maybe he still had feelings for Amy and didn't know how to tell her. Maybe the kiss was his way of telling her good-bye. Oh, how foolish she was to think he could care for her!

Although he was tired, he took the scenic route home. He needed to think about what had happened. He'd kissed Emily and then apologized. *What was I thinking apologizing like that? Emily probably hates me now. God, what do I do?*

Seth got out of his car and headed into the house he and the guys were renting from a friend.

As Seth entered the house and was greeted with a warm welcome. He gave them details of his trip home and showed them the goody basket his mother had sent to them. Greedily they dug into the brownies and cookies before realizing there was lasagna. Logan and Zack each took a slice of lasagna and heated them in the microwave.

"Your mom is the best cook, Seth! I hope Emily cooks as well, or you'll be sending her back home for some lessons!" Heath teased. Logan and Zack laughed as they left the kitchen with their plates and returned to the media room.

Looking at the long face of his friend, Heath realized something was amiss.

"Hey, man," he queried, "What's up? Did something happen between you and Emily while you were gone?"

Seth shook his head. The trip had been more than what he had expected and still less than he wanted. He had been avoiding establishing a relationship with Emily beyond friendship. Thinking back on it now, he had grown more attracted to her while they were away. Truth was he still didn't know how to accept Emily could be the woman God had intended for him. She had been raped. She had a baby. Was this really what God wanted for him?

Heath sliced them each a large piece of pie and set them on the table. He motioned for Seth to sit.

"So…do you want to talk about it?" He sliced his fork through the meringue.

Seth ran his fingers through his hair as he took the seat across from Heath. "I'm not sure." He hesitated for a moment. Pushing back the dessert, he leaned back in the chair and gave an audible sigh. "I kissed her."

Heath froze, mouth wide open, fork halfway to his mouth. "Seriously?"

"Seriously."

Heath placed his fork back on the plate. "Well, it's about time! I thought you'd never get around to it!" Heath jested.

"Yeah, but…after the kiss…" Seth scratched his head and leaned his elbows on the table. He looked down at his hands. "I apologized."

"You what?" Heath couldn't believe his ears. Here was Seth, completely and totally in love with this woman or so he believed, and yet he apologized for kissing her. "Why?" he asked.

Seth stood up and paced the room. He looked directly at Heath and shrugged his shoulders. Truth was he didn't know why he apologized. The words just seemed to slip right through his lips.

Heath somewhat understood why Seth had apologized. "So you think you pushed her into a kiss she wasn't ready for?"

Seth looked out the kitchen window at the darkened sky. He nodded his head.

Heath took another bite of pie. "Tell me, how did she respond?" He picked up his glass and downed half the milk.

Seth turned, incredulous. "What do you mean, 'how did she respond'?" Seth gestured with his hands.

"Just what I said. How did she respond?" Heath said matter-of-factly.

Flustered, Seth sat back down at the table. "Well, uh, she, uh…seemed to enjoy it. I had to practically hold her up on her feet!" Seth smiled at the memory.

"Enamored," Heath said. "Then she wanted the kiss as much as you, man. It seems to me she was ready for the kiss more than you probably think." He finished off the last bite of pie and milk before turning to Seth. "If she allowed you to kiss her, she wanted it as much as you did. Don't beat yourself up for apologizing. Just call her and make amends. Or, better yet, go back to her house and beg forgiveness." Heath could imagine his friend on his knees right about now.

"I don't think that would be such a good idea."

"Why not?"

"I don't want to lead her on."

"How would you be leading her on?"

Seth confessed. "To be completely honest, I don't want a woman who has been with another man."

There it was. "So the truth is finally revealed!"

Heath was incredulous. "Man, I can't believe you! Here you are completely enamored with Emily and yet you are rejecting the very gift God is giving you!" Heath sighed. "I can't believe you are so close-minded to think you are too good for her. You are such a dunderhead. Do you realize how shallow you sound?"

Seth squirmed at the portrayal Heath described. Was he really that obtuse? Did he really believe Emily was unworthy of him? Was she the woman God wanted for him?

The Long Ride Home

Seth thought long and hard about Heath's comments long after their conversation ended.

Later that evening, Seth received the call he and the guys had been waiting for. Art Fields, the agent they had met with at the concert, called to tell them they were to meet with a record producer the following day to discuss a contract.

They had a possible contract! Seth was certain of it. And the first person he wanted to tell, to see, was Emily. Yet he didn't call.

❧

Early the next morning, Seth, Heath, Zack, and Logan drove to the office of Arthur Fields.

The receptionist stood and greeted the men. "Hello, you must be Seth." She reached out her hand across the high countertop.

She motioned to the waiting area. "You're early. Mr. Fields has a client right now. Please have a seat, and he'll be with you as soon as he is done." She came around from the opposite side of the counter. "Can I get you anything?" She was talking to everyone, but her eyes remained on Seth. Seth could tell she was interested in him, but he could care less. All he could think about was the smoky-blue eyed beauty he'd offended the day before.

The guys politely refused her offer and sat down to await Mr. Fields. As soon as they were comfortable on the leather sofa and wingback chairs, Art's office door opened and out stepped a renowned music artist and Art himself. They shook hands and said their good-byes.

Seth was impressed. This artist was on the latest cover of *Christian Music Magazine* as one of the most sought after singers in the industry. He hoped that one day he and the guys would be following in his footsteps.

Art saw the man to the main door and turned to face Seth. He reached out his hand as he walked toward him. "Seth"—he looked at the others to acknowledge them—"I'm so glad you are all here."

They all stood and shook hands with him.

He explained he had sent their demo CD to some of the best-known labels in the area and several had shown interest. "But why discuss it out here?" With a sweep of the hand, he motioned toward his office door. "Shall we?"

The office was handsomely decorated. Books lined up on one wall from floor to ceiling. Two other walls displayed dozens of pictures of Art with another person or persons holding silver and gold albums.

In one photograph, a well-known Christian celebrity held a Dove Award, one of the most coveted awards for Christian artists. The wall behind the desk boasted a large degree from George Mason University. Some charming built-in shelves on either side of the certificate displayed various artifacts from several different countries.

Upon the deep cherry desk sat a single eight-by-ten portrait of a striking woman with two equally attractive teenage boys and a beautiful little girl who appeared to be ten or eleven years old. A small lamp sat off to the other side, while a laptop was situated in the middle. He sat behind his desk.

The sofa and chairs of burgundy leather were set on one side of the room with a small coffee table in the center exhibiting several Christian magazines sporting the very celebrities presented on the walls.

The strapping older man, every bit of fifty, motioned for the guys to have a seat.

Art welcomed the young men exuberantly. "I can't tell you how much I appreciate the opportunity to represent such talented young men as you." Pointing to the pictures and magazines, he commented, "As you can see, I've represented many clients who have succeeded in your business. Sadly, some were not so successful."

His eyes widened, and a smile that showed off perfect white teeth spread across his face. "But you…you have what it takes to make it in this business. I could hear it in your music. I felt it in my spirit too."

Seth, Heath, Zack, and Logan all thanked him for his kind words. They wanted to get down to business much faster than the agent was willing to divulge. So they sat there listening to his repertoire of successes and failures.

"As I said earlier, I've had many successful clients in the past." He named off a few of the hottest Christian artists in the business and claimed them as his personal friends as well as clients. "Then there have been a few that didn't quite meet my expectations, so I had to let them go." He shook his head, stood, walked over to the empty wingback chair, and sat down. "The last man you saw is one of my newest clients. You may have heard of him."

Seth and the guys nodded their heads.

"Yes, well, he's already made a name for himself in just a few short months. He's had several hit songs and is nominated for this year's Dove Award."

Seth was impressed at the news. *One day I pray we will be nominated for the Dove Award.*

"I believe you have what it takes to make it big in the business." He pointed to them. "And I'm here to make it happen!" He clapped his hands together. "I have no doubt in my mind that you will be a Dove Award winner in the near future."

Changing the subject, he asked, "Have any of you heard of Victor Bagley?"

They shook their heads.

"Well, he is the owner of the most popular labels in the industry. He has signed on many of my clients. Those whom he has signed on have all gone on to make it big!"

They listened anxiously for more than half an hour as Art described his experiences in detail, when a knock sounded on his door.

"Oh, that must be him now." The guys looked at one another questioningly. *That must be who?* Seth wondered.

Art stood and walked over to the door. On the other side stood a man dressed to the nines. He shook the hand of the stranger and welcomed him in. With considerable fanfare, he introduced the group to the man. "This, my good fellows, is Mr. Victor Bagley, the producer I told you about."

They stood and shook his hand as they were introduced individually. They returned to their seats once Victor took his. Unbuttoning his suit jacket, he sat back and crossed his ankle over the other knee. He gave the appearance of complete confidence.

Victor took the lead. "Men, I've heard your demo and love your sound. It's exactly the quality and excellence I am looking for." Victor's smile spread across his tanned face. His impeccable look and flawless hair emitted class and prominence.

"Thank you," they said in unison.

"Guys, what I'm trying to say is"—Victor paused for effect—"I'd like to sign you on to Sharp Records."

They looked at one another, completely amazed.

"Wow," Seth said, "we didn't expect to sign on so soon! This is a fantastic opportunity. Have we had any other offers?" He looked over at the pristine gentleman. "No offense."

Victor lifted a hand. "None taken." His smile displayed perfect white teeth.

The group looked at Art questioningly.

"There are other offers already. But Victor has the best and most renowned label on this coast. And Sharp Records has the biggest recording studio on the East Coast. He can offer you more than the smaller labels. Chances of you getting a contract from a more renowned label in the west are slim at this juncture of your careers."

Seth, Heath, Logan, and Zack looked at one another. All facial expressions were positive. So they nodded their heads in agreement. Seth took the lead. "We are all in agreement. Yes! We'll sign on with Sharp Records!"

Victor and Art were pleased. Sharp Records had the clout to get this group up and running in the right direction. The next few weeks would be gruesome with recording and photo ops, but the men were up to the task. Victor reached into his breast pocket and withdrew the recording contract. He handed it to Art.

Art stepped in to say that the group needed to review the contract and they would get back with Victor. "Is tomorrow good for you guys?"

Looking from one to another, they agreed.

Art turned. "And for you, Victor?"

"Well, I was hoping to sign them on now and start recording immediately…but I guess it can wait one more day. But realize there is a desire for your kind of music, and we need to jump the gun and get moving on their debut album as soon as possible," Victor commented.

Art clapped his hands together. "Great!" He glanced from person to person, "Then we'll review the contract immediately and will have it signed and back in your hands first thing tomorrow morning." He reached out his hand as he stood from his chair. Everyone else stood simultaneously.

Victor took Art's hand and shook it as he stood to leave.

Victor turned to shake hands with Seth, "It was nice meeting you, and I look forward to doing business with you all." He shook their hands and then nodded to Art. "I look forward to doing business with you again, Art. Gentlemen"—he looked each of them in the eye—"it is a pleasure meeting you, and I'm anxious to see you bring it on!"

Art allowed Victor to let himself out and then took a few moments to review the contract. "Looks like a standard contract." He explained it in detail to the guys. "As for my rate, I get fifteen percent of your sales and bookings."

Art walked over to his desk and pulled out the bottom drawer. He retrieved a file marked "unknown group" and handed it to Seth. "It's a standard contract as well."

Art pointed to a blank line in the agreement, "This is where your group name will be inserted. I just need to know what you've decided on and I'll complete the contract." They took their seats again and began scanning the agreements.

The guys chuckled. "It's been a bit difficult to decide on a name. I mean"—Seth paused a moment—"we haven't been able to agree on anything except Brothers for Christ."

Art shook his head. Although it was a good name, he felt they needed something more "hip," as they say. "So what have you disagreed on, may I ask?"

"Nothing very good or that's not already taken," Logan piped in. "I like 2God, but the guys say it sounds like we are worshiping two gods."

"Well, I like 4HIM," inserted Zack. "But it's already taken."

"I prefer something from the Bible, like Judges," said Heath.

Seth just shrugged his shoulders. "See what we mean?"

"Hmm. They're all good suggestions," agreed Art. "But why not something like Native Song. I understand some of you are from Native American decent, so I thought it would be appropriate."

"Actually, only Seth is Native American," said Zack.

Art clasped his hands together, index fingers propped under his chin. He sighed. Then it came to him. He threw up his hands. "How about CrossPointe?"

The guys looked at each other. They liked it. Each nodded his head in agreement. "Great! CrossPointe it is!" Art exclaimed.

The guys wanted to take their contracts and read them thoroughly. Art agreed and recommended they have them executed in front of a few witnesses. When they explained they were new to the area and didn't really have any friends to call upon as witnesses, Art said not to worry. "Just bring the blank contracts back here after lunch and I'll have my receptionist, Shanyn, and secretary, Mrs. Dodge, witness them for you."

They walked out of the office with an exhilaration they had never felt before.

But still, all Seth could think about was Emily and how much he wanted to share this moment with her. Once the contract was signed, then he would break the news to her. He didn't want to jinx anything just yet.

"I can't believe we are finally going to be recorded by professionals!" Zack pumped his fist as Logan pushed the button to the elevator.

"Let's go have some lunch and review these contracts. Then we can return here to Art's office and sign them," Seth recommended. Everyone concurred as they donned their jackets and sauntered into the elevator.

The day was frigid. Mid-October promised a cooler-than-normal autumn for northern Virginia. Outside the sky was a brilliant blue, without a cloud in sight.

On days like these, Emily liked to get outside and do some gardening. However, this year she had very little time to plant annuals and perennials with a newborn keeping her up night and day. She would have to make do with the fall azaleas and the petunias she had planted back in the spring.

Emily sat on the overstuffed blue floral sofa drinking a cup of tea. On the sofa table, light filtered downward from a blue and white lamp. Family photos were displayed proudly on the table's surface. On the coffee table, she had some papers and a birthday card.

It had taken her the better part of an hour to pick out the card. After all, it was only once a year that she poured her feelings out through a card. Compared to last year, there was more joyfulness in her heart, so getting the right card was important to her. The card wasn't the typical "To Dad…from Daughter" because none of them impressed her. This was a romantic birthday card that simply stated what she wanted to convey to her father.

Emily leaned back on the sofa pillows and pulled her knees up to her chest. She inhaled the aroma from her mug of tea and sighed. Normally on a day like today, she would get outside and enjoy the crisp, cool autumn air. However, today there was too much on her mind.

It had been a week since the eventful kiss with still no word from Seth. All kinds of thoughts had passed through her head. *Is he unhappy with me? Is there someone else? Is it over?*

Was it over? The thought seemed to inhabit her mind more than any other. Nothing else seemed to matter. She just didn't understand why Seth had not called. Maybe he was sorry he had kissed her after all. Maybe he wasn't as interested in her as she had hoped. Maybe he was still in love with Amy. Maybe…so many maybes.

Chapter 26

Seth was so excited. He couldn't wait to tell Emily the news. Only he'd been up too early to call each morning and arrived home too late to call at night. He longed for some private time to contact her, even if it was just to hear her voice.

The last several days had blended into one. Meeting with a record producer, one of the most respected names in the business, the group played and sang several songs for him. Victor set them up with an orchestra and conductor. They all worked on the music from early in the morning to late in the night. It was a gruesome schedule, but they had to get the music ready for recording the next week because Victor wanted to debut their album on Thanksgiving weekend, just in time for the Christmas shoppers.

After church, he drove out to Ashburn to tell Emily the news and explain why he had apologized for the impromptu kiss. He zipped his leather jacket as he exited his car. As he walked in front of the beautiful home, he noticed Emily sitting in the living room drinking from a mug. He ascended the stairs, two at a time, onto the wide porch. Quietly he walked up to the window, weaving through the porch furniture, to immerse himself in the sight of her.

She was the most beautiful woman he had ever seen. He noticed how slender she appeared. She had lost weight. Was he the cause of her losing weight? She looked as fragile as a porcelain doll. He should have called her. He chastised himself for not getting in touch with her at least once over the last week. But he wanted to tell her about the contract in person. Had he waited too long? Would she forgive him for his neglect? He vowed to himself to never disregard her again.

Emily was engrossed in thought. She sat motionless and serene. He wanted to know what was on her mind. He wanted to tell her everything on his. Just as he determined to knock on the window to get her attention, he noticed the card that sat on the coffee table.

He wondered who the card was for. Could it be a way for her to tell him good-bye? With that thought, he was caught off guard and lost his footing. He fell onto the back of the porch rocker just behind him.

Emily looked up and saw him. She was surprised to say the least. Gram had heard the commotion and came running into the room.

"Are you okay, honey?" Gram asked Emily.

"Um, yes. It was Seth. He's out on the porch." Emily pointed toward the windows as she placed her mug down on the coffee table.

"Well then, let's let him come inside." As Gram went to the door, Emily snatched the card and placed it in a magazine on the table. Just a small portion of the corner stuck out, but there was no time to push it in all the way, as Seth was walking into the house. She didn't want Seth to think her ridiculous because she gave her deceased father a birthday card each year.

Trying to appear composed, which was nothing like she felt, Emily greeted him nonchalantly. Bracing herself for the heartache she was surely going to receive, she stood at the sofa as Gram led him in the room. Emily welcomed him with aloofness in her voice and sat back down. Her hands trembled; she clasped them together and placed them on her lap.

Seth took a seat in the chair across from her. He could see apprehension in her eyes. He wanted to relieve her of the anxiety she felt, if only he understood why she was so stanch.

He wasn't quite sure where or if he should start. Should he wait on her to initiate the conversation? Should he start with an explanation for his apology of the kiss? Should he just skip over the kissing thing and go straight into what he'd been doing the last few days?

The Long Ride Home

He decided to tell her about the contract; after all, this was his reason for coming over without notice.

"We've signed a contract with a record producer!" Seth blurted out. "You may have heard of them. Sharp Records?"

She nodded her head. "Seth, that's great! Sharp Records is a huge corporation. What wonderful news," Emily cautiously responded. She remained on the sofa, uncertain how to react.

Her response wasn't exactly what he was hoping for. All he wanted was to hold her again, to feel her warm breath against his neck, and to kiss her sweet lips once more, but she sat stock-still, her face unreadable. He couldn't ascertain if he was even welcome anymore.

Emily glanced down at her tea. Remembering her manners, she offered Seth a cup. He readily accepted. After she left the room, Seth reached over to the coffee table and pulled out the card from the magazine. It read, "Happy Birthday to the man I love."

He didn't bother to read the words on the inside, just her signature: – Me.

It wasn't his birthday for several months, so the card definitely wasn't for him. Who was this man she loved? Was it George, Marissa's father? Was she secretly in love with him? Footsteps in the hallway brought his thoughts back to reality. He quickly replaced the card.

When Emily returned with his cup of tea, Seth stood. "Thanks for the tea, but…I've got to go." With that, he turned and walked out of the house.

Gram sat at the breakfast bar reading her e-mail as Emily rounded the island sink and vigorously poured out the tea from the extra mug. "Where's Seth?" Gram asked.

Tears fell from her eyes as she explained how abruptly he left. "He didn't even say good-bye."

Gram stood up and walked over to her granddaughter. She took Emily into her arms and allowed her to cry. She didn't understand. "Did something happen on your trip to make him so aloof?"

Emily told her how well they gotten along during their time in North Carolina and on the return ride home. "I've gone over it a thousand times in my mind. Nothing stands out as abnormal—except the kiss from Amy."

"Who's Amy?"

"Seth's high-school sweetheart."

"You didn't tell me about her, or the kiss."

Emily described what she had seen through the kitchen window at Seth's family home. "When I liken their kiss with ours, well," she shrugged, "there's no comparison.

"Oh Gram, what am I going to do?" she cried. "I love him so much."

"Oh, my dear child, I know you do." Gram gently rubbed her back. "He loves you, too. I'm sure of it."

Emily pulled away from her grandmother and looked her straight in the eye. "Then why is he acting this way?" she asked.

"I don't know, sweetheart." She stroked Emily's shoulders. "Maybe he's just not ready. Give him time, and trust God will take care of it. Everything will work out fine. You'll see."

Emily prayed she was right because she didn't have the strength to continue on her own.

Gram reached in her pocket and pulled out an envelope. "This came in the mail for you." She handed it to Emily.

"Who's it from?" She accepted the parcel and flipped it over to look for a return address.

"I don't know. You won't find a return address."

Emily sat on the stool at the bar and opened the envelope. Inside she found fine linen paper. She unfolded the single page and saw the Baxter letterhead. She flipped it over and read the signature line. "It's from George."

Emily tossed the letter onto the island. She couldn't believe he had the audacity to write to her. She picked it up once again and viciously crumpled the paper in a ball.

"Why don't you read it, honey?" Gram asked.

"Why should I?" She asked incredulously. "He's probably asking me to drop the charges against him." "You may be surprised." Gram recalled the phone call from a few weeks back. "You know, he called you while you were visiting Seth's family."

"Why was he calling me?" Emily's voice rose a few decibels higher than she intended, but she was livid. She stomped on the pedal of the trash receptacle and vehemently tossed the ball of paper and envelope inside.

"I have nothing to say to the man." Emily hurled herself into a seat with a thump.

"No, but he has something to say to you." Gram calmly withdrew the letter from the container, smoothed it out and set it on the counter. She pointed to the letter. "Why don't you read it? You may be surprised." Gram turned and walked out of the room leaving Emily to decide on her own.

Emily inhaled rapidly then exhaled slowly. She reluctantly reached for the letterhead and began to read.

Dear Emily,

It is with great trepidation I write this letter, but somehow I must ask your forgiveness for the sin I committed against you.

I realize now what I've done was wrong.

I can never give back what I took from you.

I can only hope you will understand my regret and forgive me.

Against my attorney's advice, I now admit to raping you. That one horrific act resulted in the conception of your baby girl.

Yes, I said your baby. I will relinquish all parental rights to you. She need never know about me and the events that led to her conception. I have, however, established a trust fund in her name for college and whatever needs she may have when she graduates. I pray you will accept this fund as it is the least I can do. She need never know from where the money originated as the account was established in your name, not mine.

As God as my witness, I wish I could turn back the hands of time and repeal what I have done. But I cannot. I have finally given my heart to God, and I promise to never *knowingly sin against another human being again.*

If you can find it in your heart to forgive me, would you please write and let me know?

Sincerely,

George Baxter

Emily lowered the letter to her lap. *Forgiveness. All he asked was forgiveness.* She thought she had forgiven him, but realized she had only said the words, not truly felt them. She prayed for God to help her forgive him. She knew it would be the most difficult act she would ever perform.

With a confused heart, Seth poured himself into his music. He wrote song after song, emptying his sentiments onto paper. It was therapeutic and uplifting, but still nothing could sever the distress in his heart.

Day after day, he struggled with the uncertainty of where he stood with Emily and if he could accept her as is: stained and compromised.

Why do I feel so fanatical about having a virtuous woman for a wife? Emily's everything I've ever wanted with that one exception? Why would God not grant this one last desire in the woman of my dreams?

Confiding in Heath proved to be futile. He needed some advice but not from the guys.

He had to call his mother and entrust her with everything in his heart. He knew she needed to know the whole story before she could advise him accordingly.

Mary wasn't surprised to hear Emily had been raped. "I felt something serious had happened to Emily. She didn't appear to be a promiscuous girl. But are you sure she has no feelings for the father?"

"That's why I'm calling, Mom. I just don't know what to think." He ran his fingers through his hair. "When I saw the birthday card, I just figured she must have some feelings for Marissa's father, or she wouldn't have purchased a birthday card for him."

"Hmm. Maybe the card is not for…what did she say his name is?" Mary thought for a moment, "George. That's it, right?"

"Right."

"Maybe the card is for someone else."

"But who, Mom? Who else could she love?"

"Honey, I'm sure I don't know. I think you should just wait and let things reveal themselves in their own time."

"Truthfully, the card is insignificant." Seth sighed, reluctant to bring up the real reason for his call.

Mary sensed there was more than what her son had admitted. "Well, what is it then?"

"There's the matter of her disgrace. I have struggled to accept God would allow my future wife to be compromised before our wedding night. Purity is such a significant attribute to me: I cannot accept God would give me such an intense attraction to a woman who doesn't possess this aspect."

"Seth! Are you listening to yourself? When did I raise you to be a self-righteous, ungracious, dimwitted oaf?"

Seth was dumbfounded. Did he really sound so odious?

"Son, you know I love you, but you need to do some serious praying about your attitude toward Emily's unfortunate circumstances. Your superior behavior has disturbed me beyond words. Emily did not give her consent to surrender her virginity. She wasn't even aware of the assault on her body. How can you judge her for something for which she had absolutely no control? It wasn't God who allowed this to happen, but it was God who made her your match. Whether you believe it or not, Emily is still innocent in her mind. She has no recollection of the incident; therefore, she carries no baggage into a relationship. Even if she had given herself willingly, would you hold it against her? Everyone makes mistakes, son, even you.

"When you open your heart and mind to the precious gift God has in store for you, then and only then, will you be able to accept all the good and wonderful things Emily has to offer.

"Until then, you're not worthy of her."

Helen Baxter and her driver, Montgomery Winston, had been found guilty of child abduction in an earlier trial.

Because of Winston's position with the Baxter family, it was determined he was an unwilling accomplice and was sentenced to two years probation and community service.

George Baxter changed his plea to guilty.

The District Attorney had arranged George and Helen's sentencing trial for the same day and time.

A few weeks later, George and Helen Baxter appeared before the court listening to the charges against them.

Emily sat in the court room anxiously waiting for Judge Roy McClellan to pass down sentencing.

She was to be given an opportunity to address the court prior to the judge assigning their punishment.

As she stepped forward, the door to the court room opened. Seth walked in and quietly took a seat in the back. He had read about the hearing in the papers and decided to attend inconspicuously.

He listened as Emily addressed the judge.

Emily stood tall and spoke with conviction...

"Your Honor, as the victim of both George and Helen Baxter's crimes, I humbly ask you to be lenient with their sentencing." She swallowed the lump in her throat before continuing, "In the beginning, I wanted nothing more for them than the harshest ruling. But after receiving a letter from George Baxter requesting forgiveness for his actions, I had to do some serious soul searching.

"You see, Judge McClellan, at first I had not sincerely forgiven George. Not before his letter, anyway. He had denied raping me, and that was unforgiveable. In his letter I read his heartfelt words and confession. It was then I realized all I honestly desired was his accepting responsibility of his wrongdoing. He did so in the letter and that was when I was finally able to forgive him. Forgiveness is not granted lightly. It is something I have to do every day. Every time I think about what was taken from me."

Emily turned slightly to see the humble gratitude on George's face.

"I know he must be punished for the criminal act, but ask you, respectfully, to consider his current physical condition. He is now sentenced to a life confined to a wheelchair. His body is paralyzed from the waist down. In essence, God has handed down a life sentence on him.

"George will need his mother, Helen Baxter, to nurture and encourage him. She kidnapped my daughter believing she had no other choice to protect her son. Her actions were conceived out of love for George. Although she has a cantankerous exterior, I believe she has a merciful heart hidden deep within.

"Helen Baxter would not survive in prison. Her standard of living defines her delicate nature. I believe if Mrs. Baxter were allowed to care for her son as a partial punishment, she would acquiesce with a grateful heart.

"However, sir, in addition to tending to the needs of her son, may I ask you to consider community service for the remainder of her sentence?"

"And do you have a specific service in mind for Mrs. Baxter?" Judge McClellan asked.

"Yes, I do, your Honor."

The judge nodded his head slowly. "Please, proceed."

"There is a homeless shelter here in the county in need of compassionate people to care for them. Maybe by serving the homeless, Mrs. Baxter will come to appreciate those who are less fortunate than herself, instead of looking down on them."

"Is that all, Ms. Wilkerson?" The judge leaned forward in his seat, hands clasped on his podium.

"Yes, sir. Thank you for your time and consideration." Emily turned to see Seth leaving the court room. *I wonder why he was here. Why didn't he tell me he was coming? Why did he leave so abruptly?* With so many confusing thoughts consuming her mind yet again, she refused to dwell on them. She returned to her seat to hear the judge's decision.

"Thank you, Ms. Wilkerson." The judge paused a moment before he passed down the sentences.

Helen Baxter was required to stand.

"Mr. George Baxter, you have committed a horrendous crime against your fellow citizen. The fact that you are now unable to execute this transgression again is a consolation. Ms. Wilkerson feels you have been administered a life sentence by God Himself. If this is so, then who am I to say it's not befitting? In addition to this Divine punishment, I sentence you to pay restitution to Ms. Wilkerson in the amount of two point five million dollars.

"As for you, Mrs. Helen Baxter, Ms. Wilkerson's proposal for you to serve the community in the local homeless shelter appeals to me. It will give you the opportunity to learn benevolence for your fellow man, who is less fortunate than you. You, Mrs. Baxter, will be living an altruistic life from this day forward. One that is a far cry from the life you have lived up until now." Judge McClellan struck his gavel against his podium to signal his decision had been rendered.

Seth had listened as Emily addressed the judge. He couldn't comprehend all she had endured to reach her decision. He chastised himself for neglecting her during her time of need.

As he walked through the courtyard to his car, he contemplated his attitude toward Emily.

Seth had abandoned her when she needed him most. He had spurned her, acting as if she had willingly given herself to another man. He had judged her as unworthy of him; when in essence, he didn't deserve her.

How could he be so blind? How could he be so judgmental? When did he become judge, jury, and executioner? Doesn't the Bible say 'Judge not lest ye be judged'?

God forgive me. I've been so wrong in my attitude toward Emily. I don't deserve such a beautiful loving woman, but I'd like to believe that I can change into the man you would have for her. Please don't let it be too late.

He could no longer afford to disregard the aching in his heart.

At the end of the recording, Victor had scheduled the group portraits for the album cover taken at the Jefferson Memorial in Washington, DC. While there, Seth decided to tour the city and its prominent landmarks for some much needed time of reflection. Time had not been on his side lately, and he relished the opportunity to be alone and ruminate.

The day was overcast and windy as the leaves fell from their trees and tumbled about on the ground. As he walked through Arlington Cemetery, in the distance he observed a young lady with a baby. His heart skipped a beat, and for a fleeting moment he thought it was Emily with Marissa.

He longed to see them both. He wanted to know what new things Marissa had discovered and to hold her in his arms.

As he walked closer, he detected a brown slip of paper in the woman's hand. She bent down in front of a grave marker and placed the paper on top.

The closer he got to this woman, the harder his heart pounded in his chest. It was Emily! And Marissa. Unable to call out in the quiet cemetery, he picked up his pace and began walking quickly as she turned to walk away.

To his dismay, there was a cab waiting for her on the street. He began to run after her. The taxi drove off before he could reach them. He reached the street, threw up his hands, and then dropped them to his knees as he bent down to catch his breath.

He looked up to see the brown paper flying across the ground, miraculously landing at his feet. He picked it up. It was a card. Instantly he knew. Without opening it he knew it was the card from Emily. He took a deep breath, releasing it slowly as he opened the envelope and pulled out the card. The words jumped out at him: "To the man I love." He didn't have to open it. He knew it was from Emily. But who was it to?

He walked along the markers until he reached the gravesite. On the headstone, it read, "Captain Tony O. Wilkerson Jr., 1959-1989." Emily's father. The card was for her father. Of course! She must give her father a birthday card each year! That made perfect sense. But what he didn't understand was why she purchased a card for a lover and not a father?

Replacing the card in its envelope, he placed it on the ground by the marker. Immediately he took off to the metro station. He had to get back to his car, and he had to get to Emily and explain himself. He loved her and couldn't wait to tell her so.

The sky promised rain, but Seth's heart soared. Emily wasn't in love with anyone else. If she needed time, he would give it to her; still he had to declare his love for her.

Emily sat on the front porch swing while Marissa slept against her chest. She swung back and forth, humming softly.

The evening was creeping upon the house rapidly. The air had become cooler. She needed to get Marissa inside. As she stood from the swing, she heard a car enter the driveway.

There pulling into the drive was a brand new, medium-brown metallic sports utility vehicle. In the driver's seat sat Seth. He disembarked the vehicle. A smile spread across his face as soon as he laid eyes on them.

Emily stared. She felt the warmth of his smile down to her toes. She didn't know what to think or say. After a few minutes, she composed herself. "When did you get that?"

Seth ascended the steps two at a time. "I'm test driving it." He laughed.

"What's so funny?" Emily asked.

"The look on your face," he replied. "What do you think? Do you like it?"

Emily didn't know what to think. She knew he loved his sporty vehicle, and didn't understand why he would trade in his dream car.

Seth leaned over and kissed Marissa on the back of her head. "I'll explain to you as soon as you get her back inside. It's getting much too cool for her out here." He placed his hand on the baby's head, leaned down, and kissed it again.

When Emily returned, Seth was leaning against the stone pillar with one booted foot propped against it, arms crossed at his waist. He looked so handsome in his black slacks, royal-blue shirt, and leather jacket it took her breath away. Even his boots made him look good.

Over the last few weeks, she had begun to question her feelings for this man. One look into his sparkling blue eyes and gone were the doubts. Gone were the questions. In their place was complete and utter confidence. She knew she loved him. No matter what he had to say, she would love him for the rest of her life. She sat down on one side of the porch swing, allowing enough room for him to sit beside her. Instead, he remained at the post.

Seth took a deep breath and began his story.

"When I first saw you sitting in the audience the night of the concert, I was convinced you were the one for me. But when I saw you were pregnant, I brushed that thought aside because I wanted a virtuous woman."

Emily hung her head in shame.

"Then I delivered Marissa. I loved her immediately. I never believed I could love a child as much as I love her."

She looked up and smiled timidly.

"When you told me about the assault, I wanted to extract my vengeance out on the perpetrator. Instead, I mucked out the stalls." He smiled at the thought.

Emily continued to sit in the swing, confused.

Seth continued, "I'm sorry I apologized for kissing you." His eyes gazed into hers. "At the time, I didn't want to deceive you in to believing I had feelings for you other than friendship.

"Then, I signed the contract with Sharp Records. I wanted you to be the first one I told, it's just that so much happened that week, I wasn't able to contact you. I wanted to tell you face-to-face anyway, which is why I came out that day.

"At first I was conflicted. I didn't know if I should've talked about the kiss and my apology or just jump right into the good news. Looking back at your reaction, I should've addressed the apology first."

Emily didn't know if she should explain her surly attitude. Instead she allowed him to continue.

"Anyway, when you left to make me the tea, I saw the card you had hidden. At the time I thought it was for George and decided you had secretly cared for him."

"How could you think such a thing?" Emily asked incredulously.

Seth shrugged his shoulders. "I don't know. All I knew was the card wasn't for me, and the only other man in your life at the time was George."

"It wasn't for him," she confessed.

"I know. I think deep down inside I knew it wasn't for him either. But it wasn't until that day in court when I realized he meant nothing to you. I listened as you professed your forgiveness for the man who assaulted you. When I left, I considered your mercy.

"You were so willing to forgive and move on with your life, and here I was pious and unforgiving. I believed God had intended me to have an unblemished woman. I was so repulsive in my thinking my own mother called me self-righteous."

He looked down at his boots. "Heath said I was close-minded. And they were right. All along I was denying myself of the love for which my heart yearned. No one has ever made me feel so alive and full of life. These last few weeks without you have been the most meaningless weeks of my life. The only thing good that came from our separation was the time I spent in prayer and searching my soul."

"And what did you find there?"

"Forgiveness."

"For who?" Emily didn't know where he was going with this, but she was curious.

"George."

"George?"

"Yes. After I listened to you in the court room, I realized I had to forgive George for taking your innocence. And then, I had to ask God to forgive me."

"Forgive you? What did you do?"

"I denied a very special gift from God."

Emily didn't understand. Her eyebrows scrunched together. "What gift?"

"You." Seth sighed. "God gave me you."

Emily pondered his words. Was she truly a gift to him? She was doubtful.

"When I saw you at the cemetery earlier today, I realized the card was for your late father. I tried to catch you before you left, but I was too late. So I ran to my car. I had to see you."

He took the seat next to her. "On my way here, the thought hit me: if I'm to be a family man, I need a family vehicle." He looked over his shoulder at the SUV. "What'd'ya think? Like it?"

The words sang to Emily's heart, "*...if I'm to be a family man...*"

"Emily?" Seth reached up and took her face in his hands. Slowly, affectionately, he leaned down and kissed her lips tenderly, with all the love he had in his heart.

Emily practically melted in his embrace. The passion and love she felt left her without any reservations. This was a man in love. He didn't need to tell her; she was keenly aware of it with every ounce of her being.

Seth slowly abandoned their kiss. He pulled away, reached into his jacket pocket, and pulled out a jewelry box. He dropped down to one knee. Slowly he opened the little black box. Inside was a beautiful Marquise diamond. Without reservation, he began his proposal.

"Emily, all my life I've waited to feel the way I do when I'm with you. You've touched my heart and soul. When I think of my life and how it will unfold, I see you there, beside me—my encourager, my supporter, my best friend, and the object of my desire. It's you with whom I want to spend the rest of my life.

And I want to be a father to Marissa. Would you do me the honor of loving me for the rest of my life?"

Silently, gently, and tearfully, Emily reached down to take his face in her hands. Leaning down, she kissed him deeply and completely. She stood and leaned on the porch railing with her back to him.

Looking out into the yard, she replied, "I can't."

He was perplexed. Was it because he had not contacted her in the last few weeks? Now that he realized how he felt about her and thought she felt the same, he couldn't understand why she couldn't marry him. Closing the jewelry box, he stood from where he was kneeling and waited for Emily to continue.

"Is it because I haven't called or maybe because didn't consult you about the vehicle? I just brought this one over for your opinion. I was hoping you would join me in shopping for just the right family car for us."

Emily shook her head. "No, it's not the vehicle. In fact, I love that one." She paused to take a deep breath and released it slowly. "What I mean is I'm not worthy of you." Emily turned and sat down in the swing and motioned for Seth to sit with her. She turned toward him and sighed. "You deserve a woman who has saved herself for marriage."

Suddenly she was chilled. She rubbed her arms for warmth.

"Don't you see, that doesn't matter to me?" He placed his hands on her arms. What mattered is that she would be his forever…if only she would say yes.

She shook her head. Turning to face him, she finally confessed, "You don't want a soiled wife."

"Emily." He sighed. "I may have felt that way at first, but now it doesn't matter. You didn't have control over what happened to you. Yes, physically you've had a baby, but mentally, you're still innocent."

Emily considered his words carefully. Unable to look him in the eyes, she moved her head from side to side. Tears fell from her eyes.

"Don't you get it, Emily?" He wanted her to understand she was not tainted. "In your heart and mind, you've never been with a man! And, even if you had, I'd still want you as my wife. I love you."

He lifted her face with the crook of his finger. He gazed deeply in her eyes, "You've got to believe me, Emily. Please, baby, say you believe me." He implored.

It was as if a light bulb went off in her eyes. She didn't have to say a word. Seth knew she understood. He wrapped his arms around her and pulled her close. He kissed the side of her head, then her cheek. Then gently pressed his lips to hers once again.

He took her hands in his and looked into her smoky blue eyes, eyes he wanted to get lost in for the rest of his life. "Emily, I love you with all my heart. Will you please marry me?"

Emily could hardly believe what she was hearing. He still wanted her for his wife. This handsome, wonderful, caring man wanted to be her husband and a father to Marissa. How could she deny him what she herself wanted?

"Will I marry you?"

Seth nodded his head, his eyes pleading.

"Seth, it would be an honor to be your wife. God knows I don't know why you would want me, but who am I to question Him? Or you for that matter." She released his hands and took his face in hers. "Yes. Yes, I'll marry you and spend the rest of my life with you." She looked deeply into his blue eyes. "I love you, Seth."

Then to seal the deal, she kissed him. It was a sweet, tender kiss that told him all he needed to know. She loved him. And he loved her.

Lovingly he took the ring out of its box and gently placed it on her left ring finger and kissed it.

"Now it's official." Seth grinned. He bent down and adoringly kissed her once again. It seemed he couldn't get enough of her. He had to stop before it went too far. "Want to go in and tell Gram?"

Emily nodded. They both walked into the house. Gram was sitting at the breakfast bar surfing the Internet.

"Gram?"

Gram didn't take her eyes off the computer screen. "Hmm?"

"Seth's here." Emily looked into his eyes and quietly chuckled. "He wants to ask you something."

Her eyes remained glued to the computer. "Sure thing. What's on your mind?"

"Mrs. Wilkerson—"

"Now, you know better," she chastised. "Call me Gram."

"All right then. Gram? I'd like to ask you for Emily's hand in marriage."

Her eyes never wavered from the computer screen. "Hmm? What's that you asked?"

"For Emily's hand in marriage."

Gram's fingers stopped typing, and she ceased to look at the computer. She turned to look intently in his eyes. "Are you serious? Or was this some trick to get me to look at you?"

"No, no trick." Seth chuckled. He put his arm around Emily's waist. "Would you allow me the honor of marrying your granddaughter?"

"Well, it's about time you came to your senses!" She stood from the stool where she had been sitting and gave them a big hug. "Of course you may marry my Emmie."

Epilogue

Three weeks later, the Saturday before Thanksgiving, they exchanged vows. Their wedding had been a quiet affair with close friends and family in attendance.

Kate was Emily's maid of honor dressed in dazzling crimson satin while Heath stood in as best man, well-dressed in a black tuxedo with a crimson ascot. The service was held at the Hylton Memorial Chapel. The church chapel was decorated in beautiful fall oranges, vibrant reds, royal purples, and golden yellows.

Emily carried a bouquet of red, yellow, and orange roses interspersed with purple Lisianthus.

The day Seth proposed, Gram had taken Emily up to the attic and showed her a trunk. Inside she found her mother's wedding gown. It had fit perfectly. Emily was a bit concerned what others would think with her wearing white, but white was now considered a symbol of tradition, and this would be a traditional wedding in every sense of the word.

Gram walked Emily down the aisle in place of her deceased father. Honored though she was, she was prouder still—proud of the woman Emily had become and especially proud of the man she had chosen to marry. Truly he was sent by God.

Mary was given the privilege of attending to Marissa, who was as good as gold that day. It was as if she knew how special the moment was. She was in the prettiest red velvet dress Emily and Gram could find. It had to be special ordered and was worth every penny. After all, Gram expected this to be the most beloved day of Emily's life.

They exchanged vows they had written to each other.

"Seth, I take you to be my husband, my lover, and my friend. I will honor you and keep you and only you until death parts us.

I will be beside you every step the Lord takes us on through our journey in life. I will be yours forever and always."

"Emily, I take you to be my wife, my lover, and my friend. I will honor you and keep you and only you until death parts us. I will provide for you and Marissa and the additional children we will have. I will take care of you in sickness and in health. I will be there for you and with you throughout life's challenges. I will be yours forever and always."

They exchanged vows and rings, were pronounced husband and wife, and then were presented to the audience as Mr. and Mrs. Seth Anthony Woods.

After the reception, Seth, Emily, and Marissa left for a short "family" honeymoon in Hilton Head, North Carolina. Seth was to begin touring with CrossPointe the following weekend. Emily and Marissa would be touring with them for some of the journey.

After a month of touring and sales skyrocketing to number one spots across the nation, the group took off for one more special day: the adoption of Marissa.

Early in the day with the sun shining down upon them and a cold wind whistling through the trees, the entire assembly of family and closest friends gathered once again, this time at the courthouse, while Seth pledged to protect and provide for Marissa. After the adoption ceremony, the family was finally whole.

The Laurel Brigade Inn restaurant was busy despite the hour of the day. In the largest room off to the left of the entrance, Emily, Seth, and Marissa sat together with Gram, Mary, and Chris, ready to celebrate Seth's adoption of Melissa. Other family and friends sat at the additional tables provided in the private room. In the fireplace, a roaring fire burned. Candles were lit on each white cloth-covered table. There was not an empty straight-back chair in the room.

The waitresses that tended the party were taken by the youngest, most adorable, and only baby in the room, Marissa. Today, she was the center of attention.

One of the servers, Britney, served the main table. She was smitten with Marissa. She took the orders at the main table, all the while looking at Marissa and then back at Seth and Emily.

"You know, little one…" Britney spoke to Marissa as if she understood. Britney looked up at Seth and asked her name.

"Well, lil' Miss Marissa," she began again, "do you know you look just like your daddy?"

Britney tickled Marissa's toes and looked up at Emily and asked, "Don't you think she looks just like her daddy?"

Emily scanned everyone at the table with raised eyebrows and then looked straight at Seth, took his hand in hers, and replied, "Why, yes, I do. She looks just like her daddy."